Wearing to the White Party

DAVID STUKAS

KENSINGTON BOOKS
http://www.kensingtonbooks.com

KENSINGTON BOOKS are published by

Kensington Publishing Corp.
850 Third Avenue
New York, NY 10022

All Kensington titles, imprints and distributed lines are available at special quantity discounts for bulk purchases for sales promotion, premiums, fundraising, educational or institutional use.

Special book excerpts or customized printings can also be created to fit specific needs. For details, write or phone the office of the Kensington Special Sales Manager: Kensington Publishing Corp., 850 Third Avenue, New York, NY, 10022, Attn. Special Sales Department. Phone: 1-800-221-2647.

Kensington and the K logo Reg. U.S. Pat. & TM Off.

ISBN 0-7582-0606-2

First Hardcover Printing: August 2003
First Trade Paperback Printing: August 2004
10 9 8 7 6 5 4 3 2 1

Printed in the United States of America

To Libby,
Who didn't sue me when she fell on my pool decking.
Don't worry, Libby, the dizzines
will eventually go away.

Acknowledgments

My thanks to John, my terrific and patient editor, who takes the insane stories I write and publishes them with nary a change. I am also eternally grateful to Bo Hewlitt, who told me the all-too-true story about seeing an enormous dildo lying on Mesquite Avenue in Palm Springs—which I shamelessly purloined for this book because it was too good to pass up. Finally, I would like to express my gratitude to Ray Lake, who gave me the adage about cigar-smoking rabbits when I desperately needed something insane.

No rabbits, dildos or settees were harmed in the making of this book.

1

All First-Class Passengers Receive Complimentary Warm Nuts

Everyone has a nightmare so terrifying that the mere thought of it sends chills running through the blood. A nightmare so hideous, it reaches into the furthest crevices of your mind and scars your very psyche. For some people, it's female bodybuilders (that hair, those outfits, those shoes). For others, it's visiting a place like Oklahoma City with less than five stiff drinks in you.

My worst nightmare involves me sitting on a plane high over the mountains of Colorado. I'm sitting in seat 12A, knowing that the luggage sitting in the belly of the plane is filled with ten pairs of red tank tops, four pairs of indecently brief red spandex shorts, and one pair of red leather shorts and a red leather chest harness—yes, I'm going to the Palm Springs Red Party.

By now you're assuming that I've made a mistake and meant to say the Palm Springs White Party. No, I mean the Red Party, but the explanation requires more time that I have here.

Anyhow. If the scenario of me in red spandex isn't scary enough (don't worry, readers; I won't get the chance to wear spandex shorts anywhere in this book), there will be far more frightening things to come. By the time my story is done, there will be two people dead, one injured, one terribly bungled burglary, and I will have been accosted by the emperor to the empress dowager of the Most Imperial and Hierarchical Order of Almost-Vestal Virgins.

But let's begin at the beginning. I am on the aforementioned airplane. Michael is sitting next to me in seat 12B—first class. I would not be sitting in first class with Michael if it weren't for him paying my way. Don't get me wrong. I am no gigolo—no one would pay good money to sleep with me. It usually works the other way around.

"So let me get this thing about the Red Party and the White Party *straight*," I started, trying to get a better understanding of the dynamics of the White Party and its effect on my life, but I was rudely interrupted by Michael covering his ears with his hands.

"Robert, please don't use that word in front of me! You know how *that word* upsets me."

"I'm sorry that I uttered the dreaded hetero-word. But I would be a little more open-minded about straights. After all, they did bring you into this world."

Michael put down his copy of *Details* magazine and looked at me with "oh, please" eyes. "I have a sneaking suspicion that my mother is gay."

"Michael, your mother may be a homicidal maniac who attended Heinrich Himmler's Bavarian Charm School, but one thing she is not is *gay*. Why would you ever think that?"

"Because she's completely insecure, hates everybody, uses money to buy favors, and spews attitude like a stuck-up volcano."

"Not all gays are like that!" I reminded him.

"All the ones I know are!"

"Well, look at the people you associate with. They act like they were raised by wolves."

"It's just that my friends have high standards, and other people don't always measure up to those standards. What looks like snobbery, arrogance, and pretentiousness to you is just their way of being picky."

"Snobbery, arrogance, and pretension. So these are the

pluses for being gay, huh? No wonder we're having so much trouble in our recruiting department."

"Robert, there are tons of reasons why being gay is superior to going strai—you know. We have sex without guilt, great clothes, we start all the trends, and we don't have to get stuck with some bawling babies to raise to adulthood. That's why we're called gay. That's why heteros hate us—we have fun and they don't. You know, I was thinking about this the other day: if one out of every ten people are gay—a number that I find far too low—then, it means that God has to make nine straight people before he gets it right and comes out with one of us."

"Why don't you write a letter to Pat Buchanan and tell him your theory—I'm sure he'd love to hear it," I responded. "Can we get back to my original question? The one about the Red Party?" I pleaded.

"I told you before. Of all the circuit parties held around the country each year, the White Party in Palm Springs is the biggie. There is the White Party in Miami, but it's different than the Palm Springs version. The guy we're staying with is Rex Gifford, and he's starting another party that's happening at the same time as the White Party."

"So," I ventured, "he can suck off all the success of the White one, right?"

"Don't you dare say something like that in front of Rex! The Red Party is going to have *synergy* with the White Party."

"Michael, in my *Dictionary of the Brutally Honest*, that means Rex's party is like a tick, hungrily sucking dollars off a very fat deer."

"From what Rex has told me, the Red Party is going to make the White Party look like a family barbecue in Paramus. The tickets are going for five hundred bucks. That's higher than the VIP tickets for the White Party!"

I was aghast. "Five hundred dollars to get into a fucking party!"

"Not just *a* party, but *the* party!" Michael corrected me.

"I don't care if Cary Grant were there giving blow jobs. Five hundred dollars for a party?"

"Why do you say five hundred dollars like it's a lot of money, Robert?"

"Because it *is* a lot of money."

"Not for me, it isn't," Michael added.

"Yes, but not everyone is the heir apparent to a herpes ointment fortune."

"Yeah, but at least I spend the money I have. You, Robert, you squeeze those pennies so hard, I can hear Lincoln screaming."

"Michael, since when is being responsible with money a crime? I work hard for my paycheck, and I like to spend it wisely and still have some left in the bank when all is said and done."

"But don't you see my point, Robert? There are thousands of gay men who make a lot less than you do, and they manage to go out and have a good time."

"I have a good time, too, Michael!" I said. "I just don't like dodging bill collectors and standing in line to pay the overdue electric bill because Con Edison is about to turn the lights off."

"You worry too much, Robert. I pay my bills late all the time, and I've only had my electric turned off once or twice. So what? I'm out there having too much fun to think about stupid stuff like paying bills and obsessively checking the burners on the stove to see if I turned off the gas, like you do."

"Yes, and I've never had my apartment go up in smoke like yours did."

"It was just the kitchen," Michael said defensively. "Anyway, I blamed it on the contractor who installed the Viking stove in my kitchen, and his insurance company paid for the repairs."

"Even though you left the burner on after making Jiffy

Pop when you had a little too much to drink," I reminded Michael.

"So what? Insurance companies are awash in premiums. It's only fair that the common man gets a little bit back now and then."

"You are hardly common, Michael."

"You can say that again. Anyway, to get back to what we were talking about, there's nothing wrong with Rex taking someone else's idea, changing it, and making it even better."

"Yes, Madonna's been doing that her entire career."

"How dare you blaspheme the sacred name of Madonna!" Michael stated bluntly. "If that guy over in seat 7D heard what you just said, he'd come over and scratch your eyes out."

"How do you know he's gay, Michael?"

"Maybe it has something to do with the fact that he took one of the glazed carrots from his lunch and gave it head."

"You're joking!" I said.

"I'm telling you, Robert, he gave that carrot a blow job while looking right at me!"

"I don't know if that's such a good indication. They were baby carrots, after all."

"I don't care how big he is. It's all about me. I have needs, Robert."

Michael wasn't kidding. Being the heir apparent to a herpes ointment fortune gave Michael plenty of free time—time that he spent on two things: pampering his body, and sex.

"For crying out loud, Michael, we've only been on the plane for three hours and you're horny already! What do you do on transatlantic flights?"

"I have sex several times. Or I use my Jellyfish."

"Your Jellyfish?"

"You jack off in it. Works like a charm," he said, lifting his carry-on bag onto his lap and producing a hot-pink gelatin sleeve eight inches long. "You should get one of these,

Robert!" he stated, brandishing it around for everyone in first class to see, the tube jiggling as though it were alive. "I do wish they'd make it in another color than hot pink."

"Michael, please put that thing away!"

"Why? It's not illegal. Women carry vibrators, so why can't men have Jellyfish with them? I only use it when I can't get the real thing—which it looks like I've got with the guy in seven D. I'll be right back. Here, you take this while I go freshen up," he said as he unfastened his seat belt and stood up in the aisle, tossing the quivering instrument into my lap.

I stared at the pink worm in horror. So did the woman sitting in 12C. I picked up Michael's Love Tunnel with a napkin and shoved it back into his bag. I then reached for the moistened towelette on my folding tray and scrubbed my hands with it until they were red.

Michael, after stretching lazily and making sure he had the attention of Mr. 7D, walked slowly up the aisle and threw him a cruise and nodded his head in the direction of the bathrooms. Michael entered one of the bathrooms and closed the door. Seconds later, Mr. 7D got up from his seat and walked toward the front of the cabin. He stood outside the bathroom where Michael was holed up. About a minute later, the door opened slightly and Mr. 7D slipped inside. I watched in amazement, half expecting the lavatory door to be blown off its hinges. Nothing. The incredible thing is, no one noticed a thing. Or at least, they pretended not to notice a thing. Michael would never have gotten away with this in tourist class.

About five minutes later, Michael emerged. If it weren't for the smile on his face, there was no indication of what had just happened as the captain announced that we were about to begin our descent into Phoenix. Mr. 7D then appeared, sporting the same smile as Michael.

Michael sat down beside me and sighed with complete satisfaction.

"Michael, you better fasten your seat belt—the plane's getting ready to land."

"I think my wheels have already touched down," he stated for the record.

After we landed, we changed planes and had a short and sex-free flight to Palm Springs. We gathered our bags and walked to the curb outside the terminal, where someone from Rex's house was supposed to pick us up.

I had never been to the desert before, but I was struck by its awesome beauty. From the mountains that towered over the city to the palms that stretched their tops toward the sky, this desert was anything but a barren wasteland.

"Michael, look at the size of those mountains!" I exclaimed.

"I'm too busy looking at the size of the biceps on that cop over there," Michael replied. "Holy moley! I'm going to go over and ask Mr. Biceps for directions."

And he did. Michael was the master of seduction. His plan to ask for directions was brilliant. The cop, in order to help Michael, had to lift his arm and point in various directions, putting his bulging arm within licking distance of Michael's tongue. Michael didn't take a taste, but he certainly did stare.

"Are you Michael Stark and Robert?" a voice from a Mercedes SUV asked.

"I'm Robert Wilsop. Michael's over there." I pointed. "Are you our ride to Rex's house?"

"I am. I'll pop the back hatch and you can throw your bags in. I just can't get out of the car," our driver said.

"Michael!" I called. "Our ride is here!" I said as I shoved my bags into the back of the car and came around to a side door, opened it, and got in the car.

"My name's Vince," Vince said, extending a hand for me to shake . . . which was attached to an arm, which was attached to a nude man.

"Hi, I'm . . . Robert. Oh, I guess I just told you that," I said, laughing nervously. I began to wonder if I was in the right car, but then again, who would rightly belong in a car driven by a nude man? The answer came to me instantly: Michael Stark. Yes, I was in the right car.

I heard Michael throw his bags into the back of the car, then watched as he got into the front seat with Vince.

Vince and Michael introduced themselves.

"Nice piercings, Vince!" Michael complimented. "Did you see these, Robert?" he said, grabbing Vince's private parts and showing them to me like he was a salesman displaying a collection of watches at a counter in Macy's.

I was in Rome, so I had to do what the Romans do. I leaned forward, trying to appear appreciative of the dozen rings that formed a row all the way up Vince's scrotum, and the three that sat in the end of his you-know-what.

"Very nice," I reported. "I'll bet you've busted some teeth in your time with those," I offered.

"Tell me about it," Michael chimed in. "I was giving this guy a blow job one time and it was like chewing on a length of chain! I chipped the crown in this tooth," Michael said as he pried his mouth open to show us his beleaguered tooth.

This vacation was off to a running start. It was like going on a roller coaster ride blindfolded—you never knew what was going to happen, but when something did, it was sure to be scary.

Vince put the car into drive, and we sped out of the airport, heading toward the very mountain that towered over the town. The car turned down several streets, leaving the desert landscape behind and entering a neighborhood of winding roads and vegetation so lush, you thought you were in a tropical jungle. It was not what I expected to find right in the middle of the desert.

"This is the movie colony area of Palm Springs. A lot of the old Hollywood stars had houses here. Now it's mostly gays," Vince said.

Vince pulled into a driveway that was blocked by a tall and imposing gate. He pushed a button on a remote control unit that was clipped to the car's visor, and the gate swung open, revealing a lush and shaded compound of Spanish colonial buildings. I was going to like this. Now I knew why it was worth putting up with vacationing with Michael: he never stayed in dumps.

The car pulled to a stop, and we all got out.

Vince grabbed two bags and led us toward what must be guest houses, the metal in his frankfurter jangling like a janitor's set of keys. "The weather here is perfect. That's why I never wear clothes—unless I have to. I'm very spiritual, and I believe that the body is a beautiful thing and shouldn't be hidden."

I begged to differ with Vince. It's not that I expected every nudist to have a perfect body. God knows, somewhere along the line, the gay community trampled on the commendable 1960s idea that everyone is beautiful as is, and swallowed the ideas of Hollywood and Madison Avenue that model perfection is not only desirable but attainable. Now, it seems, you're summed up by how you look and not who you are. An honest, warm, sensitive, and caring person is tossed aside because he doesn't have a thirty-two-inch waist and rock-hard pectorals. Ironically, the same gay men who toss others aside because they don't measure up to strict physical standards are the ones who cry to their therapists that the only men they meet are shallow and unable to commit beyond a sexual encounter. Duh! Anyway, I agreed with Vince that the body is indeed beautiful, but I had to defer to my eyes and recognize that Vince had a very *ugly* penis. I mean ugly. I won't go into detail, but trust me, it was ugly.

"You're here, Robert . . . and Michael, you're in that one right next door."

Vince set the bags down and opened the door on my casita, revealing a sanctuary exquisitely decorated with a mixture of gigantic overstuffed furniture, rough-hewn tables, cool Mexican tile flooring, and exposed ceiling beams large enough to hold up the Chrysler Building. No kitschy Southwest faux-adobe crap with rusted metal candlesticks in the shape of coyotes here.

After deciding that I would just move in here for life, I realized that I was only looking at the living area. The bedroom sat behind a massive oak door that looked like it came from the Spanish Inquisition. The same careful decoration here, including a bed that could easily hold a small Marine garrison. No wonder Michael wanted to stay here.

I settled in, then went next door to ask Michael what he planned to do. I knocked on the door and entered, only to find Michael in the embrace of a rather hunky-looking man who was, like Vince, naked. I quickly surmised what Michael had in mind for the rest of the day.

"Oh, God, Michael, I'm sorry. I just didn't expect you to . . . to . . . be getting, you know, so soon."

"Robert, stop being so Midwestern. This saves me the time of introducing you to Rex. Rex, this is Robert," Michael said, pointing toward me.

I shook Rex's veiny hand. He had the grip of an anaconda and the muscles of one, too. He was built like a proverbial brick shit house and had a gruff, no-nonsense look about him. His chiseled jaw, aquiline nose, flattop haircut that ran down seamlessly to the beard on his face, plus the tattoo on his arm that depicted the Marine bulldog mascot with the letters *U.S.M.C.* underneath, completed the look of a refined but swarthy gay trucker.

"Glad to meet you, Rex," I said, shaking the hand that, just thirty seconds ago, was on a certain part of Michael's anatomy. I would wash my hand later.

"Why don't we all go out to the pool and cool off?" Rex instructed us.

"Sounds like a good idea," Michael said, dropping his pants faster than you can say "George Michael."

I knew I had no choice. If I didn't go with the flow, I would look uptight and guilt-ridden—which I was. But there was no sense in making that clear to Rex—he'd figure that out after spending five minutes talking to me. I peeled off my shorts and underwear and followed Michael and Rex toward the pool.

The pool was magnificent and enormous, with hot tubs on either end of the rectangular pond, and completely private, thanks to the ever-present greenery, which poked out of every inch of available planting space. The water was as warm as bathwater, a fact that I felt worth noting out loud.

"I have it heated all year long. I do laps every day, and I don't like the cold," Rex reported.

"So, Rex, I can hardly wait for your Red Party," I said. "Michael has told me so much about it!"

Michael broke in. "Boy, Robert, your opinion of the Red Party really has changed!"

"Changed, Michael? What do you mean?" I asked, a flush of embarrassment washing over me.

"Back in New York, when I was trying to get you to come with me to Palm Springs, you said 'Why would anyone in their right mind want to attend a nonstop narcissithon infested by drug-crazed, hairless post-adolescents with the depth of a Petri dish?'"

I eked out a nervous laugh, trying to downplay what I had indeed said. "Oh, for gosh sakes, Michael, the things you say!"

"And on the plane you told me the Red Party is like a tick, hungrily sucking dollars off a very fat deer."

Rex glared at me as I shifted into damage-control mode. "Michael, I said that some people *perceive* circuit parties as being drug-infested and narcissistic and that I wanted to see for myself before I took anyone's word for it." Somehow, as the words were quickly formed in my head and headed out of my mouth, I began to realize that they didn't sound that much better than what Michael had quoted me as saying.

Right then I decided to cut my losses, swallow my foot gracefully, and dive under the surface of the water, where I hoped I'd drown.

When I came up for air, I felt that the damage had been done, so the best way to handle an awkward situation was to do what I had practiced all my life: denial. I launched into more questions, designed to calm Rex's feathers by stroking him gently.

"So, Rex, how is your Red Party coming along? It must be exciting to take on a challenge organizing something that big!" I said, trying to make conversation.

"I have a lot of balls," Rex bragged.

I could plainly see that.

"Organizing and planning is a cinch," he continued. "The difficult part is dealing with all the assholes who are trying their damnedest to keep the Red Party from becoming the success that it will be."

"You mean people are trying to sabotage your party?"

"As sure as I'm standing here," Rex said with complete conviction.

"Who would want to do a thing like that?" I inquired.

"Lots of people. Jimmy Garboni for one."

"Jimmy Garboni? Don't tell me. He's the mob boss who controls the circuit party Hello Kitty concession stands."

"Good joke, Robert. You're as funny as a road accident," Rex barked.

Feeling as though I had just been slapped across the face by one of Rex's meaty hands, I guessed that I had gone too far in my kidding. This guy really didn't take any guff. "I'm sorry if I upset you, Rex. I know you're probably under a lot of stress."

"You have no idea," he said, sounding oddly vulnerable and powerless—an odd situation for a man who had the physical build and drill-sergeant demeanor that should be afraid of no one. "I have no doubt that Jimmy Garboni has been pressuring party-planning people not to work with my company. Darlene Waldron is trouble, too. She has an exclusive contract with the White Party, and she stands to lose the most when the Red Party is a success. What I don't understand is why someone would threaten me when the Red Party is designed to work *with* the White Party. I planned that guys would go back and forth between the two."

"Threaten you!" I exclaimed. "Physically?"

"Yes, but not exactly. Let me explain. Someone sent me threatening letters. You know, with the letters cut out of a magazine and pasted to form words."

"What did they say?" I asked.

"Bunch of horseshit. They want two and a half million dollars or they say they'll prevent me from throwing the Red Party."

"How do they propose to do that?" I asked.

"Kill me," Rex said as if he had just told me that the capital of New York was Albany.

"Whew!" I said, whistling the word. "Somebody is very serious about this stuff, Rex. Did you tell the police about this?"

"I don't want word about this to get around. It could ruin ticket sales. Let's face it: no one is going to buy tickets to the Red Party if they think there's a chance it might not happen."

Michael didn't care a fig about Rex's problem, but I was clearly concerned—especially since I was staying in his house and didn't want to die in a hail of bullets fired by masked men with thick necks and gold pinkie rings. "So what are you going to do about it?" I asked.

"Nothing," was his answer. "I mean, what can I do? Two and a half million would take about everything that Rex Productions has. Listen, I've run up against tougher competitors than this. Sometimes you just gotta stare them right in the face and wait for them to blink first."

"Well, Rex, suit yourself, but I think that it would be better if the police at least knew about this. You did keep the threatening notes, didn't you?" I asked.

"Of course I did. I'm a careful businessman. That's one of the reasons I'm so successful. I'll show 'em to you at dinner tonight."

"Why else are you so successful?" I inquired, just to be nosey.

"Brass balls . . . and I can be ruthless when I want something. I can be driven, too. Red Party tickets are almost all sold out because they've seen the publicity and they know it's going to be big. A once-in-a-lifetime thing."

"I see." I was beginning to understand Rex's character quite well, what little there was.

Clink, clink, clink, clink. Vince's body jewelry jingled and jangled as he approached the pool with a phone in hand. "Rex, it's Leo. He's having some problems with some sound equipment or something." Vince handed the phone to Rex and walked away. Clink, clink, clink-a-tink. It seemed like a fair assumption that Vince would never be able to sneak up on anyone.

"Excuse me, guys," Rex announced. "I have to take this call inside. I'll be right back."

I turned to Michael, who was floating around on a raft, sunbathing as if he didn't have a care in the world.

"Did you hear what Rex said about those death threats?" I asked excitedly.

"Yes, I heard about them. So?" Michael replied, reeking with indifference.

"So? You don't care that your friend is being threatened by some lunatic?"

Michael turned his head toward me but didn't lift it from the raft—*don't strain the neck muscles, because it might leave lines in the skin.* "Rex isn't a friend, per se."

"Then what is he?"

"A fuck buddy."

"I see. Then what does that make me, since we've never had sex?" I needed clarification.

"You're a friend. The only one I have. Everyone else either hates me or is jealous of me. True friends are hard to come by."

"Michael, are you getting all mushy on me? Stop it before I start puddling up!" I said, dabbing my eyes with the edge of a towel.

"I'm serious, Robert. I really do think of you as a friend. I would never think of you in the context of sex."

"Thanks, Michael. I think."

Michael continued. "Rex is just a fuck buddy. He's a hot guy, and we enjoy each other's company."

"So what place does Vince play in all of this?"

"He takes care of the place and does stuff for Rex. As far as the rest goes, I don't know and I don't care."

"Okay, back to the death threat part. Aren't you concerned?" I asked.

"No."

"Why not, Michael?"

"Why should I be? Let Rex take care of his own business. I've got myself to think about."

"Ah, that's the old Michael that I know well. For a minute, you were sounding human there, and it scared me."

"Don't you have something to do, Robert? Weren't you going to call Monette and meet up with her?"

"I left a message for her, but she's out hiking."

"So she's at some lesbian White Party?"

"She's at the Dinah Shore Classic."

"The equivalent, from what I hear."

"I think Monette would agree with you. It's become the same thing."

"Don't push it, Robert. Lesbians are not going to put on skin-tight spandex shorts and get up in go-go cages and dance with glow sticks stuck into their orifices."

"I guess they'll just have to face the fact that they'll never match gay men in terms of the cultural legacy they leave to the world."

"You know what I mean, Robert. Lesbians can't party like gay men do. They're more nurturing."

"I tend to disagree, Michael. Monette can drink you under the table and outdance you any day. She did win that lesbian charity dance marathon, you know."

"Robert, let me remind you that winning a dance marathon to eradicate vaginal itch doesn't hold a candle to my two-day dance frenzy at the Pink Party in Miami. It's still the talk of the town."

"I think that what they're talking about isn't your dancing. It has something to do with that part where you collapsed and had to be taken to the hospital—that and the fact that you were screaming about a thirty-foot bird that you said pecked off the head of Sandra Bernhard, who, by the way, wasn't even at the party."

"I blame those Chinese herbs that this guy gave me."

"Michael, when was the last time you saw Chinese herbs that came in pill form?"

Michael was getting that exasperated look that rose to his face when confronted with a reality he couldn't deny. "Could we change the subject?"

"Fine, change it."

Michael was about to change it when Rex returned, tossing the phone into the pool.

"Goddamn it!" Rex bellowed. "Fuckin' ass-wipe Leo. The dumb shit can't get his hands on a fuckin' amplifier that a trained monkey could order! Do I have to do everything for this party?"

Michael, seeing that his fuck buddy would be in no mood for love—at least while he was in a hostile mood—tried to calm Rex's anger.

"Rex, why don't we go inside and have a cocktail and get you to relax?" Michael offered, rubbing Rex's ample pecs with his hand.

Rex complied and led Michael away, excusing the two of them and instructing me to enjoy the pool as much as I wanted or to call Vince and have him make me a cocktail.

Sitting around a pool for a whole week before White Party begins, drinking cocktails, and just soaking up the sun.

I decided I was going to enjoy this.

2

If a Tree Falls in the Forest . . .

I eventually left Michael and Rex at the pool and decided to head back to my casita to take a nap. I was deep in a dream in which Russell Crowe and I were Scottish peat farmers. We had just gone into our barn to get some wood for our fire when we discovered first lady Laura Bush spanking a five-year-old boy who had the head of actress Renée Zellweger and was eating liverwurst sandwiches as he got spanked.

I was saved by the bell. The phone that sat on my night-stand began ringing, so I picked it up and listened.

"I'm coming to you live from the Dinah Shore Classic, also known as lesbian central!"

"Monette?" I spoke into the phone.

"Boy, you thought you were in for a golf tournament, but it's already turned into a battle of the heavyweights. Which dyke will wear the crown? Gina got into a virtual smack-down with her lover, Mary, on the third fairway because Mary looked at another woman. Tricia, who is still sporting dyke hairdo number three, also known as the mudflap, the squirrel cut, or sometimes called the Rod Stewart, has no self-esteem and lives in a perpetual state of cowering in the shadow of her girlfriend, Martha, who looks like she could wrestle Kodiak bears and win. And on the approach to the tenth hole are two power lesbians sporting the latest footwear from Kate Spade, thereby confusing Tricia and Martha, who have never worn anything more than petroleum-based utility shoes that are flat, sensible, and butt-ugly. There's more going on in the spectators' area than on the greens. Are gay men this insecure?" Monette wondered.

"Of course they are. It's just that the men cover it up with a dash of attitude and a dollop of trendy clothing."

"So how are things where you're staying?"

"You should see this place, Monette. It looks like some mammoth hideaway Cary Grant used to escape to with Randolph Scott in the nineteen-thirties."

"There's no proving that there was anything between them, Robert."

"Yeah, sure. And I suppose that the two well-paid *bachelors* lived together to save on the rent. And wore matching sweaters and had cocktails together?"

"It's just wishful thinking on your part."

"What sane gay man wouldn't have wanted Cary Grant as a lover? Anyway . . . it's just too wonderful for words. The pool, which looks bigger than the reservoir in Central Park, is heated to bathwater temperature, they leave the air-conditioning on and the doors open all the time, and there's a full bar in my casita."

"So that's your idea of luxury, Robert? Wastefulness and alcohol?"

"You know how those things appeal to me since I feel guilty every time I waste something."

"I'll bet you turned the air on in your casita and left the door open, then went back and shut it, right?"

"You know me too well, Monette."

"So you're in paradise, huh?"

"Well, there is one fly in the herpes ointment."

"And what's that?"

"Someone's trying to kill Rex, our host."

"And I take it that this is not normal for Rex?"

"Well, to be truthful, Monette, Rex is the kind of prick

who should be killed, but wanting to do it and doing it are two different things."

"So why is he a target? Did he steal some queen's parking space at the grocery store?"

"No. He's throwing the Red Party, and I think some people associated with the White Party don't like the idea. He's gotten threatening letters asking him to stop or something. No, they want a lot of money before they'll stop the attempts on his life."

"Interesting. Any suspects?"

"Yeah, some gay mafia guy and some woman who has the circuit-party-items market sewn up. There are probably more."

"Are you worried?" Monette asked.

"Not too much. Rex doesn't seem to care—not that he lets on. He seems more pissed off about it."

"Well, keep an eye out for Rex. I wouldn't stay too close to him for the next few days—just in case."

"Michael's face is beaming in anticipation of sex with Rex tonight, so I don't think we're going anywhere; and I don't have a car, so I'm staying close. Maybe a night swim, then early to bed. Can we get together for brunch tomorrow? Why don't you come over and pick me up since you've got a car?"

"Sounds grand," she replied. "How's eleven sound?"

"Just fine," I replied. "And while you're at it, could you pick up a Kevlar jacket for me on your way over?" I pleaded.

I swam some more, showered, and got dressed for dinner. I assumed that clothes were called for, but you never knew since no one here seemed to bother. I just hoped that Vince would put on a little something—anything—for dinner. The thought of his body jewelry jangling against the table and dragging through my mashed potatoes as he reached across the table, offering a serving to Rex, would surely put a damper on my appetite. As I knocked gingerly on the door to the main house and entered, I found the dining room table aglow with dozens of candles and a floral arrangement that was unlike anything I had ever seen before. It was suspended in midair over the table from tiny monofilament fishing lines and contained a piece of bark with flowers cascading down toward the table in a splendid show of Japanese design and minimalism that took my breath away. There was a noise in the kitchen, and Vince emerged, drying a dish with a towel. He had nothing on at all.

"Oh, it's you, Robert," he said. "Come on into the kitchen and I'll fix you a cocktail."

"Thank you, Vince," I replied, following the clink-clink of his stairway to heaven. "The table looks beautiful, Vince. Did you do that yourself?"

"Everything but the flowers. A guy named Gil does them. He moved here from San Francisco and started his own shop. He does only the best houses in town."

"I've never seen anything like it. Just beautiful!" I commented. Not only was Gil supremely talented, but Rex obviously had the taste to appreciate his skill—and had the deep pockets to afford it. "The table looks incredible, Vince."

"Thanks."

"So this is what you do—make guests feel at home here?" I asked.

"I try my best."

"You do a good job," I offered.

"Thanks. Rex is one of the few people who really appreciate my talents. I cook and clean and run his private life. I'm kind of like a naked valet and estate manager. That's all I want out of life, and Rex hires me to do just that. I travel around the world, I make my own hours, I can be naked all the time, and I never have to worry about where my next paycheck is coming from. I may not be the sharpest knife in the drawer, but I think I live a pretty good life."

"I'd trade your life with mine in a second, Vince. Living in this beautiful estate is a lot better than writing advertising copy for feminine-hygiene products like I do. So, may I ask you a personal question, Vince?"

"No problem."

"Rex has told you about the threatening letters he's gotten over the past few weeks?"

"The ones asking for money or else?" Vince asked.

"Yes, those. Who do you think is behind them?"

"It could be any number of people. These people in the circuit party field can be so vicious. There's so much money at stake. Millions," Vince stated.

"You don't think that someone would resort to violence unless Rex paid up?"

"I wouldn't put it past them. These circuit parties are big money. More than you can ever imagine. And Rex is raising the stakes considerably. The Red Party is going to be part circuit party, part Cirque du Soleil. And it's going to be bigger than any party ever. He has skydivers parachuting out of planes carrying self-contained laser light shows, a J-lube slip-and-slide party, dancing go-go-boy holograms forty feet tall, bungee-cord air dancers in black-light bodysuits, and hydrogen fireball cannons. Guys are going to be talking about it for years. And they're not balking at paying five hundred dollars a head to be there, either."

I was about to ask what a hydrogen fireball cannon was when I was startled by an outburst of laughter behind my back. It was Michael Stark braying about the length of some unspecified thing.

". . . So I said to this guy, what do you want me to do with it? Fly it?"

"Michael," I started. "So nice to see you! I'm sorry I interrupted your conversation about airplanes."

"Dinner's ready. If you'll take a seat, I'll get the date soup out of the refrigerator," Vince said.

Michael was about to grab a chair when I made a grab for it first. The one I wanted had its back to the wall, just in case a bullet came crashing in through the window—I wanted to see it coming—plus, whoever sat across from me would take the bullet for me. I contemplated maneuvering Michael into that seat. His ego alone would stop a mortar shell fired from twenty feet away.

"Michael, I'm very feng shui and I need to sit with my back to the wall."

"Since when are you into feng shui?" Michael asked with an equal mixture of surprise and disbelief.

"I got into it just recently. Like a few seconds ago."

"Whatever," Michael replied as he picked the chair next to mine and sat down. Rex seated himself in the death chair, then tossed some pieces of paper toward me.

"These are the extortion letters I received. I said I'd show 'em to you."

"Oh, thanks," I replied, not knowing exactly why Rex wanted to show them to me. It must be because of the curiosity that I showed earlier. I unfolded the letters and looked at them one by one.

YoUR Red PaRTy WiLl nOT
HapPEn UnlEss You PaY
$2.5 MilLIOn to us
TiE HANkerCHief on TrEE
By YouR MailBoX to
SIGNal you AgReE
We'Re noT KIDding

The next one was more specific:

Pay UP or YOU'Re a
DeAd MaN

The last one was brief and to the point:

YOU're AbOut
TO SEe ThaT
We MEan BUSineSS

Vince entered with a tray of four soup bowls filled not only with date soup but with a Phalaenopsis orchid bloom floating in the creamy brown broth. It was a work of art.

"There we are," Vince remarked as he placed the soup bowls just so.

I couldn't believe that people actually lived like this; it was hard to imagine. My apartment in New York looked shabby no matter what I tried to do to it. I bought expensive soaps, luxurious towels, beautiful wine goblets, and exotic flowers, but it was like putting great actresses on shitty stages: no matter how hard they tried, they just couldn't overcome their surroundings.

"The soup looks marvelous, Vince!" I exclaimed, trying to get the conversation ball rolling. Rex had ideas of his own.

"I got another of those threatening letters today," Rex remarked to his soup.

"Another one?" Vince replied. "What are you going to do, Rex? You're not going to pay them, are you?"

Rex snorted and laughed out loud. "Over my dead body."

As we were all contemplating the intended irony of Rex's response, there was a tremendous bang as something large and heavy hit the French doors behind Rex. The suddenness of whatever it was that hit the window startled all of us, but no one more than Rex, who jumped so suddenly, his soup spoon flew out of his hand and into guess-who's lap: mine.

As Rex calmed himself and apologized to me, Vince got up and jangled over to the doors and looked outside, trying to ascertain what it was that had attacked our peaceful dinner.

"It's just a palm frond," Vince reported. "The wind can really kick up here in the spring and just tears the dead fronds off the trees. These date palm fronds can be surprisingly heavy. Thank God it didn't break the window!"

Rex tried his best to show that he had recovered like the rest of us, but the incident had clearly shaken him.

"Don't worry about your shorts, Robert. Vince will send them to the cleaners in the morning," Rex added, trying to steer the dinner conversation back to more innocuous topics.

Michael broke the uncomfortable silence. "You know, I once had sex with this guy in a palm tree. We both had on pole-climber lineman boots with the cleats in the bottom. We both had those fall-prevention belts on. It was one of the hottest scenes I've ever had."

I just had to know more about this. "Michael, so this guy likes to have sex in palm trees?"

"No, but he had a boot fetish and he had hundreds of pairs of boots that he liked to wear. We tried some on to have sex in, and I saw that he had two pairs of the telephone lineman boots. I just made the suggestion that we put the boots to good use and have sex in a tree."

"Why?" I asked.

"Because I had never done it in a tree before. Haven't you ever wanted to do it someplace wild?" Michael probed.

"Not really, Michael. I find that a nice, clean bed suits me just fine."

Michael was not about to be halted by my answer. "C'mon, Robert, you're not being honest. What's the kinkiest place you've ever had sex?"

"Michael, I just told you—a bed. Does that make me a freak?"

Michael kept up his goading. "C'mon, Robert, you can tell us! C'mon, c'mon."

"No, Michael."

"C'mon, c'mon. I won't stop asking until you tell us," Michael clarified for me.

"Oh, all right, Michael . . . in a barn."

Michael was stunned. "In a *barn?* That's it?"

"I think that's pretty kinky," I said, defending myself.

"Did you do it with an animal?" Michael asked, with saliva almost falling from his lips.

"Sweet Jesus, no! I just had sex in a barn."

"I wanted to hear something like 'the confessional booth at a Catholic church,' or 'while hanging upside down from a chain,'" Michael said, expressing his disappointment.

"Michael, not everyone has to have outrageous sex for it to qualify as a good time."

"You are the only one who's never had anything but vanilla sex," Michael shot back.

"Okay, Michael, let's test your theory," I stated, turning to our host. "Rex, what's the kinkiest place you've ever had sex?"

Without hesitating a nanosecond, Rex said, "On horseback at full gallop, wearing a wrestler's outfit and knee-high rubber boots."

"Okay, so I'm boring. Where were we?" I asked.

"Getting horny," Michael added.

"Me, too," Rex replied. "Vince, do you mind if Michael and I finish our meals later?"

"No, not at all. Go on; I'll put your dinners in the refrigerator and you can reheat them when you're finished. I'll have dinner with Robert," Vince finished.

"Yes, go have fun; I'll just sit here completely rejected," I added, trying to play the martyr but to no avail. Rex's hand on Michael's ass indicated that nothing else in the world would matter to Rex and Michael for the next two hours.

The minute they were out of sight, I asked Vince who he thought was sending those extortion letters.

"Hard to tell. There are so many suspects. The first one that comes to mind is Jimmy Garboni, gay mafia miniboss. He runs one of the largest catering businesses in Southern California. You don't throw a big event without using him."

"You've mentioned his name before. I just can't believe he's gay *and* mafia. It conjures up all sorts of pictures. It's too funny!"

"No, I'm serious."

"I know you are, Vince, but I can't help but laugh. Jimmy Garboni? It's too funny!"

"Believe me, it's no joking matter. I've heard about too many party production company owners who had 'accidents' with meat cleavers for daring to use another catering company."

"Let me guess, those accidents didn't happen anywhere near a kitchen?"

"The man gets one thousand dollars for the correct answer," Vince replied, pointing his finger at me.

"I've never heard of a gay mafia boss. I suppose that when he gives the kiss of death, he trades tongues?"

"No, it means that his gun always matches his handbag," Vince added.

"Well, I think he makes our list of suspects, doesn't he?"

"He seems a natural choice. He's not the only one, though," Vince cautioned. "There are plenty of people who'd do just about anything to protect their share of the circuit party."

"I guess the next obvious choice would be the guy who throws the White Party."

"Kip Savage is his name. He backs it, but he doesn't own it. No, he wouldn't stoop to something like this—I know him very well. Why would he threaten all that he's built up by extorting money from Rex? No, I just can't imagine him doing anything like this."

Vince seemed too sure of this Kip Savage for my comfort. How much does anyone know anyone? I continued. "Vince, I once befriended this guy who was the nicest person you ever met. But I later found out that he wasn't what he seemed."

"And he turned out to be what?" Vince inquired.

"A woman."

"Oh."

"Don't get me wrong. I have nothing against transsexual

women. It's just that they don't fit the bill for a gay man. It's why I moved out of HeteroWorld in the first place."

"Yes, I bet that this made things difficult."

"So can you think of anyone else who stands to lose money if the Red Party becomes a great success?" I asked.

"Darlene Waldron. A royal cunt. She owns Circuit Toys for Party Boys and has big concession stands that rake it in, not just at the White Party but all year round on the Internet. Darlene and Rex have almost come to blows before. Well, to be truthful, they *have* come to blows before."

"You mean he hit her?"

"No, she hit him—with her car! Or tried to . . . just a few months ago. She tried to run him down when he came out of his office. He was crossing the parking lot to his car when she screamed by in her Toyota Landcruiser, missed Rex, and took out two Miatas and one Lexus. She said her heel got wedged under the gas pedal."

"And let me guess. She said she was coming over to his office to discuss a business arrangement that she couldn't give a shit about."

"Something like that. Rex said he didn't want Darlene to be associated with the Red Party. Rex is very moral and says she was overcharging for laser gloves and glow-stick belly jewels."

"Whoa, Vince. Now slow it down. Laser gloves? Belly whats?"

Vince looked at me as if I had just told him I didn't believe the world was round. "You've never heard of these things?" he remarked.

"No, Vince, I can't say I have."

"Oh, God, they're the latest things. Laser gloves are just what they sound like. They're gloves that you put on with lasers in the tips of each finger. You dance around and fire the laser beams in any direction your fingers point. Fun stuff. Glow-stick belly jewels are just the thing to show off your washboard abs. They're round glowsticks with an adhesive backing that you peel off and stick on your belly button. Puts a light right in the middle of your abdomen."

"And this stuff sells?" I asked incredulously.

"Like hotcakes."

I shook my head and rested my chin on my hand. "I'm in the wrong business."

"What do you do for a living?" Vince asked. Silly him.

"I write ads and brochures, mostly for feminine-hygiene products," I responded.

"I'd think that selling laser gloves would beat douches hands down."

"Don't remind me. But it could be worse, Vince."

"How's that?"

"I could have to write ads for the Snuggle fabric-softener bear."

"Yes, that would be about the bottom of the barrel. Could you hold a minute, Robert? I'll tell you more just as soon as I clear the soup bowls and bring the entrées in," Vince proposed.

Vince cleared the table with the efficiency of a seasoned waiter and puttered in the kitchen while I stared out through the glass doors of the dining room. I knew we were inside a walled compound, but I couldn't help the feeling that I was being watched.

In a few minutes, Vince returned with our entrée, which was as striking as the soup before it. I took one bite, proclaimed it delicious, and started my line of questioning.

"So who's involved in Rex Productions, Vince?"

"T-Rex Productions," Vince corrected me.

"Tyrannosaurus Rex. Very clever—and appropriate."

"Rex is the president and he has several investor partners. Leo Thomas is vice president and is the biggest bodybuilder you will ever see. He's just huge . . . very sensitive, too. Of course, Rex can be a little gruff."

I almost swallowed my fork. "A little?"

"Rex is Rex. Sometimes the stress gets too much for him and he'll do something careless and call Leo a steroid-freak muscle-fuck."

I took a bite of my goat-cheese-stuffed chicken breast, nodding my head as I chewed. "I have no idea why Leo would get upset about a comment like that. You're right; he's too touchy."

"Rex likes Leo a lot—he just doesn't always show it."

I continued. "So Leo does what?"

"He takes care of all the arrangements, from the flowers, backdrops, sound systems, tables, audio-visual systems—you name it. Without Leo, this company wouldn't move an inch."

"Okay, who's next in line?" I asked.

Vince looked puzzled. "In terms of investment or title?"

"There's a difference?"

"Oh, yes. David McLeish is a big investor, and he doesn't really have a title. He's just an investor to the tune of a few million. You do know who he is, don't you?"

I squinted my eyes, looking for an answer behind Vince's back. "I can't say that I do. Irish?"

"Close. He's a famous soap opera star. Handsome, well-endowed, and completely closeted—until he's off the soundstage at ABC, then watch out!"

"Watch out for what?" I replied.

"You'll find out. He should be out here tomorrow."

"Pretty wild?" I ventured.

"You could say that, in a matter of speaking," Vince answered.

I wasn't quite sure what Vince was getting at, but I wanted to know so I wouldn't be shocked when David started eating bugs or flashing his genitals at little old ladies driving oversized Buicks.

"Don't ask any more, Robert," Vince cautioned me. "You'll find out tomorrow."

"Okay, who else works with Rex?"

"Marc Baldwin. Sweet as can be—kind of like you. No, *a lot* like you."

"A lot like me?" I asked, surprised. I had lived with myself for over three decades and wondered how others perceived me.

"Like a cuddly, gay teddy bear," was his answer. "Brown hair, blue eyes—like yours."

"Well, thank you, Vince, I'm flattered. So nothing about me makes you think 'muscle stud' or 'hunka-hunka burning love'?"

"Don't take this the wrong way, but no."

From the look on my face, Vince could tell that I had indeed taken it the wrong way. So he tried to retreat from his declaration—but I beat him to the punch.

"Don't worry, Vince, I've been going through bioenergetic therapy lately. I'm really starting to like myself."

"Bioenergetic?"

"Yes, it focuses on releasing the true self through physical acts that counter the mind's attempt to suppress feelings. It sort of undoes prior hurts to the psyche."

Vince seemed intrigued. "And how is this accomplished?"

"I throw dinner plates at a mannequin that I've dressed up to look like Michael Stark and shout 'Shut up!' as I fling the china at it."

"And you feel better afterward?" Vince asked.

"Like you wouldn't believe," was my response.

"Well, Michael is quite a character, isn't he?"

"Character? I was thinking that he was more of a bottom-feeding slut."

Vince laughed while nodding his head in agreement. "I think deep down, he's got a heart of gold, but he really is self-consumed."

"Tell me about it. I once bought him a silver-plated hand mirror and had the words 'you are so beautiful' printed on the surface of the mirror."

"And?" Vince implored me to go on.

"And he uses it all the time. I once came into his apartment and he was sitting on a couch and staring into it."

"He was making fun of your sarcastic gift!"

"I wouldn't lay odds on that conclusion if I were you," I cautioned Vince. "So is there anyone else with T-Rex Productions I should know about?"

Vince thought a second, then scrunched up his face in disgust. "The Cunt-tessa! How could I forget?!" Vince said in amazement.

"The . . . ?

"Cunt-tessa! It's what Rex calls him."

"Him or her? I'm confused," I said.

"Not a she. He's a he . . . sort of. Colorado Jackson."

"Colorado Jackson?" I remarked. "He sounds like a windswept cowboy who lights matches for his Marlboros on the backs of rattlesnakes while watching reruns of *Gunsmoke*."

"Far from it, Robert. Colorado is a vicious queen so toxic, even the EPA won't touch him. *Gays* bash him."

"He sounds charming. So if he's so nasty, why would Rex tolerate him? Rex doesn't seem like he has a lot of tolerance for irritating people."

Vince took another bite of his chicken and continued. "I don't know. I guess Colorado has some kind of in to the party production community here. Or, has some way of getting favors from the Palm Springs City Council—I don't know. It mystifies me. Well," he said, getting up and clearing my plate, "you seemed to appreciate my chicken."

"Vince, it was delicious," I said as I thought I saw someone run past the window in the distance. "Vince?"

"Yes, Robert?"

"Is there supposed to be anyone on the grounds besides Michael, Rex, and you and me?"

"No, why?"

"Well, I thought I just saw someone zip through the yard a second ago."

Vince emerged from the kitchen to look out the window. He peered into the darkness while he dried a plate.

"I don't see anyone," Vince replied. "Maybe it was a plastic bag or a tarp flying through the yard. You'd be surprised how strong the winds can get around here."

"It wasn't a bag. It was tan and sparkly."

Vince screwed up his eyebrows at my report. "Tan and sparkly? Maybe it was Liberace's ghost. He had a house here for years."

"I don't know. Maybe you're right, Vince. It was probably the wind," I conceded, finally giving up the chase.

"Are you ready for dessert? I've made chocolate raspberry baked Alaskas."

"Oh, God, Vince. I'm going to gain so much weight here, they're going to have to fly me back to New York on the back of a Boeing 747—like the space shuttle."

"Don't worry. Tomorrow we go back to low-fat cooking. I just wanted to do something special for your first night here."

Vince slipped back into the kitchen for a few minutes, the clattering of pots and pans interrupted by periods of silence. Was he praying that his Alaskas would come out all right? After about ten minutes, he reappeared with the individual baked Alaskas. I dug in and was in heaven.

"Vince, this is wonderful! It's like an orgasm."

"How do you think I get the Alaskas so creamy?" he replied, eyebrows arched in a suggestive manner.

I couldn't help but think of his body jewelry as my spoon halted in midflight. "Oh, gosh, Vince, this is so rich I don't know if I can finish it!" I said, pushing my Alaska a safe distance away. "Now, who were we discussing?"

"Colorado Jackson. The face that launched a thousand surgeons' knives."

"Face-lifts, huh? Sign of trouble."

"Numerous, Robert. Colorado has had more work done on his face than Interstate five."

"And let me guess. He came from some tiny town where

they didn't even have running water, but he moves here and sets up a . . ." I said, grasping for a career.

"An inferior decorating boutique in Palm Springs," Vince supplied.

". . . yes, an inferior desecrator and he makes a little money, and all of a sudden, he's descended from Russian royalty and gives you attitude because he picked out the draperies for Edie Gorme's half-sister."

"Exactly. You don't need to meet him, since you know all there is to know."

"I'd rather meet Saddam Hussein."

"He's probably nicer," Vince added. "Well, unless you're dining out tomorrow, you're going to run into him. He comes here all the time. Plus, Leo is throwing a kickoff party at his house tomorrow night, and he's invited—along with everyone who works with T-Rex Productions. I did the invitations."

I was just about to add that I would bring my AK-47 when there was a tremendous crash that made the entire house shudder. You could hear wood cracking, glass shattering, and items toppling onto floors. Fearing we had just been through an earthquake, I looked at Vince for clues of what to do.

"Jesus Christ!" Vince shouted as he got up and ran into the living room.

I figured that I'd rather face whatever happened in the other part of the house than run outside and face the mysterious person I suspected lay in wait for me, so I hightailed it after Vince. There in the middle of the living room was a palm tree, and this was no houseplant.

"Oh, my God!" Vince said as he stood there in a state of shock.

"This wasn't an earthquake, was it?"

"No, the wind must've blown it over." A look of worry swept over Vince's face. "REX? MICHAEL? ARE YOU TWO OKAY?"

Nothing.

Vince was clearly scared. "REX? CAN YOU HEAR ME? IF YOU CAN, JUST FOLLOW MY—"

"Yes, I can fuckin' hear you!" Rex bellowed back as he came up behind us, surprising me. "I crawled out through the door from the bathroom into the yard and came in the front door. I couldn't get out through the bedroom doorway!" He pushed aside palm leaves like an irritated Tarzan—except that this Tarzan didn't have a loincloth on. Rex was wearing medical scrubs and a stethoscope around his neck. Michael, who staggered into view behind Rex, took his place at my side to survey the damage. He was wearing a hospital gown—on backwards. While Vince stood looking at the tree in shock, he didn't make the slightest mention of the way Rex and Michael were attired. I, however, just couldn't cast a blind eye toward this. I just couldn't.

"Michael?"

"Fucking amazing!" he responded, shaking his head in wonder.

"Michael?" I asked again.

"Yes, I heard you, Robert! What is it!?"

"Why are you wearing a hospital gown—backwards, no less?"

"We were playing doctor. Isn't that obvious?"

"I thought it was, but I just had to ask. Could you please close your gown a little?" I asked, averting my eyes.

"I can't believe this!" Michael exclaimed. "It ruined everything!"

"I know, the room is a total loss," I added.

"Not the fucking room, Robert! Our sex! Our sex. I was really getting into the medical scene and this tree came crashing through the room! Knocked the medical tray over and everything on it!"

"Michael, I'm sorry this tree had the temerity to spoil your Marcus Welby sex scene, but this is serious. Do you realize that this didn't happen by coincidence?"

"What do you mean? The tree blew over in the wind."

Rex looked over at me, suddenly interested in the conversation that Michael and I were having.

"I don't think it did, Michael," I commented, realizing that my audience now included Rex and Vince. "While Vince and I were eating, I thought I saw someone run past the windows just a few minutes before the palm blew over."

"And you think the two are connected?" Michael remarked.

"No, Michael, I think it was a Jehovah's Witness putting a *Watchtower* on our front door."

"You *saw* someone?" Rex inquired with eyes so wide, you felt you could climb through his pupils.

"I swore I saw someone outside in the yard—about forty feet away."

Rex was still looking spooked, but he managed to get out another inquiry. "Did you get a good look at this person? Was it a man or a woman?" he asked, restrained but still exuding desperation.

"No, I couldn't say. I just got a fleeting glance."

Rex looked at me for an answer, which I'm sure was sketchy. "What was the person wearing?"

"I'm not quite sure. Tan, brown . . . something like that. With something sparkly."

"Sparkly?" Rex asked. "What do you mean, 'sparkly'?"

"Well, I saw flashes of light coming from something."

"Flashes of light?" Rex probed.

"I don't know. Just bursts of light."

"Bursts of light?" Vince asked. "It could be a spirit. The local Indians believe the spirit of Tahquitz roams the canyons west of here."

Rex rolled his eyes and looked deeply into mine to get more answers.

I couldn't stand the cross-examination anymore. I was swept back in time to third grade, when I felt the laser-beam eyes of Sister Mary flashing her instant disapproval. Sister Mary was the nun who terrorized me for one hour each

Sunday before church. She would make me stand and challenge me with questions that would stump most Catholic adults. How old was Jesus when he died? What is the shortest sentence in the Bible? And what was Jesus' favorite color? There was, of course, no answer to the last question, but it was one that I would always fall for, and Sister Mary would greedily pounce upon me to humiliate me for answering. My only revenge for this inhumane treatment came years later from the mother superior, who reported over the classroom loudspeaker that Sister Mary, who had moved to Ghana to teach the unbaptized heathen, was "encountering great difficulties" and that we must all say a prayer for her soul. That same day, a fellow classmate/inmate said that he heard that she had been roasted by pagans and eaten. Had I only known that this fate would befall hateful Sister Mary, I would've sent her tormentors a case of barbecue sauce.

I was awakened when I felt Rex's powerful hand on my arm, tugging at it for an answer.

"So you didn't see who it was?" he pleaded.

"I'm sorry, Rex. I just caught a glimpse of whoever it was. I didn't get anything definite."

Rex looked strangely relieved. "Well, then. Maybe this was all something you thought you saw and the palm just happened to break in the wind. After all, most of the palms in this area are very old."

I decided to play Monette for a minute and ventured forth. "Rex, do you have a flashlight?"

"A flashlight?"

"To see why the palm fell in the first place. There's little reason to sit around here wondering why the palm tree made its unwelcome entrance, unless we're sure it decided to pay us a visit on its own or whether someone helped it along."

"Sure. I have one in my office. Let me go get it," he answered, then disappeared down the hall. He returned shortly, holding a flashlight that looked like it could illuminate Pluto.

I led the search party outside, and we approached the remaining stump of the aforementioned intrusive palm tree. I shone the light on its base.

"Look! Sawdust! Someone cut the tree so it would fall down in the direction of the house!" I reported.

No one said anything, but right in front of their eyes was the indisputable evidence that someone had intentions on Rex's life. The trunk of the tree bore the unmistakable signs of having been sawed. I looked up at Rex and told him that I thought it was time he called the police.

Rex snorted and nodded. "I guess I can't pretend any longer. It looks like someone is serious about me paying up if I want the Red Party to get off the ground. T-Rex just doesn't have that kind of money to spare. If we pay up, we'll be operating right on the edge—if something unexpectedly goes wrong, we won't be able to cover it. It could bankrupt us."

"Perhaps this is what someone has in mind. Whoever is behind this may be trying to make a lot of money and bankrupt you at the same time."

"I'm afraid you're right."

"And," I added, to make a point very clear, "this person is willing to kill to get what he or she wants." I pointed to the fallen tree. "Now, I think we better go inside and call the police."

As we all walked back to the house, Michael bent toward me and whispered into my ear, "I think I'll wear a helmet to bed tonight," Michael said.

"Sounds like good protection, but won't that be uncomfortable?"

"Not really," he answered. "I've worn one before. I was dating a biker guy—"

I put my hand to Michael's lips. "Not another word,

Michael," I said. "There are enough things that I just don't understand tonight. I'm afraid that the tale you were about to tell would put me over the deep end."

The police arrived in a matter of minutes, their sirens screaming and wailing, no doubt alerting people as far away as Phoenix that something nasty was afoot here in the Old Movie Colony.

The police swarmed all over the ground like uniformed ants, some staying outside to investigate and perhaps arrest the date palm, the others coming inside to examine the rest of the tree and to ask questions. Vince was trying unsuccessfully to remove some of the immense palm tree with a kitchen knife and set things right, but he was stopped in midchop by an officer who waved him away, saying that the evidence mustn't be disturbed. Michael was sitting in an oversized chair, thumbing through an issue of *The Advocate*, paying no attention to anyone until his eyes lit on the same thing mine did: an officer with arms as big as most people's thighs, talking to Rex. Michael was on him faster than Shirley MacLaine on a previous life. Michael pretended to be intensely interested in what Officer Biceps was doing, all the while practically licking the bulging biceps with the irises of this eyes.

Rex, on the other hand, was telling the police about his Red Party, his party production company, and who his partners and employees were. He then mentioned the threatening letters to the questioning officer.

"This whole thing started with these threatening letters a few weeks ago."

"Could you tell me what was in these letters?" the officer asked.

"I can do better than that. I can show them to you, Officer . . ." Rex hesitated.

"Gorski. Sergeant Gorski."

"Gorski. Fine. Just give me a minute and I'll get the letters. I've got them in a safe in my office—which, thank God, didn't take a hit from the tree."

Rex walked off, leaving me with Sergeant Gorski. He didn't waste time in Rex's absence, asking me what I knew about this freak coincidence of gravity and botany.

"I can't tell you much, but I did see someone run through the yard just a few minutes before the tree hit the house."

"Could you describe what you saw?"

Again, the same grilling that Sister Mary Appetizer and Rex had put me through. I told them I only got a glimpse of someone in a tan shirt and pants and something glittery. It was as if they were asking me to do an artist's rendering of the criminal when all I saw was a flash of the person from over forty feet away—in the dark, no less. No, I couldn't tell them what height the person was. Or how old. Or what race.

Rex returned shortly with the letters in hand. He handed them to Sergeant Gorski and sat down across from him. "Would you like something to drink?" he offered.

"No, nothing," came the reply.

"Well, I think I could use one," Rex reported. "Robert? Care for anything?"

"I'll take a gimlet," I said, wondering if that was man enough of a drink to ask Rex to make.

No comment from Rex. A liquor bottle rose and fell in the air, followed by a bottle of Rose's lime juice. Rex looked like he had mixed cocktails as a child. Perhaps he had. It was a skill that must have come in handy in later years. Rex returned to his place on the couch, with a gimlet for me and a manly glass of an amber-colored liquor with two large ice cubes. Probably scotch. Exactly what you'd expect a gay playboy stud to drink.

"Mr. Gifford, these letters aren't threatening letters!" the sergeant said, shaking the evidence at an imaginary jury.

"Great. I feel better already," Rex snidely added.

"No, these are extortion letters! Why didn't you call the police the minute you got the first one?"

Rex looked at Sergeant Big Arms as if he were a pitiful moron—a look that I'm sure Rex cast at just about everyone in his path. "Sergeant, first of all, I didn't take them seriously at first. I mean, asking for two point five million dollars? Now, who in their right mind is going to pay someone that kind of money and have no assurances whatsoever? And asking me to tie a handkerchief on the trunk of the tree by the mailbox to signal that I was going to pay? Now, come on! It sounds like a thirteen-year-old writing these letters."

"Well," the sergeant started, "it wasn't a thirteen-year-old who cut down a palm tree with the intent of killing you."

"Well, it didn't kill me," Rex said to set the record straight.

"Mr. Gifford, whoever cut this tree down knew exactly where your bedroom was, and you have to admit, they had pretty good aim. Whoever this person is knows what they're doing, and they might not miss on their second try."

"Tonight was not their first attempt," Rex said, causing every head in the room to turn toward him.

"You mean this is the second attemp?" This question came not from the sergeant but from Vince, whose tone said that this was the first time he had heard this truth.

"Yes, Vince, there was a suspicious attempt about a week ago."

"I can't believe it, Rex!" Vince exclaimed. "You never mentioned anything about it to me."

"At first I didn't think it was intentional. I mean, the way it happened, it looked like a freak chance of nature," Rex finished.

Sergeant Big Arms looked like he was falling behind in the line of questioning, so he jumped in with a question of his own. "Mr. Gifford, could you tell us why you thought the first attempt—which I hope you will give us a description of—was a chance of nature?"

"It happened a week ago. I went for a short hike instead of making my usual trip to the gym."

"You what?" Vince blurted out, unable to believe what Rex had just said.

Rex held up his hand in an attempt to stop Vince dead in his tracks. "Now, now, Vince. I know that it seems fool-hardy to go out alone when all this is going on . . ."

"No, that's not what I was going to say," Vince explained.

"Well, could it wait until I'm done with my story?" Rex asked, eyebrows raised slightly to let it be known that the master of the house was speaking.

"Fine, Rex. Whatever you say."

"Good. I was hiking on Spitz Trail. I needed to get out and clear my head, and the gym was just too much of a dis-traction—with all those men, you see."

"I see," Sergeant Big Arms said, although from the wed-ding band on his finger, the George Bush Sr. aviator-style glasses, and his hopelessly out-of-date haircut, I doubted that he did see what Rex was talking about.

"I had been walking for about a half hour, thinking about some details of the Red Party, when this huge boulder came crashing across the trail only a few feet in front of me. I looked up and saw someone running away from the edge of the cliffs far above me."

Gorski looked at Rex with complete disbelief in his eyes. "A boulder misses you by a few feet, you see someone run-ning away from the spot from where the rock came from, and you thought it was an accident? Mr. Gifford, excuse me for sounding a little snide, but it doesn't take Colombo to figure this out. Why did you wait so long to call the police?"

The sergeant had a point. I was wondering how such an astute businessman could fail to see such obvious connec-tions.

Rex stared at the ice cubes in his empty whiskey glass as if the answer were written on fortune cookie slips of paper frozen inside the icy prisms. "I really don't know what to tell you, Sergeant. I guess that I didn't want to believe that this was really happening. If news of this got out, no one would want to attend the Red Party. People would be afraid to come for fear that something might happen to them."

"That's understandable, Mr. Gifford, but how did you think you were going to handle this on your own?"

"I hadn't gotten that far yet," Rex replied, the *über*-businessman apparently out of ideas.

"Well, that's all for now, Mr. Gifford. We'll post an officer outside on your grounds in the meantime for your protection. Here's my card. Give me a call if you think of anything, no matter how insignificant the detail."

Vince had the look on his face that indicated that he was about to speak, but Rex needed a little something to calm him down first.

"Vince," Rex said, holding out the empty glass in front of him, "could you pour me another double shot of scotch? I think I need something to calm my nerves."

"Sure, Rex," Vince said, suddenly concerned that the undefeatable Rex Gifford, the king of party productions, was meeting his match.

As Rex sat in a leather club chair talking to Vince, and Sergeant Big Arms gathered up his official-looking briefcase and went out the front door to join his comrades, I wondered where Michael had gotten to. I went outside, around the house, and into Rex's bedroom through the side door, feeling that since the palm tree had left several gaping entrances to Rex's bedroom, it wouldn't be rude to enter without knocking. After all, there was little to knock on.

I entered the bedroom only to find Michael putting his hands around the arms of another cop—whose arms weren't anywhere near as big as Mr. Big Arms' were. But to Michael, a cop is a cop, and a cop blew air up his codpiece more than anything. Michael didn't notice me standing there watching him, so I remained silent and watched. I wanted to see if Michael could break his previous record for seducing a real, live cop. The previous record stood at two minutes, five seconds.

"Wow," Michael said in faux amazement. "How big did you say they were?" he asked, copping another feel of the amazing biceps—pun intended.

"Twenty inches," the cop said with great pride.

"Twenty inches!" Michael swooned. "That must be at least three inches bigger than mine," Michael lied. I knew that Michael's arms were twenty-one inches around—a fact that he continuously drummed into my head. Michael took his hands off Mr. Policeman's biceps and goaded him to give Michael's arms a squeeze. And to my amazement, Mr. Twenty Inches complied.

For as long as I have known him, Michael has exhibited an amazing skill for seduction. He wasn't always subtle, but he was almost always successful. I still couldn't quite figure out how he managed to get people to carry out his will. He said that every man has some gay gene lurking deep inside and that he just has a talent for finding and bringing it out. It was a trait that I noticed in a cross-section of the population. There would always be those who could twist others around their little fingers. These people, I noticed, had a flair for charming and flattering people endlessly, an inability to take "no" for an answer, and the chassis that enabled them to take people on the ride of their choosing. Maybe it was as simple as the fact that popular people swallowed it.

"You're just going to have to tell me what routine you follow to get your arms that big," Michael continued. "I eat three hundred grams of protein and hit the arms every two days, and still I haven't got the results you have."

Officer Twenty Inches was starting to launch into a discussion of his biceps-triceps routine when Michael interrupted him.

"The biceps are great, but what I really want to know is about your abs. How many crunches do you do daily?" Michael asked, his right hand slipping onto Mr. Arms' lower abs and just a fraction of an inch from his duty belt. "I'll bet you have an eight-pack instead of the usual six," Michael added.

Like so many straight men, Mr. Abs hadn't the slightest idea that he was being cruised by a gay man—that is, until now.

"Mr. . . . ." Officer Twenty Inches started, obviously never having gotten Michael's last name.

"Stark, Michael Stark," he supplied.

"Thank you for the information you've supplied, Mr. Stark. If we need any more information, we'll call you," he said, squirming like a CEO of Enron at a Congressional hearing.

He managed to wriggle out of Michael's grasp and head hurriedly for a doorway—any doorway—while running right into an expensive side table in the hallway with a shin-busting crack. He grabbed and steadied the square glass vase filled with calla lilies that stood on top of it, and cautiously pushed the table out of harm's way.

"Damn!" Michael uttered when Officer Twenty Inches was out of sight. "Robert! How long were you standing there?" he asked.

"Just long enough."

"Long enough to scare my policeman away," he accused. "And I was doing so well."

"Not from what I saw. Yes, you may have had his arms on you, but that doesn't mean you had him in bed. And furthermore, your date, Rex, the man you flew across country to sleep with, is outside. I think he's upset about a tree or someone trying to kill him or something petty like that. You could go in there and give a little support, you know."

"Do I have to?" Michael whined. "All through sex, his

mind was on his stupid Red Party. He barely looked at me the whole time."

I pictured the air rushing out of Michael's ego, leaving behind a pint-sized Michael in its place—one that you could easily step on.

"Michael, go *in there!*" I implored.

"Oh, for God's sake," he complained. "I came to the White Party, like everyone else, to have great sex and I end up playing nursemaid to a forty-five-year-old baby who's upset because a tree falls on his house. Just last winter I had a tree fall on my penthouse, and you didn't see me crying, did you?"

"Michael, that was a ten-foot Japanese maple that blew over in its pot and broke a single pane of your window glass . . . and then blew off your balcony, almost flattening a shih tzu who barely escaped taking the last crap of his life."

"I gave the owner fifteen thousand dollars for the inconvenience."

"I'm sure she could've gotten more," I moralized.

"Yeah, until she found out who my lawyers were. She was lucky to get what she did. When my lawyers finished with her, she would've been happier sewing Tommy Hilfiger knockoffs in a Singapore sweatshop."

"Go *out there!*" I repeated.

Michael let out a sigh with a great rush of air that should have collapsed his lungs, then headed out to Rex like a snail suffering from low blood sugar.

I, for one, had had enough for one day. I was really looking forward to getting into my little casita, cranking the air conditioner up to maximum, then pulling the covers over my head and forgetting that there ever was a Red Party.

I was about to make my wish come true when Rex approached me.

"Yes, Rex?"

"I have a favor to ask."

"Yes, anything, Rex."

"Could Michael and I sleep in your casita tonight? It's the only room in the house that has a queen-sized bed, now that mine is under a two-ton palm tree."

"Sure, Rex," I answered. After all, what could I say? I was sleeping for free.

"You can sleep in my office. It has a couch that folds out into a very comfortable single bed."

"Sure, Rex. Let me move my luggage."

"Thanks for understanding. I'm sorry to put you out."

I was about to correct him by saying that it was Michael who was putting out, but decided that this was no time for a joke.

I went back to my casita and kissed its luxury good-bye, gathered up my clothes and shaving kit, and came back into the house, following Rex to his office. It was actually quite comfortable, complete with a flat-screen television, several lounge chairs, and a full bathroom—with black granite everything and a Jacuzzi that Rex showed me how to operate. Yes, I thought, I would be quite comfortable here.

"In case you want to watch anything," Rex said, opening the door to one of the exotic-wood built-in cabinets, "there's plenty to choose from. Just help yourself. If you need anything, Vince's bedroom is just down the hall. First door on the right."

"Thanks, Rex. I think I'll do just fine," I admitted quite truthfully.

I closed the door to the room and just stood there, taking in my surroundings. The lighting system, combined with the thick carpeting and the whisper-quiet air-conditioning, gave the room a hushed feeling like an extremely comfortable church. Since I was still a little wound up from the events of the past two hours, I walked over to the cabinet and glanced at the video choices before me.

They were all porn titles. I checked the next cabinet, and it contained more of the same. No *Auntie Mame* or *All About*

Eve or even an Alfred Hitchcock title to lull me to sleep. I looked around the room guiltily, as if someone might have been watching me in the windowless room, then closed my eyes and reached out to randomly grab a title. This was a gay vacation, and I could watch a little porn if I wanted to. Other people did.

I opened my eyes and saw that I had chosen *Caned and Able*. On the cover was a huge man dressed in military fatigues, bearing the shiny nametag (blown up for all to see) that said *Corporal Punishment*.

I looked at the other titles and they weren't much better—not that I was sure what kind of title I was looking for. I relented and popped the tape into the VCR, which sparked to life, feeding the monstrous flat-screen TV at the same time.

I climbed into bed and watched with amazement. I was just about to fall asleep from the pathetic dialogue and piss-poor acting when I saw something that made my eyeballs pop farther out of my head than Barbara Bush's.

There on the screen was a very naked Michael Stark, his buttocks begging for punishment.

If the palm tree wasn't enough already, I knew that what I saw would give me horrible nightmares tonight. And for many years to come.

3

Waiting for the Other Sandal to Drop

Somehow, I survived the night. I woke up, put on a bath-
robe, and ventured forth into the living room, hoping that I
wouldn't find a palm tree lying there. I was to be disappointed.
The recalcitrant palm was, however, much smaller than it had
been the night before, thanks to a team of gardeners, who were
busily sawing up the enormous *Phoenix dactylifera* and cart-
ing it away by hand. Vince was overseeing the palm tree's
dismemberment, clothed; very tight shorts were the one concession to the gardeners.

"Well," Vince commented, "you're up early. There's coffee in the kitchen."

"I could certainly use a tankard right now. Boy, you've
really gotten a lot done this morning."

"It's nine-thirty!" Vince said, as if I had been sleeping off
a three-day alcohol binge.

"I could pitch in if it would help, Vince," I offered.

"Just rest. Besides the pruning shears that I keep out on
the porch, there isn't anything that would do much good."

"With all these trees on the premises, you don't even
have a small saw?" I asked.

"Nope. Rex hires people to do everything for him."

"Speaking of Rex, how is he this morning?" I inquired.

"Hasn't gotten up yet," Vince said as he raised his mug of

coffee to his lips and sipped. On the side of the mug was obviously Vince's life motto: *I was born naked and I intend to stay that way*. Rex must have picked up this mug as a gift for Vince the last time he dined at a Cracker Barrel restaurant. "I walked by the casita about an hour ago. It sounded like two moving men delivering a grand piano to the top of the Matterhorn, so I assume they're alive."

"Rex must be tickling Michael's ivories," I added.

Vince laughed at my little joke. "There are some pastries on the dining table. I'm going to whip up breakfast as soon as Rex and Michael get up."

I took a gulp from my mug, downing the coffee in one quick motion. "Don't wait for me, Vince. I'm having brunch with Monette, my lesbian friend, at eleven. Can you suggest a good place to go?" I figured that with Vince's astounding culinary skills, he must know of somewhere to eat.

"You might try the Pesca. I also know for a fact that the food is very good at The Garage—it's in a former auto garage. Don't worry; it's clean."

"Thanks for the tip. I'll be back later this afternoon."

I put down my coffee mug and started to leave the room when Vince gave me a last piece of advice. "Whatever you do, don't go to Bathsheba. It's terrible."

I headed to Rex's office, shaved, showered, and got dressed. I stood outside the compound gate and waited for Monette. She showed up ten minutes late in a Chevrolet Metro, no less. Seeing Monette's six-foot-four-inch frame jammed into the tiny subcompact made me think of a tiny circus car full of clowns—an observation that I kept to myself, owing to Monette's mortal fear of them.

"Get in," she shouted, shoving her elbow into the rear seating area in order to unlock the door and let me in.

"Couldn't you get anything smaller, Monette?" I joked, getting in and letting my chin rest rather precariously on my knees. It was that or I would have to put my chin on the dashboard—a prospect that seemed even more tempting to fate, owing to Monette's notoriously bad driving skills. They were so bad, I harbored the belief that she learned to drive a car in Cairo, considering sidewalks as viable right-turn lanes and pedestrians as something to swerve around—like potholes. I fastened my seat belt and hung on for dear life. When Monette got behind the wheel of a vehicle, it was her id that did the driving. Her superego was told to get in the backseat and keep its mouth shut.

The tiny car zoomed off like a cockroach suddenly finding itself under the blaze of kitchen lights. Despite two-lane streets that were wide enough to land a Boeing 747 (a curious fact I discovered about Palm Springs), she so closely hugged the yellow line separating our tiny car from certain death, the line frequently disappeared under the car and occasionally showed up on my side of the vehicle. I said nothing.

"Where are we going—so fast?" I managed to squeak out.

"I can't go any slower. My legs are so long, they're wedged between my pelvis and the gas pedal. Your only choice is idling in park or doing sixty. Get used to it!"

Okay, okay," I relented. "I asked Vince, the naked manservant and cook, about a few places to eat."

"Me too. I got the girls to suggest somewhere to have brunch. They raved about Bathsheba."

Just then there was a loud thump as the car drove over something large in the road.

"Ah, I think we just hit something," I offered. "It might have been a buzzard," I suggested. "Or maybe an old lady."

"I don't know what it was—I wasn't looking," Monette replied with more than a little irritation showing.

A driver who wasn't watching what was lying in the road as she drove the car over it. I now had my confirmation that she had learned to drive a car in some Middle Eastern country where the idea of an automobile hadn't quite yet caught on.

Monette circled and drove back toward something very large and black lying in the middle of the road. She pulled over to the side and we both got out, the two of us expecting far more exotic roadkill than the rats and pigeons (was there a difference?) we were used to seeing pulverized into the blacktop streets of Manhattan.

"Oh, for fuckin' crying out loud!" Monette yelled in a voice loud enough to be heard in Los Angeles. "Whatever the fuck it was, it blew out the tire! I hope it's dead, whatever it is—serves it right!"

"I'm not surprised," I said, looking at the deflated tire. It had that sad look that tires get when they let you down. "It was huge, whatever it was," I said, thinking the object in question was one Gladys Whippleman, age eighty-seven, who had wandered away from the Death Valley Retirement Center for the last time. "Since the car's not going anywhere for the time being, maybe we should find out what we hit."

Monette nodded her head in angry agreement and carefully approached the object lying motionless in the road, my mind racing to figure out this strange creature. Was it some kind of bizarre desert animal, like a black armadillo or an escaped potbellied pig? Or something even stranger like a roadrunner lizard.

"It's a dildo," Monette said, as if she had just told me that today was Monday.

And quite a dildo it was. The size of a small fire hydrant, it must have measured close to two feet in length and had a diameter that was just plain obscene.

We looked at each other and burst into laughter.

"Now, what would a monstrous black dildo be doing lying in the road in the middle of the day?" I asked.

Monette couldn't take her eyes off the thing. "Maybe it's God's way of saying 'Welcome to Palm Springs.' I was warned that some pretty outrageous stuff goes on here, especially during White Party." Monette took a pause; then her mind changed gears. "What I can't get over is that it's just so . . ."

"Big?" I suggested.

"No, incongruous," she said.

It was the perfect—and only—word to describe the situation. Here in the street, in front of suburban ranch homes with perfectly manicured green lawns and tidy sidewalks, was a behemoth latex penis complete with balls big enough to keep the object from accidentally slipping into a manhole, let alone an orifice.

"Maybe Madonna's in town," I suggested.

"No, I got it!" Monette ejected, the tone of her voice saying that she had solved the mystery and we were about to hear the stunning answer. "Two gay men—a couple—are having a fight in their car. The one says he's not going to play second fiddle to Mr. Fireplug anymore. He takes the creature and heaves it out the window, much to his lover's dismay. Case solved."

"You're not fooling me, Monette. You saw this exact same thing in an episode of *Murder She Wrote*, didn't you?"

"I've got to take a picture of this!" Monette exclaimed, running back to the car and fetching her camera. She snapped a few pictures as cars passed and slowed down to see what was lying in the road. When they got close enough to discern that this was no ordinary roadkill, the drivers would hit the gas, trying to spare the wife and kids from the imposing monster. I could hear the conversations now.

"Daddy?" little Sybil asked.

"Yes, Sibyl. What is it?"

"What was that in the road? It looked like an elephant poop that I saw at the circus!"

"Yes, dear, that's exactly what it was."

Monette waved at me to get closer to the device. "Get down next to it so I can get you both in the picture."

Get *you both* in the picture, I thought. The latex battering ram was now on a par with me in Monette's eyes, the two of us being photographed by a six-foot-four-inch redheaded Irish lesbian Avedon.

"I'm not going near that thing!" I said in disgust. "It still looks greasy, which I think answers the question 'I don't know where it's been.' "

"Oh, for God's sake, Robert. I'm asking you to stand next to it, not mount it."

I finally relented, and Monette began snapping photos like a *National Enquirer* photographer catching Laura Bush facedown in Lynne Cheney's crotch. No matter how you viewed it, it wasn't a pretty sight.

"Have you gotten enough photos?" I pleaded.

"I think that will do nicely," she replied.

The moment she said the word "nicely," I knew that I had just wandered into a trap. Monette was going to use the photos to embarrass me. We had met in Palm Springs just minutes ago, but she was all ready to launch the first salvo in our ongoing war of fiendish practical jokes. I decided to say nothing and would hope to get my hands on her camera and open the back, exposing the film and her nefarious plot at the same time. She must have read my mind, because she reached into the car, put the camera into her purse, and latched it shut.

We stood next to the car, trying desperately to project our helplessness, which eventually worked when a Palm Springs police officer pulled over and changed the tire on the car, putting the spare on like he had been doing it all his life—which, apparently, he did. I suppose that we could have changed the tire ourselves, but being New Yorkers for many years, it never occurred to us that the car came equipped with a spare tire. When a tire went flat, the solution was simple: pay the cab driver, get out and find another cab, leaving him or her to take care of the tire. I'm a New Yorker! Not my problem!

When the spare was on, we thanked Officer Blake end-lessly and categorically denied that we had anything to do with the rubber Godzilla.

As we drove away, we turned to see Blake pushing the dildo off to the side of the road with his nightstick. He had little intention of picking it up, and I didn't blame him.

Fearing that we might run into more trouble the farther we drove, I agreed with Monette that the first recommended restaurant that we passed would be where we'd eat. No sooner had we shaken hands on the deal than Bathsheba came into view.

We went inside and sat down.

"Tell me what has been going on in your compound of hedonism," Monette said.

I told her. By the time I had finished the entire story, our brunch was ordered, eaten, and cleared away, leaving us a clear table for discussion. And yes, Bathsheba was terrible.

"So someone is trying to extort guarantee money from Rex, and they've made two attempts on his life, huh?" she ventured.

"That's about the sum of it," I said.

"It seems that there's not much we can do right now . . . although . . . although . . ." She trailed off.

"Oh, God, don't tell me you're intrigued by this whole situation."

Monette ordered more coffee. "And you're not?"

"To tell you the truth, I couldn't care less. My only con-cern is that Rex's assassin might miss and get me along with Rex. Other than that, I don't give two hoots. Rex isn't ex-actly a shining example of humanity."

"Just do me one favor, will you?" Monette asked ever so nicely.

"What is it? Find where Lily Tomlin stays when she comes to the desert?"

"No, although that would be nice to know. I was thinking of something different."

"Spill it," I said.

"You're sleeping in Rex's office, aren't you?"

"Yes. What has that got to do . . . ?" I saw where Monette was going with this, and I didn't like that it involved mostly me. "Oh, no, you don't! I am not going to rummage through his office in order to turn up something that would shed light on this whole extortion thing."

"Oh, c'mon, Robert. I'm not asking you to dynamite his safe. Just kind of peek in drawers, look through files—that sort of thing."

"There's no guarantee that I'll be there after last night. He might move me again."

"Then convince him that you're just fine where you are."

I resigned myself to the fact that I would have to play the role of Agatha Christie's Miss Marple again. "So what am I looking for?"

"Anything that looks suspicious. Bank statements with large sums of money being transferred, overdue invoices or legal actions Rex has taken against stubborn suppliers. Partners with an axe to grind with Rex. Stuff like that."

"And what do I do if I find anything?"

"Photocopy it and bring it to me. There is a copier in his office, isn't there?"

"Strangely enough, there is. So what if Rex tries to enter his office and finds the door locked with me on the other side and the sound of his copier whirring away?"

"He'll think you're making copies of your butt and faxing them to friends as a joke. How do I know? Make something up."

This feeling of dread came up over me as we left the restaurant—maybe it was the atrocious food. As Monette drove back to drop me off at the compound, we passed the spot where the black dildo would be lying in wait for another subcompact car. It was no longer there. The thought that someone had actually picked it up amazed me no end.

When I thought about it, my life was kind of like that dildo lying in the road. Where either of us was headed right now was a complete mystery no one could predict.

4

Third Time's a Charm

When Monette dropped me back at Rex's compound, she gave me a hug and asked if I wanted to go out on the town tonight; I told her I would call her back.

She waved good-bye and careered down the road until her little Metro disappeared—a mere six seconds.

I slipped my plastic security card into the card reader, and the imposing gates magically opened. I headed toward my casita, then remembered that I was camped out in Rex's office for the time being. So I entered the house and went for Rex's office. I opened the door, never thinking that he might be working inside, let alone that there would be a crowd there.

"Oh, gosh, Rex," I said, still quite startled at having an audience. "I just came in to get a few of my things."

Rex was sitting behind his butte-sized desk, in command of the room. "Help yourself, Robert," he said before plowing on.

"The thing I am not going to do is give in to this extortionist! Fuck him—or her! Let 'em kill me. The Red Party will go on, and it will be a huge success!" Rex exclaimed as he hit his meaty fist on the table.

I went over to where I had my nylon luggage, only to find that an extremely inconsiderate queen had dropped cigarette ashes all over my bag and had even managed to produce two burn holes. Even worse, the queen was still there flicking ashes from his Virginia Slims onto my suitcase—even as I was digging through it.

"Ah, excuse me," I said, the anger rising in my head enough to put me within seconds of making him eat that cigarette. "Could you not do that? This is my bag that you're dropping your ashes on!"

"Oh, sorry, dear," he said, rolling his eyes and elevating his chin a half inch higher so that he wouldn't have to look at me. As he turned his head toward Rex, he flicked his cigarette one more time onto my bag in the most intentional act of bitchiness I have ever seen.

My assertiveness training has taught me to stand up in a situation like this. So I did what an evolved, rational, and self-assured person would do: I reached into my shaving kit, retrieved a pair of hair-trimming scissors, and stealthily prepared to snip a small but noticeable cut in the bottom of the queen's trendy microfiber (why not just call it nylon, people?) shirt. To make sure it was irreparable, I was going to make sure the cut was nowhere near a seam.

Just as I was reaching for the bottom of the untucked shirt, I looked up and realized I was being watched by a man about my age, whose eyes were clearly egging me on to finish my task. If the message that the eyes were telegraphing to me was mistaken, his intention was clear when he nudged his head in the queen's direction. His body language said, "Do it; c'mon, do it!"

So I did it. And I felt so good, too. Apparently my admirer agreed, because he gave me a very subtle thumbs-up signal, followed by a mischievous smile.

I gathered up a few things and started to make my way out of the room, when my partner in crime got up from his cushy chair and grabbed me by the arm. I thought that he was going to arrest me.

"This meeting will be over in half an hour," he whispered in my ear. "I really would like to see you!" he said, grabbing my arm again, but this time his grip was surprisingly tender yet had just enough force to make it clear that passion was also at play here.

His eyes locked with mine, then traveled down deep inside my soul. The way he looked at me made me feel that I was about to experience the vapors.

I left the room, stealing one last glance at my mystery admirer. He was looking right at me still. I closed the door behind me and stood there taking short breaths and smiling idiotically to myself.

God, did this feel good!

When the meeting broke up in Rex's office, I was conveniently sitting in what was left of the living room, reading an issue of *Party Production Weekly*. Mr. Mystery Man would have to pass my chair in order to reach the lunch that Vince was setting up on the porch outside.

Sure enough, he approached my chair, stopped, and kneeled at the arm and pulled the magazine gently downward to reveal the surprised face I had practiced for the past half hour.

"Listen, if we're going to hit it off, you've got to realize I wasn't born yesterday," he said like James Bond to an archenemy in one of his verbal cat-and-mouse games. We each knew what the other was up to. It was just a question of who would blink first. Luckily, *he* did. "No one in their right mind would read something so boring unless they absolutely *had* to. My name's Marc. Marc Baldwin."

"No, it's really fascinating! I didn't know there were so many types of confetti!" I said, offering my hand to shake. "Robert Wilsop."

He wasn't pretty-boy handsome—a relief on my part— but solid and wholesome. Brown hair, about average height, blue eyes, and with a teddy-bear-like cuteness. In fact, he kind of reminded me of me. I skated past the narcissistic implications of dating myself (something Michael Stark would do if he could) and pushed further.

"So how long will you be in Palm Springs?" he asked.

"Marc, if we're going to hit it off, remember that I wasn't born yesterday, either. Your question sounds like a pickup line."

"That's because it is," Marc added.

This was too weird. I fought tooth and nail against coming to the White Party/Red Party with Michael, and now no one was going to drag me away from this event for all the money on God's green earth. We were like two femme fatales (is there an equivalent for a male femme fatale? An *homme* fatale? A drag queen?) bantering with smart-aleck questions and responses learned from some tough scrapes of a life living by your wits on the streets of New York. I loved it!

"Well, what are you waiting for?" I asked. "Aren't you going to pick up me up?" I quipped.

To my surprise, he did just that—picked me up. He wasn't Charles Atlas, but he scooped me up with surprising ease and carried me outside. I, of course, protested and laughed my darn-fool head off. He approached the table that had been set for lunch, and then continued past it, making me wonder where he was taking me in front of all these other people. He walked to the edge of the pool and threw me in. I hit the water like the asteroid that destroyed the dinosaurs, sank under, then popped to the surface like a champagne cork, spitting a stream of water for effect. Marc just stood there at the edge of the pool, then jumped in right after me, resurfaced like a horny submarine, and kissed me like Burt Lancaster in *From Here to Eternity*. This promised to be even better than my last relationship, to Count Siegfried von Schmidt—a long story. Don't even ask.

We carried on like lovesick schoolboys, ignoring the crowd,

who pretended to ignore us. Marc eventually loosened his mouth's grip on mine and suggested that we get out, dry off, and join the others for lunch.

Marc stripped my clothes off and wrapped a towel around me, then did the same to himself. We exchanged small talk and knowing glances as we drew near the table and sat down. Vince was ever the gracious hostess.

"Just grab a place at the table, guys. I've got drinks and appetizers to tide you over while I fire up the grill for the chicken."

Michael had apparently joined Rex's crew and was the first to speak.

"Well, if you two are through fornicating in the pool that others have to swim in!" he said, pointing an accusing finger at the two of us.

Michael was defaulting to his usual juvenile personality whenever a man didn't fall head over heels for him. What bugged me most was the fact that Megaslut Michael was pointing a moral finger at me. It was like Dean Martin lecturing on the evils of drink.

"Michael, I can't believe that you're lecturing me about public displays of affection when I know for a fact that just last week you went dancing at Texture clothed merely in trash bags."

Michael looked at me in horror as if I'd had the gall to consider his sartorial garb questionable. "Hey, my costume was a big success," he reminded me.

"Michael, I thought that the message conveyed by your outfit was redundant," I said, lobbing a mental grenade across the table in his direction. "Oh, and since we're on the subject of trash, I saw you get your butt beat last night."

Michael looked at me quizzically. "I didn't leave the door to the casita open, did I?"

"No, I mean your debut on the silver screen. *Caned and Able?*"

"Is that the one where I'm taken to this abandoned bomb shelter by six California Highway Patrol cops and forced to lick their motorcycles clean?"

"No, but now that you mentioned it, you will have to tell me about that one some snowy Christmas Eve. No, this is the one where Corporal Punishment discovers that there's cum on your combat boots, and he wants to know how it got there."

"Oh, yeah, *that* one." Michael swooned.

"*That* one? I thought you said you did only an occasional cameo role."

"I've done several now. But I really excel where my butt plays center role."

"I'm feeling in love right now. I won't even touch that line, Michael."

"Oh, stop being so puritanical, Robert. I've been a butt model in lots of flicks. Did you like my butt in *Caned and Able*?" Michael asked proudly, as if I spent each night watching gay porn movies about corporal punishment.

"So I suppose you let some guy dressed in military BDUs whip the hell out of your butt?"

"No, not mine," Michael explained. "My butt was the one you see before they began the caning session. When it came time to whip, they brought out a stunt butt. They cut the camera, I walk out, and the guy who really takes the caning takes my place."

"Michael, you're rich. Why do you do these movies when you have a butt-load of money? No pun intended."

"Robert, for the millionth time, my *mother* has the money. And she dribbles it out as she extracts concessions out of me, one by one, like some insidious torture. So I have to make some money on the side because I can't live on forty thousand a month. It's too confining."

I interrupted. "Concessions? What concessions? I can't imagine you changing your behavior for anyone in the world." I'm sorry, but it was true.

"My mother is constantly trying to get me to cut back on my spending!"

"I hate to agree with your mother on anything, but she's right. You spend like the CFO of a crooked Dallas savings and loan."

Michael looked like I had just taken an unflattering photo of him for *Out* magazine, but said nothing. After all, there was nothing he could say. Michael was trashier than the Staten Island landfill and damned proud of it.

Rex interrupted our derailed train of conversation. "Vince, I'll go start the grill while you bring the appetizers and drinks out."

Vince looked puzzled, then spoke. "Oh . . . well . . . thanks, Rex!"

I looked around the table and helped myself to a glass of wine after Vince brought out a magnificent collection of chardonnays. Small talk started around the table and continued politely. I sat there smiling, not knowing anyone there save Michael, Rex, and Vince—and now, thankfully, Marc. He saw my discomfort and began a round of introductions.

"Robert, Michael, this is—" he began, but was interrupted by a huge explosion off to the side of the pool. We all jumped like hypercaffeinated rabbits, and Rex, who was walking toward us at the moment all hell busted loose, hit the pool deck like a trained Marine.

It seemed like an eternity before anyone left their crouching positions to see what had happened. As we got over our shock, we turned to see Rex getting up, blood streaming from his elbows, knees, and chin. It wasn't a pretty sight, but neither was what was behind him: what was left of the stainless (and imaginably expensive) built-in outdoor grill was engulfed in flames.

"Boy, Vince should go easy on the jalapeños," I joked, trying to relieve the graveness of the situation.

No response. Everyone was too stunned. Vince, always

the restorer of order, motioned for me to go out and help Rex up while he ran inside and got a fire extinguisher. "I've already called the police and the fire department," he said over his shoulder.

I ran to help Rex up and steady him. I immediately saw that he was crying uncontrollably. I didn't know what to do, so I put my arms around him, his waterworks running onto my shirt like the East River. As he sobbed and sobbed, Vince ran by, stopping to pat Rex on the head with a "there, there" moment of tender sympathy, then dashed to the grill, trained the nozzle of the extinguisher on the flame-broiled grill, and unleashed a torrent of white, gassy blast, putting the flames out in a matter of a few seconds. The grill looked like it had been hit by a Scud missile; its twisted lid lay some distance away at the bottom of the pool. The pool deck and even parts of the yard were scattered with pieces of chicken. It never rains in California in the summer, they say, but sometimes you can get a brief shower of chicken. Followed by a downpour on your shoulder from a big, strong man.

I continued to hold Rex for some time, that is, until the tremors from his sobbing stopped. I helped him over to the lunch table, where he sat down. Michael, true to form, didn't lift a finger to help.

Vince examined the grill fully, checking to make sure the fire was completely out. Then he put the extinguisher down and joined us. "Rex, I'll go get some disinfectant for those cuts. Maybe he should have a glass of wine just to calm things a bit," he suggested before he clinked and clanked into the house, his body jewelry bobbing back and forth in the sun like a dozen sailboats in a sea of flesh.

"I am not going to let those sons of bitches scare me out of the greatest coup of my life! Over my dead body!" Rex declared emphatically, banging his fist on the table for extra emphasis.

The guy sure loved banging his fist on tables.

The bitchy queen, whose name I was about to learn in a

matter of seconds, peered over at Rex as if he were a pathetic fool and said, "Over your dead body? My goodness, Rex, wise up. I think that's *their* plan!"

"My God, Colorado, you can be so cold sometimes—no, make that *all* the time!" Marc shouted angrily at the puff adder in his tacky clothing.

"My dear, I'm only saying what seems obvious to everyone here at the table. You're going to fault me for telling the truth?" he hissed back at Marc.

"Colorado, shut the fuck up, will ya?" Marc fired back. "No one wants to hear your goddamned bitchy comments right now."

Colorado looked surprised that anyone on this earth not wearing a crown should talk to him in this manner. He folded his arms, lit another cigarette, and poured himself another glass of wine.

Colorado is what Monette called a human Cuisinart—a bitchy queen who will slice and dice anyone unfortunate enough to step in the way of the whirling blades of her tongue. This one was a doozy. His short hair was dyed that ashen dog-doo white that even Annie Lennox abandoned a decade ago. Although the rest of humanity had moved past Y2K years ago, Colorado still put styling mousse in his hair in order to punk it up on top. He seemed completely unaware that the hairdo of the moment was the circuit-boy close-crop with the tiny Pee-Wee Herman flip in the front. Colorado wore at least a dozen gold neck chains dangling various pendants and an unbuttoned microfiber short-sleeved shirt in Day-Glo colors, complimented by microfiber red pants. It looked like he bought his wardrobe at McDonald's. This was no Hawaiian-shirt-wearing queen who would don funny hats in gay bars on Easter Sunday and hurl catty insults at others. This queen was as deadly as a coral snake—and dressed like one, too. I suppose the garish colors Colorado wore were an attempt to get attention from a world still clinging mercilessly to black, but I noticed that nature also colored its most lethal creations brightly as a warning to others. Why is it that people never see these unmistakable don't-touch signs?

While Marc's angry outburst had temporarily shut Colorado up, I knew it wouldn't last long. The tongue that tasted blood would soon be out for more.

Vince soon returned and began pampering Rex's battle scars with disinfectant and bandages—just about the same time that three police cars came screaming in through the open gates of the compound, followed by a huge fire truck, its sirens wailing like an opera diva with a too-small dressing room. Kathleen Battle to the rescue.

Within minutes the police were swarming over the grounds, while the firemen examined the grill like they would a routine car-becue on the freeways of nearby Los Angeles. They poked the grill, examining its innards, trying to figure out what sent those flightless chicken breasts into orbit.

While two of the policemen talked to the firemen—whom, I noticed, Michael was watching intently—the third came up to Rex and sat down next to him. It was none other that Sergeant Big Arms.

"Someone's trying to scare the shit of out of you, huh? Third time's a charm?" he said, actually getting a few laughs out of the table, whereas a few minutes ago my little joke had produced none. I guess it's all in the timing.

Of course, you're more likely to get a laugh—or anything you want—if you're a bona fide cop wearing a uniform that clings tighter to your bruiser body than Saran Wrap. Having a rather substantial tattoo on a bicep the size of most people's head will get you a few coerced laughs, numerous dates, or a Mercedes SUV.

"Scare me? They just tried to kill me!" Rex stammered. "But I'm not giving in . . . never."

"Mr. Gifford, I don't think that whoever is behind this is trying to kill you . . . yet. Kill you, and they have nothing to leverage. No one's going to pay them if they kill the goose that lays the golden eggs, if you follow."

While Sergeant Big Arms' conclusion seemed to make us feel that murder had been again forestalled, it sent a chill up my spine that perhaps attempt number four would be successful. I began wondering if there were any rooms available at the Motel 6 down the road.

"Mr. Gifford," Sergeant Big Arms continued, "I believe that these attempts on your life are just that—attempts. They may seem well planned, but to tell you the truth, they're sloppy. Rolling a boulder at you? C'mon. And the palm tree? If they wanted you dead, they wouldn't miss. These attempts are meant to scare you into paying them off. Plus, if they murder you, they're facing first-degree murder charges, which are a lot more serious than trying to extort money, no matter how large the figure."

The table, who listened with rapt attention, seemed to feel a little better upon hearing Sergeant Big Arms' theory—like a turkey discovering that Thanksgiving was still three weeks away.

Sargeant Big Arms continued. "I'm going to have an officer on your grounds for the next few days. Twenty-four-hour protection—starting right now."

"Starting now?" Rex asked with strained elation.

Having a cop on the grounds, I surmised, would certainly put a damper on nude sunbathing and screwing poolside. But I was wrong about Rex's hesitation.

"That makes me feel a lot safer, Sergeant," Rex confessed, "but you must keep this a secret. I can't have this leaking out to my competition, or it could ruin me!"

"We'll keep as low a profile as possible, but we want your attacker to know that we're here."

"I appreciate your help, Sergeant. My associates and I have a lot of work to do before the Red Party opens on Thursday. My associates," he said, sweeping his hand toward the gang seated at the table, "won't have trouble getting in and out of the compound, will they?"

"No, the only one we want to prevent getting in is your assailant," Sergeant Big Arms commented. "Anyone wanting to enter the grounds will be searched and must be okayed before they're allowed to enter. Feel better?"

Rex looked immensely relieved. "Much! Now maybe we can get our minds back on throwing the greatest party the world has ever known."

Rex's associates applauded mildly, their enthusiasm tempered by a fireman who approached us with a worried look on his face and a sorry-looking piece of black pipe in his hands.

"So what do we have here, Jim?" Sergeant Big Arms asked.

"I'd like to know how old this grill is," Jim said.

Sergeant Big Arms turned to Rex, who turned to Vince for the answer.

"Rex, we just got that put in last fall, didn't we?" Vince asked.

"It seems like so long ago. Yes, I guess you're right. The first meal you grilled on it was for Halloween." After determining the age of the grill, Rex looked up at the fireman. "Why? Does it matter?" he asked.

"A great deal. If you had told me that the grill was, say, eight years old, I'd probably say that the desert heat and lack of humidity had dried out the propane supply hose, which leaked gas into the compartment beneath the grill until enough of it escaped and came in contact with the flames above and kapow!" he said, waving his arms skyward in imitation of the grill and the chicken.

"Now that you know that the grill was almost new, what would you say then?"

The fireman answered without having to think about his answer. "That it was tampered with."

Vince, who seemed to be fighting the obvious truth almost as energetically as Rex, searched for a logical explanation for exploding outdoor grills—besides extortion or murder. "But how do you know that it wasn't improperly installed? Or maybe the hose was loose or something."

"Because these propane tanks are now built so they don't release gas unless the hose is fastened tightly to the tank."

"Maybe the tank was leaky."

"Nope," said the fireman, again without an ounce of doubt.

"How do you know?" Vince asked again. "I mean, don't get me wrong Mr., er . . ."

"Bud."

"Thank you—Bud. I'm not questioning your training. I just want to understand what's going on here."

"Me, too. I wouldn't be standing here in ninety-degree heat in these overalls unless me and my buddies were after the same thing."

"Oh, I think you look wonderful in your overalls," Michael added, then under his breath, but not so low that those seated near him could not hear, "which I'd love to be all over me!"

The fireman—excuse me, Bud—smiled at the first part of Michael's comment, ignored the second part (which you could tell he heard), then continued. "If you look at this delivery hose, you can see that it's burnt more in this area than the other lengths, leading us to conclude that . . . ?" Bud asked as if we were supposed to supply the answer.

"Because it's made of a more flammable material," came one answer.

"Because it was nearer the fire," came another.

While these answers were fallacious, Michael's was so far off that it was no wonder that his mother had to keep donating building funds to the private college Michael attended so he could earn his degree. Or should I say, *buy* it.

"Because black absorbs heat and that made it the hottest. I know this for a fact since I wear a lot of black, and it can get really hot in summer!"

Even Bud was stunned by Michael's answer. Bud stared up into the clear blue sky and probably hoped that Michael wasn't a member of any engineering team that built bridges and tunnels in California. "No to all your answers."

Before Bud could give us the correct answer, I, a person who knew that yak milk was pink, as well as a million other useless facts, blurted out my answer.

"That spot that you pointed out was where the gas leaked from the hose, so when the compartment caught fire, that spot burned the longest, so it's charred the most. In fact," I said, getting up and examining the hose up close, "this weird ridge on that part of the hose indicates that the hose was probably slit with a sharp object, so when the hose caught fire, the portion on each side of the slit melted and curled back, leaving a deeper ridge in the hose than the slit itself."

Bud looked amazed. "That's exactly right. You can go sit down now—this is my show and I don't share the spotlight easily. Plus, this is definitely a tough audience," Bud said.

We had a fireman with a sense of humor. I was impressed.

"This man is correct. The hose was cut here in the middle, and I think that it was done deliberately."

"And your reason?" Sergeant Big Arms inquired.

"Because if the hose had been damaged when it was installed, you would've had an explosion long before now. And I suppose that you use the grill frequently?"

"All the time," Vince confessed.

"So there. And as for the propane tank, it sits in a separate compartment than the hose, and it didn't detonate—which, if it did, you'd have known it. If these tanks get very rusty, they can leak, but yours is brand-new. Leaks also leave a frosty residue near the leak, none of which is present on your tank. End of investigation. Sergeant, I'll give you a copy of my report in a few minutes and you can add it to yours."

Bud went back to the grill to check over a few things and add it to his report. Michael decided to get up from his place at the table and seat himself next to me.

"Yes, Michael?" I asked, knowing exactly what he was up to. "You saw that my knowledge impressed Bud, and you want me to use my in to Bud—which is tenuous at best—so you can do a quick pressure test on his hose, right?"

"Something that like," he assented.

"I can't believe you, Michael!" I said in an agitated whisper. "You come here because you said Rex was sex personified. Then, as soon as you arrive at Rex's house, you start salivating all over Sergeant Big Arms. Now you've got your sights set on Bud. I can't believe your lack of morals. What happened to Rex?"

"All this murder stuff is becoming a real hard-off. Plus, he cries too much."

There was Michael's theory to dating. His interest in certain men lasted about as long as an ejaculation. As Mae West once said, find 'em, fool 'em, and forget 'em.

"So what's the big deal with the fireman? I thought cops were your fetish."

"No, *all* guys in uniforms—unless it's a Salvation Army uniform. Cops, firemen, garbage men."

"Garbage men?" I asked, completely astonished. "What's so sexy about that?"

"The orange uniforms, stupid!" he replied.

I think that the kettle just got called black by the pot.

"Michael, I can't find anything even remotely erotic about a guy who has three teeth and smells like certain parts of New Jersey."

"Jesus, Robert. I wouldn't have sex with someone like that! God! No, when I get a guy with a killer body, I make him wear the orange uniform. That's sexy."

"But the uniform seems so unnecessary, Michael. You could put a guy with a body like that into burgundy polyester Sans-a-Belt pants and he'd still look sexy."

"You just can't understand the erotic power of a uniform until you wear one. Give it a try sometime; you don't know what you're missing. That's why I have an entire closet full of uniforms."

"Before I met you, Michael, I never would have given cops a second glance. But now I catch myself staring at them all the time. I guess something of you has rubbed off on me—and I don't need a cream to treat it," I said, laughing.

"Very funny. See, if you listen to me you start expanding your sexual horizons. You need to stop being so literal about things. That's why the most erotic encounter you had was with barnyard animals."

"It wasn't about bestiality!" I exclaimed. "I had sex in a hayloft!"

"But that proves my point exactly. You think a hayloft is way-out sexy? C'mon! When it comes to wild sex, you have to think outside the hayloft. Get your mind going. Have sex in a church, on top of a skyscraper, underwater, or tied up to a child's merry-go-round at a public park—use your imagination!"

"What was that last one?!" I demanded.

"Nothing," Michael said. "Could we change the subject?"

"Can we leave Michael's 'Little Shop of Whores' and get back to Rex and his problems?"

"Oh, God!" Michael whined. "We all have to sit and listen to his problems again. This is not my idea of a fun vacation!"

For once, I had to agree with Michael.

*   *   *

Once the police and firemen left, we were all sitting around the table feeling lower than Death Valley.

No one wanted to speak or cared to. But Colorado, never one to pass up the chance to twist the knife after it was already squarely between two ribs, started by lobbing a live grenade on the table, then lit a cigarette.

"Well, I guess that someone has crashed the party and that someone's name is Death."

Big strong, strapping Rex burst into loud sobs again. "I don't want to die!" Rex wailed, turning the waterworks into a flood of biblical proportions.

None of us knew quite what to do, so we looked down at our still-empty plates and wondered if Death had indeed taken his place at the lunch table, and if so, then he could've had the decency to pick up a bucket of fried chicken on the way.

Just then, Death did indeed crash the party, when two meaty hands the size—and tanned color—of two hams landed on either side of Rex's neck and looked like they were going for his neck.

"DEATH!" Rex yelled so loudly and suddenly that Michael dropped his wineglass.

Rex turned around to find that Death didn't look like, well death, and that Death was actually quite healthy. In fact, Death seemed to lift weights on a daily basis.

"Oh, Leo, thank God it's you!" Rex said, began blubbering, then burst into tears again.

"What is going on here?" Leo said like a person who had no idea what had gone on at the compound for the past hour. "You all look like you just came back from a funeral."

More bawling. I tried to be as understanding as I could. Rex was definitely hurting, but his crying was starting to annoy me a little bit, too. Was I becoming as shallow as Michael?

Marc took Leo aside and explained the latest events at

Casa Rex—or was it Casa Wrecks? I could see Marc pointing to various people around the table and then at the grill, his arms flying up in the air very similar to the way Bud's had done to explain the explosion. Once Leo was brought up to date, they both returned to the table with weak smiles that they hoped would pass off onto the rest of us. But as Bud had commented earlier, this was one tough audience.

Vince popped his head out of the house and told us that he'd have an improvised lunch ready in about twenty minutes. As my stomach prepared itself for lunch, my eyes were gazing at our newest arrival, Leo. Everything Vince had said about him was true. Leo's polo shirt could barely contain his massive chest and arms, his neck was as big around as my thighs, and the shorts he was wearing were worn along the seams where his thighs rubbed together. The things that you have to put up with to have the body of Hercules.

But after you got past staring at his oversize body, the next thing that struck you was his hair—and gold jewelry. Leo's hair poofed up into some kind of one-piece pompadour that results from combing fine, black hair backwards and spraying it in place with tons of shellac. The jewelry was no better—he could have been a used-car salesman in a former life.

Figuring that Michael's bubble had been burst, I leaned over and offered my condolences.

"Sorry about the hair and the jewelry, Michael. It's like putting a polyester tube top that says 'I'm with stupid' on Michelangelo's *David*."

Without taking his eyes off Leo's arms, Michael muttered out of the corner of his mouth, "You think I'm going to let a little tackiness get between me and those muscles? You gotta be crazy! I can always have him take the Sarah Coventry off."

"Yeah, but what about the hair-don't?"

"I'll just put a hood on him."

"You're joking!" I muttered back.

"No, I always carry one. I run into a lot of guys with great bodies but with faces straight from a kennel club...."

"... or the hair is French poodle," I said, pointing at Leo.

"Exactly," Michael continued. "I put a hood on them and I can go on imagining that they're gorgeous."

As with most of the stunts that Michael pulled in this world, I should not have been surprised—but I was. Maybe that was my attraction to Michael—there was something new all the time. "Your dates actually let you do this and they don't complain?" I asked.

"Oh, sure; in fact, some of them don't want me to take it off of them—usually the ones who don't want me to put it on them at first."

"Michael, if you don't mind, I'm going to hitch a ride on the mother ship and get back to reality. Plus, I've got my sights set on Marc, so don't get any ideas."

Michael's ego seemed to give off a malevolent aura, as if I had just asked him to wear something from the Liz Claiborne collection for men. "Robert, you can rest your pretty little head. I am not the least bit interested in Marc—he reminds me too much of you."

Yes, dear reader, I was used to Michael insulting me to my face, but I decided to let his comment slide for two reasons. One, I was head over heels in love with Marc and didn't care about anything Michael said, and two, as I often did, I would put Michael's transgression on the huge tote board inside my brain, to be given the appropriate penalty when the opportunity presented itself.

"You know," Michael whispered in confidence to me, "this place is getting me down—and hungry. I'm going to take Rex's car and get something to eat downtown. You know any place good to eat in this town?"

Fate, like many things in this world, is a very tricky thing. Sometimes Fate is so against you that you just have to bend over and take it like a man. But every once in a while, she smiles down on you and tosses you a bone. This was one such moment.

I leaned over and took one tick mark off Michael's tote board.

"Bathsheba. I hear the food is great!" I whispered excitedly to Michael.

5

That's the Great Thing About Wearing Red—It Doesn't Show Blood!

Lunch was uneventful, if you don't count the fact that Rex fought back tears most of his way through the meal, Colorado got off a few more parting shots throughout the meal, and Leo threatened to knock Colorado's front teeth "so far back in your head, you'll have to stick a toothbrush up your ass to brush your teeth." Other than that, it was just your ordinary, everyday lunch.

After lunch I called Monette, but she wasn't there, so I left a message.

"Monette, I've landed right in the middle of a mystery here, entitled *Death By Barbecuing*—no, make that *Martha Stewart Serves Up Death*. I'll tell you the details later. Call me."

Leo was throwing a party at his house later that night, so in the meantime, I decided to spend the afternoon walking through downtown Palm Springs. Rex's house wasn't that far from all the action, so to avoid running over errant dildoes, I walked.

The temperature was hovering around eighty-eight degrees, but the air was drier than a gin martini, so it didn't have the oppressive humidity (and the aromas) of New York summers. The town (you couldn't really call it a city) was filling up fast with circuit boys. The desert was in bloom with brightly colored outfits stretched tightly over gym bodies, carefully tanned by countless hours spent in ultraviolet-ray cancer boxes. All this artifice was why I hadn't wanted to come to the Red Party, and I began to wonder why I had let Michael talk me into this. But moments later, I realized that I wouldn't have met Marc if I had stayed back in the city.

I poked in a few shops, then stopped at a Starbucks and had iced coffee outdoors under the spray of the outdoor cooling system. I gazed at passersby, amazed that gay men and women were everywhere. I was told by Rex that Palm Springs was becoming the number one place for gays to move to. I didn't doubt that claim one bit, allowing for some overinflation by the deluge of lesbians already here for the Dinah Shore Classic, and the gay men pouring in for the White and Red Parties. As I sipped my coffee, a drag queen who announced herself as Petal Luma stopped in front of her captive audience at Starbucks and performed *You Can't Catch a Man with a Gun* to the boom box she daintily placed on the sidewalk. She sashayed back and forth on the sidewalk, lip-synching and firing cap pistols into the air at appropriate moments during her song. All in all, it was a very professional number. When Petal Luma was finished, she took off her Sunday-church-testifying-for-Jesus hat and held it out for donations. I got up from my table and threw ten dollars into the hat, prompting a sly wink and a Marilyn Monroe airblown kiss from Petal. What could I say? I loved drag queens. Plus, her version of street entertainment had one small advantage over the kind I was familiar with in New York: it was better than another goddamn mime.

I walked around town for an hour or so more and felt that it would be nice to take a swim and a nap before the party at Leo's house that evening. Rex had gone with Vince to supervise the Red Party setup, so I had the house to myself.

No one was in the pool, so I had an afternoon of complete luxury all to myself. I was lying on a float, with a gimlet in a martini glass sitting at the edge of the pool, under an improvised shade to keep it frosty cold. I was staring up past the surrounding palm-tree tops and into the endless blue sky when I felt that there was something that I was supposed to do. I closed my eyes and saw a photocopier floating in the sky and wondered what it meant. Perhaps it was one of those inexplicable mental images that floated in front of your eyes and you never knew why—like seeing an Airedale or an eggplant. Perhaps it was a portentous sign from the oracle at Delphi. Perhaps it just meant that I had had one too many gimlets.

Then it occurred to me what I was supposed to be doing. Monette had asked me to rummage through Rex's office to see if I could find anything suspicious. There wasn't a better time, either. No one was around, so I could lock the door to Rex's office and pretend that it was taking me a long time to change my clothes.

I jumped out of the pool, dried off hurriedly, and ran to Rex's office, where I locked the door and glanced around the room, wondering aloud that if tasked with rifling an office, where did one begin to rifle?

I sat at Rex's desk and started pulling the top drawers open but found little more than office supplies, an odd photo or two, and one condom. The bottom drawers were locked. The shelves above Rex's desk were filled with row upon row of photo books of Rex's past parties, trade magazines, and supplier catalogs. Nothing suspicious there. I scanned the room again. The computer! That was where Rex probably kept his correspondences, his accounts, and, perhaps, secret information.

I pushed the *on* button on his powerful-looking computer, which welcomed me in a loud voice and roared to life. I cringed, worried that someone had come back to the house and heard me start the damn thing up, but the house remained silent. After the computer booted itself up, I sat there staring at the screen, looking at a multitude of files, wondering which to open first. I looked down the long list and then found one that said *Jobs*. I opened that folder and found another list of folders inside, but one was clearly marked *Red Party*. Now we were getting somewhere. I found a list of documents that probably would've taken a year to comb through, so I just double-clicked on one marked *Catering*. The document took its good old time to open, and when it finally presented its contents to me, the worst thing that could possibly happen, happened. The doorknob jiggled violently, and someone tried to open the door.

Fuck! Fuck, fuck, fuck, fuck, fuck, fuck, fuck, fuck! I was about to be caught red-handed.

"Robert?" came the voice on the other side of the door.

"Rex?" I said, hoping that it was not, in fact, Rex.

"I'm sorry, Robert." Without a shadow of a doubt, it was Rex's distinctive voice. "I didn't know you were in there. I need to get something from my desk."

Think fast. Say something stupid! "Ah, I'm changing. I'll be out in a few minutes," I managed to squeeze out of my hyperventilating lungs.

"That's fine," Rex replied. "I'll be out in the kitchen."

Silence. Thank God he left. Or was he standing there with one ear to the door, wondering why his computer was on? Had he heard the guilty tone in my voice? He was a savvy businessman, so did his list of management skills include smelling bullshit from thieving employees and cheating suppliers? There was no time to shut down his computer the proper way, so I dove underneath his desk and tore at the spaghetti-mess of wires that connected his computer to the surge protector. It was the old horror-movie cliché. The hero, being chased by a killer, finds himself at a locked door with the key. In the excitement, he acts like a virgin groom on his wedding night: no matter how frantically he tries, he just can't get his key in the hole. I got so flustered, I had to go back to the computer and retrace the power cord until I could find the plug. Four hours later—or so it seemed—I yanked the plug from the surge protector. I waited a few seconds and was about to plug the computer back in when I noticed a folder that had fallen behind Rex's desk and probably been forgotten long ago. I pulled it out and stared at it. It was marked *A.D.*—after death. This was important. Inside was just one piece of paper. It was a drawing of a building—an extraordinary building in the shape of a pyramid. Below the exotic building were just two words: *Butia A.D.*

I had no idea what the drawing was for, but it seemed significant to me by the way it practically vibrated in my hand. Maybe it was a prop for a party Rex had handled or was proposing, but there was no time to figure that out. I plugged the computer back in and hustled it over to Rex's copier and copied the drawing, intending to put the drawing back in its graveyard of forgotten documents. I did do one smart thing: I turned on the clock radio and set it to a station where festive music played.

The doorknob jangled again. *Fuck, fuck, fuck, fuck, fuck!*

"You're still in there, Robert?"

No, asshole, I thought. *I let all of the air out of me like a cartoon character and slipped under the doorway, leaving the door locked with no one inside.* What I said was something different altogether. "Sorry it's taking me so long. Just a second." I grabbed the photocopy of the drawing, threw the original behind the desk, and slipped on a pair of underwear. I then walked leisurely to the door so that I wouldn't be out of breath when I opened it, not wanting it to look like I had been helping Mr. Happy throw up via my right hand and a porno tape from Rex's collection.

Rex smiled when he entered the room, carrying a very large briefcase. He walked over to his desk, which made me shiver at the thought that I had left some telltale clue of my clumsy investigation.

Nothing yet. So far, so good.

Then, however, my alibi started coming apart faster than the Enron Corporation. The tune that the clock radio had been humming stopped, and an obnoxious announcer started screaming like a baritone banshee, "*Sabado, sabado, sabado . . .*"

I was too scared to concentrate on what was being said, but I did manage to catch the words "*desfile*" and "*Santo Louis.*"

Rex looked at me strangely. I wondered why.

"You understand Spanish?" he probed.

"Oh, yes," I said mistakenly. "I just wanted get a taste of the culture," I said, beaming with international enthusiasm.

"I speak a little bit, too. Let me hear you translate," Rex asked, with eyes that said, "you liar."

"Well, I'm a little rusty. He seems to be talking about El Salvador and all the problems they're having there. Some woman has been having these feelings, you know, like seeing a vision of Saint Louis—no, the woman who saw the vision is from Saint Louis."

Rex waited until I had dug my grave deeper, jumped in, and pulled the dirt in on top of me. "I guess you understand the Castilian Spanish, because the announcer said that there's a parade this Saturday at Saint Louis Church."

I turned the radio off, explaining that I'd "had enough music right now."

Cher could not have felt more exposed. Rex looked at me without saying a word, expecting me to break down in a torrent of confessions. But none came, just a silence that was so profound, I could hear the blood pounding through the veins in my head—which, coincidentally, were about to explode. He continued to look straight into my eyes, then turned his head toward a sound that was coming from behind him. It was the fan on the copier, still whirring from one goddamn photocopy. I hadn't noticed it before, when the radio was on.

Fuck, fuck, fuck! Think fast again—how did spies do it?

"Oh, you're probably wondering why I was using your copier—I hope you don't mind!" I said with a politeness that would have charmed the pants off a celibate eunuch. "I was making a photocopy of my ass, you see. My friend Monette and I play these practical jokes on each other—just ask Michael—and I was going to sit on the glass, copy my ass—hey, that rhymes—and fax it to Monette, who is staying here in Palm Springs. She would really get a kick out of it."

I finished my story, but Rex didn't seem like he was buying it. Just when I thought he was about to order the Gestapo to come in and arrest me, Vince stuck his head in the door and announced that dinner was ready.

And just like that, I was off the hook for the time being.

Dinner that night would have made a person with bipolar disorder feel right at home. On the one side, were Michael and I. Even though it was about as easy as rolling a four-hundred-pound boulder uphill on roller skates, I tried to keep the conversation going. Michael, in his usual state of self-absorption, chattered ceaselessly, expounding on the marvels of Palm Springs' attractions, but from the smile on his face and the energy that radiated from it, it was clear that he had been trolling around the Sunny Dunes area—a place where dozens of gay hotels stood elbow to elbow. (Michael told me that during the evening, men cruise up and down the area, going from one hotel to another in an endless parade of gay men that left a permanent slick of testosterone on Warm Sands Road. He even told me about an incident he caused two years ago, when he was staying in the area. Michael, always buff and always tanned, strode out onto the streets wearing only a minuscule thong. His presence on the street caused two elderly gay men in Cadillacs to collide head-on at five miles per hour. Michael refers to the incident as "When Queens Collide"—a loving reference to the play by the late, great Charles Ludlam.)

Rex and Vince represented the dour side of dinner. Rex

was a mess of contradictory emotions, looking like he was about to shatter at any moment, while his face emitted long, slow waves of despair like a weary ocean. Vince, who was usually rather chipper, peered at Rex with grave concern.

Dinner was cleared, and we prepared for the trek over to Leo's house for the Red Party kickoff. All the vendors, suppliers, and associates of T-Rex Productions were invited, and Michael said it would be one of the biggest parties of the weekend.

Michael might have been correct in his estimation, but I had the gnawing suspicion that *notorious* was the word that would describe it best.

Gay society, while appearing monolithic to the casual observer, is actually complex and fractured—more so than the San Andreas fault. In addition to gym bunnies, flaming queens, and butch types, we now have bears (hairy, supposedly masculine men), cubs (a smaller version of bears), otters (I will hazard a guess here: furry, lithe, playful young things) and of course, the main attendees of the Palm Springs White Party: circuit boys. This group is made up of gay boys who are, for the most part, young, hairless, buff, and several months behind on their electric bills. But with years of partying under their belts and having passed the dreaded age of thirty, those circuit boys who haven't forsaken weekly body shaves and eight-pack abs and passed into beardom become a new class of gay men: short-circuit boys. Excessive partying and bill-collector dodging have taken a visible toll on these gay men, making them look old before their years and unable to pick up a check at dinner.

From the looks of the crowd filing into Leo's party, we had a bumper crop of gay men who looked like they had more than a little resistance in their wiring.

Michael and I drove up to Leo's mid-century modern house in Vince's car, while Rex and Vince followed in Rex's.

(Rex felt that two cars were better in case Michael and I wanted to stay longer.)

Leo's house was an Alexander, judging from the architect's butterfly roof, which seemed poised for flight at any moment. What amazed me about Palm Springs was how well everyone lived here. For an amount of money that wouldn't even buy a mediocre one-bedroom co-op in New York, people here lived in rambling houses embodying the wacky exuberance of 1950s architecture, complete with pools and stupendous views of the mountains that encircled the town. I'm sure that I was not the first New Yorker to question the wisdom of living in New York, and I'm sure I won't be the last. The relaxed lifestyle, the sheer numbers of gay inhabitants, and the promise of a secluded lifestyle complete with pool and year-round outdoor living, all made Palm Springs a very seductive place.

Being a die-hard modernist, I couldn't wait to see the inside of Leo's place. I was hoping for orange and lime-green walls with Technicolor sailfish leaping over George Nelson Ball wall clocks and welded-metal wall sculptures.

No such luck. Leo's house had been done up in a style I like to call "Archie-Digest." Take classic pieces from the Regency or Empire period, add tired opaque washes and faux animal-print fabrics and throw in about two thousand tortoiseshell tchotchkes, and you have a look that has to be dusted daily, is guaranteed to make guests feel completely uncomfortable, and can be destroyed in just seconds by a spilled glass of anything liquid. Nothing could be more out of place, but it occurred to me that I might be wrong—perhaps Leo's furniture went with his hairdo.

The party was in full swing, with thumping music and hordes of people all dressed in red. From the bar in a corner of the living room, it looked like a red tide bloom had erupted in a shallow sea, leaving desperate fish surfacing and gasping to escape the toxic waters. I saw people in red thongs, red caftans, red Chinese mandarin robes, red leather, red wigs, and one man nude but covered entirely in red paint-on latex, giving him the appearance of a large balloon sculpture. I thought I had seen it all when I spotted a man dressed as a dog, complete with paws, a tail, snout, and floppy ears. He was crawling around the ankles of the partygoers, sniffing their shoes and barking. People laughed at his antics, probably the same way that patrician Romans did as their city was being sacked by the Visigoths.

I threaded my way through the crowd and made my way toward the floor-to-ceiling windows that overlooked the pool. Michael had ditched me at the bar to go off with a severe-looking man with a goatee so pointed, you could open cans with it. So I stood there, looking for Marc, when a shock of red hair grabbed my attention and consequently made me the happiest guy alive.

"Monette!" I shouted through the crowd.

"Robert!" Monette shouted back.

We forged our way across the pulsating crowd in slow motion, like two lovers who hadn't seen each other for decades. The only thing missing was the daisy-covered field.

"I didn't want to let you know I was coming," Monette shouted in my ear. "I wanted to surprise you!"

"You certainly did. I don't really know anyone here, and Michael abandoned me faster than a fag-hag in a gay bar at last call." I was about to tell Monette what was going on at La Casa de Mort when a man came up to me and fastened his lips on mine and dipped me backwards until my head almost touched the floor. I had been dipped!

It was Marc.

Monette pointed toward Marc and asked, "Do you know this guy?"

"I've never seen him in my life," I said.

"We Palm Springians are very friendly," Marc reported.

"What are you waiting for, Robert?" Monette asked in amazement. "Introduce me!"

"Monette, this is Marc. We met this afternoon."

"Glad to meet you, Marc. I'm Monette. Well, well, Robert," Monette commented, making the situation between Marc and me sound dirtier than it was.

"I'm just trying to live up to the lesbian joke," I replied.

"What joke is that?" she asked.

"What does a lesbian bring on a first date?"

"Let me guess, Robert. A U-Haul?"

"Very good, Monette; you receive two hundred dollars and a year's supply of Summer's Eve feminine deodorant spray."

"Robert, that joke is older than Steve and Edie."

"Marc and I just met," I started, "but I'm selling all my things and moving to Palm Springs, where we're going to raise organic Chihuahuas."

"I see," Monette said, pulling thoughtfully at the swirls of her flaming-red mop. "And what was it that brought you two together? The Red Party?"

"No," Marc said, jumping headlong into the conversation. "I think it was assault and battery on a vicious queen who deserved it."

"Anyone I know? George Wayne? Andre Leon Talley?"

"No, Colorado Jackson. He's a party planner and sometimes interior designer."

"You're pulling my five-foot legs," Monette exclaimed, the disbelief showing clearly on her face. "A queen with the name of Colorado Jackson? What does he do—decorate riding stables?"

"You're close. You should see the work he's done. Oh, mercy!" Marc cried with a lisp so heavy, you had to towel yourself off after hearing it. "It makes Leo's house look pretty tame."

"So you assaulted this queen? What did you do? Scratch his eyes out? Loosen the stitches behind his ears and let his face fall back into place?"

"He was purposely dropping cigarette ashes into my luggage, so I sliced up the bottom of his trendy microfiber shirt," I confessed.

"I'm gunna tell," Monette shrilled.

"Marc made me do it," I said, pointing to Marc, who was by now laughing quite hard.

"No I did-ent!" Marc responded, pointing back at me.

I looked over at Marc and realized that of all the qualities I prized in my friends, having a quick and sardonic sense of humor weighed in the heaviest. It's a quality that I got from watching a lot of black-and-white movies as a kid. I couldn't imagine anything more glamorous or sophisticated than William Powell or Myrna Loy standing around a New York penthouse, slinging one-liners and cocktails with equal gusto at platinum blondes and hard-boiled coppers. Those were days that you couldn't bring back, but I felt that at least you could relive those times by whizzing off a good retort in their honor.

"Speaking of the she-devil, there's Colorado now," Marc said, pointing out The Evil One.

True to his reputation, Colorado made his way slowly through the crowd, holding his cigarette out in front of him menacingly enough to make people clear the way for him.

"You know, the more I think about Colorado, the more I realize that Michael has a lot of the same qualities. But how is it that I can tolerate Michael's self-centeredness when Colorado makes you want to pull out a gun and do the world a favor?"

"Probably because while Michael will push people out his way to get somewhere, he doesn't kick them when they're down like Colorado would. You also tolerate him because he lets you use his house on Fire Island and he invites you to a lot of parties."

"That might have a teensy-weensy bit to do with it," I acquiesced. "But remember, I saved his life, Monette. That creates a bond that you just can't break."

Marc looked at me with approving astonishment. I bowed

as humbly as I could. Marc and I liked each other from the start, but with each little complimentary tidbit that we learned about each other, the closer we grew—and we hadn't even known each other twenty-four hours yet.

"Marc, did you see the guy dressed as a dog? Monette, you should've seen it. Puppy paws and nose, ears—the whole shebang."

"I didn't have to see it. I was standing there wondering if I was witnessing the fall of Western civilization when I felt something bumping up against my crotch, and I look down and here's this guy in a dog suit sniffing my vagina and barking. I wanted to kick him, but I'm an animal lover. I swear to the goddess, that bumper sticker is so true."

"Which one is that, Monette?" I inquired.

"The one that says the more I learn about people, the more I love my dog."

"But you don't have a dog," I reminded her.

"I'm about to go and get one—just not one like that one you saw here."

"I hate to tell you, but that dog is David McLeish, the soap opera star, extreme closet case—and the largest investor in T-Rex Productions," Marc said.

Monette and I glanced at each other to see who could have their jaw open the widest.

I spoke first. "He's a soap opera star and he dresses like this in public?"

"Well, first of all, this isn't exactly public. And second, you didn't recognize him, did you?"

"I don't watch soap operas, Marc," I answered.

"Fine, but you didn't recognize him, did you?" Marc pressed on.

"No, and I get your point. It would be difficult to recognize anyone in that getup—unless you were a beagle."

"It's amazing that someone would act like this in public yet act so straight for his fans. In fact, it ticks me off. Hey, why don't we out him?" Monette suggested.

"No, no, no," I replied. "You know what happened to Armistead Maupin when he outed Rock Hudson back in the eighties? He got shit from a lot of gays who said Armistead had no right to do that. Not for me."

"We call him David-on-a-Leash behind his back," Marc responded. "He's invested millions in T-Rex because Rex gives him terrific returns on his money and David doesn't get involved much in the day-to-day. He puts up a lot of money and doesn't interfere, and he gets returns like thirty percent."

"Very impressive. I've got a 401(k) that isn't doing much—maybe I should invest with you guys."

"Sorry, Robert, but the minimum starting investment is five hundred thousand—and I don't think Rex is taking on any more investors until the Red Party is over. This is our biggest gamble, but if it turns out the way we expect, we will be in the big leagues."

As David McLeish came into view again, he was followed by a strikingly handsome man who grabbed David's leash and jerked him back confidently, causing David to lower his tail and come whimpering up to his "trainer" full of remorse. The trainer was wearing skin-tight pants tucked into knee-high boots, with a white button-down shirt and three open buttons (I counted) to give just a peek of a rock-hard chest. I instantly thought, *ringmaster*.

Marc, seeing that Monette and I were watching this spectacle with the intensity of Cher eyeing a comeback vehicle, felt the need to explain further.

"That's his trainer, Hans, from Germany," Marc offered. "He does this full time with David and gets paid quite handsomely."

Both Monette and I forgot completely about David and stood staring at Hans. To think that people did things like this and got paid a lot of money for it. I had heard of outlandish occupations that you and I, dear reader, would kill for. I had read about a guy who retouches impressionist masterpieces, a man in England who thatches roofs the way they have been done for hundreds of years and makes enough to take the summer months off and drive an Italian sports car, and now we had Hans, house-trainer to the stars. Where were the college courses like these when I was at Michigan State University? Huh?

"Uh-oh, here comes more trouble," Marc warned us. "That's Darlene Waldron. She owns the largest circuit party concession, Circuit Toys for Party Boys. She hates Rex and the rest of us because we're giving her some competition. Don't let her appearance fool you—she waits for you to get your guard down and wham!" Marc exclaimed, pounding an imaginary Rex flat in the palm of his hand.

"She doesn't look very intimidating," I countered.

"Just watch this. I'll introduce you," he said, grabbing Darlene lightly by the arm—and I do mean lightly.

Darlene spun around as if she had been grabbed from behind by a mugger. A flash of hatred and anger flooded her rosy, china-doll face and disappeared as quickly as a desert rain. Now you see it, now you don't.

Marc pulled Darlene toward us. "Darlene, I'd like to introduce you to Robert and Monette."

Darlene extended a fragile, lily-white hand and laid it in mine where it remained like a dead sparrow. "Nice to meet you," she said in a voice so soft, it was difficult to hear above the roar of the party.

I shook her hand carefully, taking pains not to crush it. As she introduced herself to Monette, I couldn't help but notice that besides her stature, everything about her was tiny. She wore a petite wristwatch, tiny belt, tiny shoes, a tiny brooch, and she sported a close-cropped hairstyle that made her pointy, henna-red hair seem as if it were in full retreat on her head. I thought it odd that a person so small would work so hard to emphasize her diminutive size; usually it's the other way around. It was as if she wanted to portray herself as vulnerable.

"So," Monette started, "Marc tells me that you own a company that sells circuit party accessories. How interesting! How did you come to be in this business?"

The way Monette said the word *interesting*, I almost believed her. But I could tell that Monette didn't like this woman for some reason and she was putting Darlene on the spot. Darlene seemed to pick up on Monette's energy, because I could see her body stiffen like a cobra, coiling itself before striking.

"I was selling variable annuities for a few years," Darlene began, "but it didn't give me the excitement I needed. I wanted to do something different, you know. I had some gay friends, and they told me that circuit party items were a big business, so I did some research and I opened Circuit Toys."

Monette decided to take one more jab at Darlene. "So, Darlene, did you find that there's a lot of money to be made selling circuit party accessories?"

Darlene looked like a cornered rat. "Could you excuse me?" she said, pulling a cellular phone from her suit pocket and dialing hurriedly. "There's a call I have to make before I forget, sorry. Maybe I'll catch up with you later."

We all watched her walk into the crowd with the unmistakable look of desperation on her face.

Monette, who seemed satisfied in making Darlene squirm and run away, smiled and shook her head. "I get the feeling that that woman would stab someone and sit down and watch television without even feeling a twinge of guilt. Marc, if she's one of Rex's enemies, why in hell is she here?" Monette asked.

"Because Rex invited her—and a lot of other people who are working the White Party," Marc answered.

"Because Rex wanted to keep things light and airy—all the while he's raising the stakes for everyone, right?"

"Kind of like that, Monette," Marc said. "Actually, it's more of a case of keeping your friends close and your enemies even closer. That's how Rex has been so successful: he's got brass balls and he doesn't like to be the first to blink. He can be pretty fearless."

"Until last night," Monette managed to slip in.

"Yes, until last night," Marc conceded.

"I see," Monette replied, which caused Marc to look at her with a don't-tell-me-I-told-you-so look. "Don't get me wrong, Marc; there's nothing wrong with a little competition, but it's something that I don't have a lot of personal experience with. I'm a graphic artist who works for the Endangered Herbs Society of America—I don't have to fend off hordes of people who are trying to take my job."

Marc scanned the revelers for a while and pointed at a squat man with thinning black hair and a face that looked like an overripe red grape about to burst. He must have been from Los Angeles, because he seemed to be always on a cell phone.

"That's Jimmy Garboni, a mafia guy who handles most of the food service jobs and garbage collection in L.A. and the Coachella Valley—or else."

"Food service *and* garbage? I've been to a few parties where it tastes like they got the two mixed up," Monette quipped.

"And over there is Martin Stevers; he's the guy you're supposed to go to when you need sound and electrical systems."

"Now, let me guess here, Marc. Rex chose not to work with Darlene, Jimmy, or Martin, correct?"

"You are correct," Marc replied. "Their bids came in a lot higher than the vendors we're working with. Rex figured that if the Red Party were going to catch on, he'd have to spend his money on the razzle-dazzle and wow everyone. The White Party already has the big-name DJs, but music is music, and if you play it loud enough and keep amazing people, they will come."

I stood there, silently compiling the list of possible threatening suspects—a list that was growing faster than Candy Spelling's Christmas wish list. Let's see: Darlene Waldron, a tiny, birdlike woman with henna-red hair, pointy business suits, and a fake smile that drew her lips so tight, they appeared to stretch around her entire face like pink bands of rubber. Next on the list was Jimmy Garboni, a Left Coast hood who probably couldn't make the grade in New York organized crime and who wore unbuttoned polo shirts and gold pinkie rings. Then there was Martin Stevers, a salt-and-pepper-haired man with a perma-tan and perma-frown. Like Jimmy, Martin was conspicuously dressed in black. No matter how you looked at the situation, Rex had pissed off a lot of people—enough to make someone want to kill him.

The party grew and grew until it appeared that every registered voter in Palm Springs was cramming into Leo's place. Rex and Vince made the rounds of the party, shaking hands and hugging just about everyone in sight. Rex seemed to be having a good time for a change and didn't seem like a man with the sword of Damocles hanging over his head. He spotted the three of us and made his way toward us, laughing and patting people on the back as he neared us.

"Enjoying yourselves?" he asked when he was finally in our faces—literally.

"Great party, Rex! A really great party!" I screamed above the ruckus. "Oh, Rex, I want you to meet my friend Monette!"

He looked up into Monette's face towering above him and shook her hand vigorously. "Glad to meet you, Monette. Even your hair is dressed for the occasion!" he said, laughing at Monette's flaming ember-red hair.

I didn't say a word, but the one thing you didn't joke about was Monette's red hair. The other was her height. Being the trooper that she was, she took Rex's comment in stride and smiled gracefully.

"There you are, Rex!" came a voice from over my shoulder. A distinguished-looking man emerged from the crowd and walked up to Marc, hugging him like a long-lost brother. "I thought you were hiding from me!" the man added.

"Hiding from you!" Rex replied with astonishment. "I wouldn't hide from the guy who's helped me every step of the way!"

Marc whispered to me that the handsome stranger was none other than Kip Savage, the largest backer for the White Party, along with Brian Keeper, his PR guy who tagged some distance behind Kip, shaking hands with various partygoers.

Rex, realizing that he was being impolite, introduced the two to Monette and me. Rex took a healthy swallow of his drink, then put his arm around Kip and turned to the three of us.

"Could you excuse us for a few minutes? I have to discuss some matters with Kip and Brian privately—if you can find anywhere private to talk. Party stuff," he explained.

"No problem, Rex," Marc said for the three of us.

Rex, Kip and Brian went off laughing and talking, clapping each other on the back and enjoying private jokes. Of all the people associated with the White Party, Kip seemed the most unlikely. From his red face that screamed heavy drinking to his unbuttoned polo shirt and receding snow-white hair, the fifty-five-year-old man looked like he'd be more at home on the eighteenth fairway or in a boardroom than surrounded by gaggles of gyrating, half-naked gay men.

When they were out of earshot, I leaned forward and told Monette who the illustrious men were.

Monette raised her eyebrows in astonishment. "Then why is it that two guys who should be Rex's biggest enemies seem to be his best friends?"

"Both Kip and Brian are shrewd businessmen, Monette. Probably the best I've seen. They don't shit where they eat."

"That's so poetic, Marc. Remind me to have that embroidered on a pillow sometime," Monette commented.

"You know what I mean, Monette. Brian is following the first rule of PR."

"Make it look like someone else's fault?" I suggested.

"No, Robert, that's rule number four. Rule number one is, don't make a bad situation worse. Just smile big and take the Fifth Amendment."

"That's why I didn't make it in public relations, Marc," I said. "I thought you were supposed to tell the truth. As Monette could attest, I have trouble lying, so I went into advertising because it tells half-truths. Take my client's product, a carbonated douche that makes your vagina smell bubbly fresh."

"You're speaking from personal experience, I take it?" Marc asked.

I didn't reply to Marc's question, but a huge smile broke out across my face, giving him the only reply he needed. I had to say, Marc's humor was a big change from Michael Stark's. With Michael, most of what you said went into one ear and out the other because he wasn't interested in what others had to say, but the part that was the most annoying was that when you came up with a real zinger, it would sail clear over Michael's head like a clay pigeon during a skeet-shooting contest.

"Do any of us know what we were talking about?" Monette asked.

"I think we were smelling vaginas, if my memory serves me correctly," I said, setting the record straight.

Monette grinned at me and spoke. "The subject was Rex and the fact that party production made strange bedfellows."

"I just want to set the record straight. You heard it from Rex himself—Kip and Brian have been nothing but helpful to us. Sure, Kip would rather be in a position where he didn't have to compete with anyone, but Rex is in the game and he's not going to bow out just because someone doesn't like

him. Kip has been a perfect gentleman the whole time—
which is a lot more than I can say about some people," Marc
said, pointing at Darlene Waldron, who was nibbling a stalk
of celery while showing that fake smile of hers.

The party continued to swell, leading me to believe that
neighbors were pushing their way inside, forcing the house
to bulge at its very seams. Fortunately, from our vantage
point looking down into the sunken living room area, we
were able to look over the seething masses without being
caught in the thick of it.

As the three of us drank martinis and scanned the crowds,
Rex popped up right in front of us, smiling from ear to ear,
with Vince, as always, nearby. His cell phone must have
rung, because I saw him whip out the tiny instrument and
talk into it. I nudged Monette to keep her eyes on Rex. I
continued watching him. I don't know how he could hear
anything above the roar of the crowd and the dance-trance-
from-France music. I managed to catch most of his conversation.

"Rex Gifford. What? What? Yes, I understand. Tonight.
Yeah, remember that if I pay, you go away. Right."

Rex hung up his cell phone, and his face fell faster than a
soufflé on an artillery range; then, a few seconds later, it was
as if his mood did a complete about-face. He stood up no-
ticeably straighter and set his jaw against an unknown foe.
He had finished his call, because he clipped the phone back
onto his belt and proceeded to talk with Vince animatedly.
Just as Rex looked as if he were about to stride off, his cell
phone must have rung again, because he answered it. But
this time his strength dissipated, leaving him looking tired,
helpless, and scared. He turned away from us, not wanting
us to hear anything he said, which seemed strange because
he said very little. He seemed to be listening mostly. Rex
hung up, then turned and swam his way through the waves
of partiers and disappeared out the front door. I was going
to say something to Marc, but he was talking to someone

else to his left. I let the matter ride. Besides, Rex was a big, strong guy—he could take care of himself.

"Having a good time?" came Leo's voice behind me. He put his meaty arms around our group, corralling us all at the same time with his formidable forearms. You could feel how hard the muscles on his arms were. I was certain they could break a man's neck with about the same effort as punching a button on a TV remote control.

Marc responded for the three of us. "Great time! Great time! Say, I haven't seen you all evening. Where have you been hiding yourself?"

"I've been out in the kitchen part of the evening, then I figured that it might be a good idea to hang around the front door to greet people as they came in."

As Leo talked, my eyes drifted over to his arms, my pupils following the bulging veins up to his almost unbelievable biceps. They just didn't seem real, because it didn't seem like a part of the body could get that big. Well, almost. When I was a kid, there was a woman who attended church who had a leg that had blown up to a monstrous size while its counterpart remained normal. My mother would fire a withering look at me if she caught me staring at what every other person in the church was trying not to see. But leg or no leg, every Sunday she clumped up to the altar to receive communion, oblivious of the leg that always seemed to be one step behind her, having to be forcibly dragged down the aisle. It was as if she were dragging it out of hiding to embarrass the leg for misbehaving so badly. I did learn a lesson from the big-legged lady, however. It doesn't matter what you were born with—you just have to make the best of it.

Once I jogged my mind onto another track, it erupted into another strange thought. For years, I had worked out in a gym almost every day of my life, yet I never seemed to get very muscular. Michael used steroids, and I suspected that Leo did too, but I wanted to know if Leo had a secret that I didn't possess.

"Leo, I was wondering if you would tell me what you do to get so muscular? I work out five days a week, and I'm nowhere near where you are. What's your routine?"

"Why is everyone asking me this tonight?" Leo remarked.

"I guess that when you look like you do, you have to expect questions like this," I said.

"Diet is seventy percent of where you need to concentrate your efforts. So you work out five times a week?"

"Five times."

"How long have you been doing this?"

"About six years," I responded.

"Heavy weights?"

"As heavy as I can safely handle."

"I can tell what your problem is," Leo said confidently.

"You can?"

"Yeah, you're not eating enough protein. You gotta eat protein until you puke," Leo said.

"That sounds like an easy rule to remember," Monette chimed in. "It's not the most picturesque, but it's easy."

Leo smiled at Monette's comment and continued like an Olympic coach training his star weightlifter for the summer games. "Make sure you have a heavy protein meal at least two hours before you go to the gym. I have a protein shake in the midafternoon and go to the gym around five. Then have a protein shake the moment you finish your workout. Remember, around forty grams of protein every two hours, six times a day."

Marc clapped me on the shoulder. "You're going to look like Arnold before you know it!"

"Not if it means turning into a Republican," I responded.

"You can be a Log Cabin Republican—and change the system from the inside," Marc commented in a voice that meant he didn't believe a word that he said.

"That is one thing I will never get," I said. "The term 'gay Republican.' It's an oxymoron. It makes about as much sense as a Jewish Nazi."

"If you're through campaigning for mayor of San Francisco," Monette interrupted, "I think we have more pressing matters."

"Like what?" I asked.

"Like the matter of Rex going out the door five minutes ago and not having come back in yet."

"Oh, he left," Leo added.

"How can you be so sure?" Monette asked.

"Because he told me when he went out the door a while ago."

"Where did he say he was going?" Monette asked, the panic rising in her voice.

"He didn't say where. He just said that he had something very important to take care of."

"If it doesn't take care of him first," I added.

The four of us, Leo, Monette, Marc, and I, stood there staring at each other for a while, suspecting that Rex was headed for trouble—if he hadn't run into it already. We found Vince and tried to get him to explain what Rex had said to him before he left. And, more important, why Vince had let Rex leave by himself. Marc suggested that we search the grounds in case Rex had run into trouble before he got to his car. Leo went to call the police. And I? I did what I did best during a crisis—I turned to Monette.

She set about questioning Vince in order to get some clues surrounding Rex's unorthodox disappearance. Like it or not, Monette and I were being sucked into this case. Michael—who could tell where he was? Maybe he was just getting sucked.

"So you said Rex got a call on his cell phone and his whole mood changed?"

"There were two calls, one right after the other. The first one . . . it was weird. Rex was scared at first, but then it was like he made his mind up about something. You know, like he pulled himself together to tackle some challenge. I know it sounds stupid, but he looked like a man going into battle."

"Go on," Monette coaxed Vince. "What about the second call?"

"He looked surprised. He spoke very little—he listened mostly. Then it looks like he lost all his nerve. I could see all the strength drain out of him. He was really shaken up. Then he said he had to go and that I could ride back to the house with Robert and Michael in my car."

"You didn't try and stop him?"

"When Rex makes up his mind, no one stands in his way—not even me."

"Did he say where he was going?"

"No, he just said he had to take care of something very important and for me not to worry—that he would be all right. He said he'd be home a little later."

Before Monette could probe any further, the thump-thump-ka-chunk of the party music was shattered by the sound of several police car sirens, producing an amazing effect on the partiers. Like lemmings, dozens of them pushed their way furiously through the house and into the backyard. Even in the dim landscape lighting, I could see wave after wave of the partiers going over Leo's wall and presumably emptying their pockets of marijuana, ecstasy, crystal, and other party contraband.

A phalanx of policemen entered the house, with Sergeant Big Arms at their head. We explained the situation to Sergeant Big Arms, trying to give a minute-by-minute account of the two suspicious phone calls. When we were done, Big Arms conferred with his buddies and instructed several of them to fan out over the grounds while he assigned two of them to hightail it over to Rex's house with Vince's gate code and house keys—which they did in a matter of seconds, sirens screaming into the night until they faded away.

"If you don't mind, Sergeant," Monette ventured, "I

would like to give you my number while I'm staying here in the desert." She offered a piece of paper, which he took, with a dumfounded look. "I have a very good detective mind and I've solved two murders involving my two friends, one involving my friend Robert, who I take it you've met before."

Sergeant Gorski stared at Monette as if she were a little old lady who frequently saw imaginary murders. "Thank you . . . I'll take that under consideration, but I can't divulge any information that is confidential."

Me, I just stood there. It's not that I didn't have some sensible courses of action to recommend, but I had a deep-seated problem with authority figures. A cop would only need to pass within my general vicinity and I'd feel that I'd done something illegal. I mean, I cheated on my taxes some-times and once in a while would keep my mouth shut when a cashier undercharged me for a bottle of wine, but other than that I was a law-abiding citizen. Perhaps that's why I wasn't getting ahead in this world—the people at the top lied, cheated, stole, and sometimes killed.

Monette broke my little daydream with a matter-of-fact suggestion to Sergeant Gorksi. "I know you're wondering who the hell I am, talking to you like this, but I think that you've wasting your time looking for Rex back at his house. He won't be at the Red Party setup area, either. I think he's out trying to pay off the person who's been threatening him. Where that is, I don't know. But I'd look for a dark, deserted road somewhere in the desert. And tomorrow morning, I'd call the bank who handles Rex's company money and check to see if there has been a large withdrawal in the last few days. I think Robert, Vince, and I will head back to the house and wait for Rex to return. Remember, call me if you need any help."

Monette suggested that we head back to the compound, and she said that she would go back to her room in Rancho Myass. She told me to call her if anything happened. I could tell that she was definitely concerned, but at the same time, she had had a taste of mystery, which was as addictive to her as sex was to Michael. She was hot on the trail of a mystery, and everything else could fall by the wayside. After all, as she often said, "When you work for the Endangered Herbs Society of America, you take any excitement you can get."

Monette left, and Marc and I went in search of Michael, who was still nowhere to be found. I passed David McLeish, who barked that he hadn't seen Michael all night. Then I passed Colorado. Oh, well, it was worth a try.

"Colorado, have you seen Michael Stark?"

"Robert, you've obviously confused me with someone who cares."

"Thanks, Colorado. You're such a team player," I fired back.

I walked past Colorado and heard from over my shoulder: "Why don't you look under a rock? That's probably where you'll find him."

Half of me wanted to turn around and force him to swallow several lighted cigarettes while the other half took Colorado's advice and thought of looking where the Bitch Queen advised. I crept around a huge boulder lying in the landscape, and lo and behold, eureka!

"Michael, if you can extract your wee-wee from your friend's mouth, Vince and I are leaving now. We're going back to Rex's house, since he's missing and it doesn't look good no matter which angle you're viewing the situation from. Meet you outside in ten minutes or you'll have to find your own ride back to the compound."

I walked away with Marc. He seemed very apprehensive about my going back to Rex's place, and I was genuinely touched by his concern.

"Don't worry, I'll be okay, Marc. There's probably several policemen there right now, and I'm sure they'll be hanging close to the compound if he comes back," I said.

Marc stared into my eyes and read my thoughts. "You

said '*if* he comes back.' You don't think he's going to come back, do you?"

I tried to conceal my fatalism, but I couldn't help it. My despair over Rex's fate sat there on my face. Only the news ticker on Times Square was more easily read. "I don't know, Marc. I just hope he does return."

"Why don't you stay over at my place in Cathedral City with me tonight?" Marc blurted out. "I feel you'll be a lot safer there with me."

"Why, Marc, that's very nice, but I think Vince needs me tonight. God knows he's not going to get any support from Michael."

"I want you to stay at my place, but I understand what you're doing. It's very thoughtful," he said, planting a tender kiss on my lips. "Here's my phone number. Now, if you need anything tonight—anything—call me. I mean it. You promise?"

"Yes, I promise."

"Okay, see you tomorrow. Sweet dreams," Marc said, then turned and left.

Vince and I headed to the car as well, neither of us saying a word but both of us hearing an incessant *tink, tink, tink* a short distance behind us. I turned to see Michael bringing up the rear, his unfastened belt buckle swaying back and forth as he walked, a frown on his face completing his wardrobe.

"What the matter. Lose your shirt?" I asked.

"Yeah, it's somewhere in the backyard. It got trampled when everyone went over the wall. It doesn't matter. I don't give a shit about the shirt. But I do mind being disturbed when I'm in the middle of something," he snarled.

"Or someone," I added.

There wasn't much conversation after that. We got back to the house, where the police were waiting inside the compound. They had searched the house and grounds and pronounced both safe.

I went into Rex's office and heard a phone ring in the

house. Seconds later, I heard Vince call out to me that Marc was on the line. "He's on line two, the one that's blinking," Vince instructed me. "Just press the button near the blinking light and pick up the phone."

"Thanks, Vince." I did as instructed and soon heard Marc's voice on the other end of the line. It didn't sound good. In fact, he was crying.

I tried to calm him down and get him to tell me what was the matter.

"There's . . . in the pool . . . with the floats . . . him!"

Marc didn't have to say another word. I instinctively knew that among the floats in Marc's pool was another float. One shaped exactly like Rex Gifford.

6

I'd Add a Little Chlorine to that Pool Water if I Were You

Vince, Michael, and I sped over to Marc's house in Cathedral City. According to Vince, Marc lived in the Cove, an area sandwiched in between the foothills of the Santa Rosa mountains. The Cove stood in stark contrast to the neat and tidy manicured gay neighborhoods of Palm Springs. It was far wilder, from its willy-nilly architecture and inexplicable zoning to the raw desert that came right to its border. And it was dark. Very, very dark. But for some reason, I liked it right away because it seemed so remote, so far away, so quiet. These were great qualities when it came to having a place to call your own, but they were not so great when you had a dead body on your hands.

When we drove into Marc's driveway, I liked his house immediately. The building was a modern white cube that sat anchored on the desert landscape, pure and uncluttered. It was the complete opposite of what you saw taking over the desert: bland, sand-colored ranch houses masquerading as Mediterranean villas, trumpeting names like River View or The Falls. (Why, I wonder, did these gated communities have to allude to water in their names, let alone squander it so wastefully?)

The owner of this house was watching for our arrival from the safety of a window. As we walked up the sidewalk to Marc's house, he came running out and latched on to me with a hug that would make an anaconda jealous.

I didn't say a word but just put my arms around Marc and held him. The tighter I held him, the more I could feel just how much he was trembling. Vince indicated that he wanted to go to Rex, but I mentioned to him that he shouldn't touch anything.

"Don't worry, I won't," he reminded me. "I want whoever did this to pay for what they've done."

Michael, always one to be uncomfortable with raw, human emotions, did what he did best in situations like this: he acted like nothing was amiss.

"Boy, Marc, you've got quite a view up here. It must be really something from the backyard!"

The backyard, I surmised, was where the pool was—and, logically, Rex, the human flotation device.

"How much did you pay for this place?" Michael asked further, inserting his foot deeper into his gaping mouth.

"Michael," I said helpfully, "this probably isn't the best time to discuss real estate. Would you go inside and fix Marc something to drink—something with alcohol?"

"Sure," he said, and went into the house ahead of us, heading for the kitchen.

I guided Marc into the living room—anywhere away from the windows that looked out onto the pool—and sat next to him, holding his hand. I heard Michael in the kitchen, opening drawers and banging metal against metal. From the noise he was making, it was clear that Michael intended to distill the alcohol himself and not just pour it from a bottle like other humans.

After what seemed like an eternity, he emerged from the kitchen walking as carefully as a tightrope walker, being careful not to spill his concoction.

He handed one to Marc and one to me, then sat back in a chair and sipped at one himself. Marc took one look at the drink and started sobbing loudly. I knew it wasn't intended, but I was sure that the coffee bean floating in a glass of Sambuca hit a little too close to home for Marc.

"Marc?"

"Yes, Robert?" Sob, sob.

"You called the police, didn't you?"

"Just as you drove up."

"Where is your phone? I think I need to place a call to Monette. She's good at this sort of thing, and I think her input would help a lot right now."

"The phone is right in the kitchen. It's a cordless. Just bring it out here and call."

I retrieved the phone and called a very sleepy Monette, telling her what had happened. She expressed her sympathies to convey to Marc and Vince but said that she wasn't surprised at the turn of events.

"Just do one thing for me before the cops arrive," she requested.

"I think that may be too late. I can hear their sirens now."

"Act quickly and do me a favor."

"Whatever you say."

"First, is Marc with you right now?"

"Yes, he's sitting right next to me. He's pretty shook up."

Monette continued relentlessly onward. "Ask Marc if there was any sign that Rex entered the house before he . . . er . . . decided to take his last swan dive."

I conveyed the question to Marc—minus the last part—and got a definite answer, which I repeated back to Monette.

"No. Marc said the security system was still on and hadn't been tripped when he came home."

"Question two: Were the pool lights on when Marc found him?"

I conveyed the question, got an answer, and repeated it back to Monette: "Yes, they were."

"Okay, good. I don't know if any of this means much, but it's a good start, because once the police get there, we might not have access to the facts. Okay, last question, Robert, and only you can answer it. Go outside and carefully check the entrances to the pool area and see if you can see any dragging marks. I want to know if Rex was killed elsewhere and dragged to the pool or if he was killed at the edge of the pool. And while you're at it—and I know that this seems grisly—but check to see if there's blood in the pool. Off you go—call me when you get the answers."

I told Marc that I had a quick mission to complete and that I'd be back in a few minutes. I went out to the pool and saw Rex floating peacefully with the pool floats, his body bumping up against them in the light breeze. Behind me, staring from the kitchen windows, was Vince. No wave, no sign of recognition, nothing. He just stared, probably wondering what the hell I was doing out there after I had advised him against disturbing anything from the crime scene. I didn't have much time, since I could see the police enter the house and talk with Marc, so I walked around the edge of the pool, heading toward the only visible gate, and looked for any clue of blood swirling in the water as I circled. No blood.

I opened the gate and looked for any sign of dragging: pieces of grass, dirt, stones, or marks on the white concrete sidewalk. Nothing that I could see. Because the police were coming out onto the pool deck, I decided to go around the front entrance to the house so they wouldn't know I had been in the vicinity of the body.

I came around and entered the house again from the front, explaining to the police that I had been outside getting something from the car. Marc was answering questions, so I decided to sit and see if I could learn anything more.

Marc said that he had come home from the party, turned off the alarm system, and gone into the kitchen to get a glass of milk before bed. He noticed the lights on in the pool and a body floating in it. He ran to the front door, locked it, and turned the security system back on so it would sound if any-one tried to get into the house. He went into the front bed-room and locked the door. He called Vince's house to report that he believed it was Rex in the pool, then called 911.

The police asked a few questions. Did he notice any strange cars in the area as he came home? No. Did he see anyone in the area? No. Did he step outside near the pool? No, he was too scared that a murderer might be outside, but he could clearly see that it was a body in the pool. Was he sure he didn't leave the pool lights on when he left for the party? Yes, he was one-hundred percent sure they were off. Last question: Why did he give the 911 dispatcher the wrong house number? Marc said he was too shook up. "I guess my mind went numb," he said.

The police asked if they could look outside around the pool now. Sure, Marc said.

There was a knock on the door. I opened the door to find a man from the coroner's office of Riverside County. I let him in and showed him the way to the pool, where he stud-ied the scene carefully before setting his toolboxes down. He looked at the body in the pool and then took a few pho-tos of Rex from different directions. Then he stuck his fin-ger into the water and withdrew it so quickly, you would have thought there was a pack of piranhas in the pool. He repeated his actions, then slowly put his hand in the water and left it there. I was fascinated with the coroner's investi-gation, mystified at what he was doing. He asked the two policemen who were watching him to help him pull Rex from the pool. The coroner, using a flashlight to examine Rex, poked and prodded him, shining the flashlight in his face and doing enough things to annoy even a dead person.

Eventually, the coroner's assistants arrived with a gurney and lifted Rex into a body bag, and off he went, out of our lives forever.

The police searched the grounds for over an hour and, to

our knowledge, found only one clue—an extension cord—and asked Marc if it belonged to him. Yes, he said that it did. That was the only other question they asked. They taped off the pool deck and told Marc not to let anyone in the area, because they'd be back to search for more clues in the morning.

When the police had gone, I looked at Marc, he looked at me, and Michael looked blank—what's new?

There was an awkward silence that permeated the room like the smell of a bad fart. Marc was the first one to break it—the silence, that is.

"Am I thinking what you're thinking?" he said to Michael and me.

Michael looked as if he had discovered the Grand Unification Theory of Physics. "Yeah, it looks like someone used a power tool to snuff Rex," he said.

I shot a glance at Marc that telegraphed the message "Please don't judge me by the people I hang out with." I looked back at Michael and agreed that yes, someone had drilled Rex to death.

Marc was much kinder to Michael, but then he hardly knew him. Spend a little time around Michael and you would inevitably be dumped in dance bars when a promising trick came along, and stiffed for restaurant checks because Michael rarely carried any money and ended up talking for hours about nothing but himself. Why did I put up with Michael, then? Simple. Down deep, I felt that he meant well, even if he didn't always show it. Plus, I liked the excitement of being around him. He went to interesting restaurants and bars, had incredible parties, and had one of the best houses on Fire Island. Not reason enough? Okay, I saved his life from a bunch of fag-bashers in the Village one night long ago. Satisfied? Life is a contradiction, and I am not above being a paradox from time to time.

But back to the story at hand.

Marc, under considerable strain himself, answered Michael

in the nicest way possible. "Michael, I think that it appears that someone threw the extension cord into the pool and Rex just happened to be in it."

"So you think he killed himself?" Michael asked incredulously.

"Eh . . . Michael, if you don't mind, it's getting late and I feel a headache coming on."

"Oh . . . right," Michael said, the light finally dawning on him. "I guess we should get going, right, Robert?"

"Michael, if you don't mind going back to Rex—Vince's house without me, I think I should spend the night here with Marc. I think he'd feel better if someone were here with him." Marc's hand moved over and grasped mine, telling me that he approved of my idea.

"Fine, I'll take the car and head home. See you back at the casa tomorrow, Robert."

And just like that, Michael left and I was here alone with Marc. Not exactly the ideal setting for a night of wild lovemaking, but you take what you can get. We could just cuddle, I figured.

Without another word, Marc led me back to his bedroom, where we disrobed and lay next to each other, him curling against me and turning out the light.

7

A Not-So-Dynamic Duo

I woke the next morning with a ringing in my ears. At first I thought it was from the music at Leo's party the night before, but it started and stopped. Then started again and stopped again.

Up and up I swam, through layers and layers of dreams, until I saw Marc standing at the side of the bed, phone in hand, saying something into the phone. He handed it to me, which was a dangerous thing to do since I was still sleepy enough to eat the phone. Not until I had my first cup of coffee in the morning would the world make sense.

I held the phone close to my ear and heard a voice that went through my skull like Kiri Te Kanawa hitting a high note in *Die Zauberflot*. Only a gay man would describe a sound like that.

"Get the fuck up!" came the voice that could crack a continent. "It's ten-thirty. I've already been up to the top of some fuckin' mountain and back by now."

"Monette?" I said weakly into the phone.

"No, it's Congresswoman Mary Bono and I desperately need your vote. The gays are taking over Palm Springs and they don't like me."

"Monette," I repeated. It had to be.

"Yes, it's Monette, dear. Up and at 'em; rise and shine; daylight in the swamp," she continued.

"Where are you?" I struggled, sitting up, trying to make sense of where I was.

"I'm here over at Sadie's house in Rancho Myass. The question is, where are *you*?"

"Where the hell is Rancho Myass? It sounds like a dude ranch for Michael."

"Rancho Mirage, Robert. The only mirage here is the *rancho* part. If someone can show me a rancho amidst all this nouveau riche gated-community bullshit, I'll eat it."

"I'm over here at Marc's house, in Cathedral City," I said, taking in the unfamiliar surroundings just to make sure that was where I was. "How did you know I was here?"

"I called you over at Vince's place, and they said you were at Marc's place and that you didn't come home."

"Who told you? Michael?"

"No, Vince answered the phone. Michael didn't come home last night."

I got a twinge of anxiety but figured that Michael was probably shacking up somewhere. He'd turn up . . . I hoped.

"So how is Marc doing this morning?"

I looked around the bedroom, but no Marc. "I don't know. We were still sleeping when you called. I think he went to make coffee. I wanted to wake up and find out that the whole Rex thing was just a bad dream, but something tells me that isn't going to be so, is it?"

"No, I'm afraid not, Robert. How are you doing?"

"I'm okay, I think. I don't know what to do, really."

"How about this? You and Marc have some breakfast, then call me and I'll come over and maybe we can get this matter straightened out. How's that sound?"

"Wonderful. I'll have two eggs, toast, and three zombies—no ice."

"Have a Bloody Mary and a helping of Marc and call me when you finish."

"Monette," I said, trying to set the record straight. "Nothing happened between Marc and me last night. You'd think that finding your business partner dead in your pool would make you hotter than Madonna in a room full of gay men, but he wasn't in the mood. We just cuddled."

"Aw, that sounds wonderful. Good for you. I cuddled with a pillow last night. That's about as exciting as it got."

I was about to hang up from Monette when Marc came into the bedroom, holding a piece of paper his hand. His jaw was open and he was as white as a sheet.

"Just a minute, Monette; hold on. Something's happened," I said, getting a bad feeling in the pit of my stomach. "Marc? Marc? What is it? What's wrong?"

Marc stood there, opening the piece of paper and dropping it in my hand without saying a single word. I opened the letter, and a pulse of adrenaline flooded through my body, my heart pounding so hard, I was sure it was going to shoot out of my chest and scuttle across the floor. I read the letter slowly, every word pushing up my pulse even higher. The message was simple and made of pasted letters cut out of a magazine:

YOU DiDN't GeT tHe MessAGE?
YOU'rE NeXt!

I looked up at Marc, and he just stood there as if he had just been hit by lightning. I took a deep breath and picked up the phone.

"Monette?" I said. "I think you better come over here right away. And bring the police with you."

Monette arrived a few minutes after the police. Marc was talking to the police out by the pool, so I let Monette into the living room, where she sat shaking her head.

"Well, isn't that the damnest thing!" she said when I told her about the letter.

"What are we going to do?" I asked, fearing for Marc's

life. I was about to get the closest thing to a real, living, non-inflatable boyfriend that I had had in over a year, and now some fucking lunatic was trying to snuff him out, too. I thought this but didn't say it.

"Let's see," Monette said, scratching her flaming-red head. "I guess that no matter what the police do, no one should leave Marc's side—not even for a minute."

"No problem there," I replied.

"I said his side, not his backside. Now, did you get to see the letter before the police took it?"

"Yes."

"What did it look like?"

"Like a piece of paper with words cut out of a magazine and pasted on the paper."

"Robert, I could get an answer like that out of Michael. You'd think that having been through several murders already, you would have learned more from your training. You're with the best, remember?"

Monette wasn't far from the truth. In the past few years, I had become involved, through no choice of my own, in two murder cases, and she had solved both of them. Her uncanny ability to see the fire when everyone else was looking at the smoke came from her voracious reading of mystery novels. She claims to have read every mystery novel ever written, and one trip to her crowded apartment in Brooklyn would dispel all doubt to that claim. It was lined from floor to ceiling with shelves jammed with thousands of crime novels, from Agatha Christie to Umberto Eco. She also gives some credit to being raised Irish Catholic—she says it made her suspicious of everything and everyone. Hers was a talent wasted working as a graphic designer for the Endangered Herbs Society of America, but so was mine. I hoped that my talents would someday make me a great author or at least a halfway decent courtesan.

I looked at Monette, who was staring out toward the pool, as if the answer to Rex's murder would slosh out and run over her. "So I'm sure you've got some suspects in mind already, right?"

"No, no, too early. Plus, I just don't have enough information about possible suspects yet, and unless we blackmail someone in the police department to let us in on what they find, we might be nowhere."

"Blackmail?" I asked.

"Yes, it worked twice before. On that guy in Provincetown and what's-his-name in Berlin."

"I forgot his name. It doesn't matter; I get your point."

Monette clapped her hands as if she were focusing her energy on picking up an engine block by herself. "Okay, now, did you find any signs that the body was dragged to the pool?"

"No. I checked around the pool. No heel marks or scratches from belt buckles or anything like that."

"Very good, Robert. I wanted you to put your catastrophizing mind to good use and imagine the worst that could happen—which is where your mind naturally goes. You're turning into a good little detective! Good. Now, what signs would you look for outside the gate, assuming there wasn't a sidewalk there?"

"No, no sidewalk. I checked the grass to see if it had been flattened or showed signs of a heavy object being dragged across it."

"Good. I'm sure if Rex was dragged to the pool from outside the backyard, the coroner would find grass in Rex's belt or shoes—information that we need to know. What else can you tell me?"

"For one, the coroner tested the pool water to see if it was electrified."

"Electrified?"

"Well not *electrified*, but with electric current running through it."

"How did you know that?" Monette asked.

"He stuck his finger in the water real fast and then pulled

it back. I couldn't figure out at the time what he was doing, but when one of the cops showed Marc an extension cord and asked if it was his, I knew what they were after."

"Was it a thick, appliance-duty-gauge cord."

"Yes, orange and with three prongs—I could see water dripping out of the holes."

"Okay, Robert. We can assume a few things. So far it looks like Rex came here—or was lured here—by someone who wanted to kill him quietly and without a lot of witnesses. It's quiet up here in the Cove—the perfect place to do it. Our suspect probably wasn't a strong person, either."

"And how, pray tell, did you come to that conclusion, madame?"

"Mademoiselle."

"Have it your way. How do you know that?"

"'Mademoiselle' is used for a younger woman."

"No, not that, Monette. How do you know that the murderer is a ninety-pound weakling?"

"Funny you should use that term, because one possible suspect is Darlene Waldron—among others. Take Rex first. The guy was big and had some very decent muscles on him. Very few people are going to be able to overpower Rex."

"How about Leo?" I asked.

"That's possible, too. I'm not sure what the motive would be, but you'd be surprised at how often the reason to commit murder isn't obvious—to the untrained mind. I'll tell you what I think happened, but this could all change when more facts and motives are uncovered."

"Shoot—er, continue."

"All righty. I think that Rex came here of his own will, or rather, that he was going to meet someone here—someone that he knew. He may have come to talk, but my guess is that he came here to pay off the person who was threatening him. He pays the person off, and that man or woman pushes him into the pool and takes an extension cord plugged in ahead of time and tosses the free end into the pool. Even with a circuit breaker, Rex gets enough electricity to knock him out, where he soon drowns. The killer turns the pool lights on now so that Marc sees the body when he comes home."

"So you think that Rex was trying to pay off this person—persons?" I grilled Monette.

"If I were a partner in T-Rex Productions, I would look into their checking account right away, because I think Rex made a big withdrawal recently—and the killer made a withdrawal from Rex."

"So you think he gave in and tried to pay someone off so the Red Party could go on?"

"I'd lay money on it. C'mon, I don't care how tough Rex tried to come off, but it all went out the window when someone cut a tree down on his bedroom and blew up his outdoor grill."

"And tried to drop a boulder on him. Don't forget that."

"Yes, the rock, too. Three attempts on his life, all planned to scare the shit out of him, yet none intended to kill him. After all, why kill the goose that lays the golden eggs?"

"That's exactly what Sergeant Big Arms said the other day."

"Sergeant Big Arms?" Monette said, almost laughing. "Let me guess: a cop with big biceps—something Michael would find irresistible. And let me make one more guess: Michael's all over him like a redneck on a six-pack? By the way, where is Michael?"

"You told me he didn't come home last night, remember?"

"Do you think he's with Sergeant Big Arms?"

"It's very possible."

Marc finished talking with the police and joined us.

"So what are the police going to do?" Monette asked.

"They advised me to stay home and they'd assign an officer to protect me twenty-four hours a day. Plus, they agreed to keep the matter of Rex's murder quiet for right now. After all, we can't afford a stampede of ticket cancellations—we owe too much to vendors, suppliers, everyone. I guess I can handle some of the Red Party setup by phone. If the setup crew runs into problems, they can call me . . . or Leo. By the way, I didn't have a chance to thank Leo much at the party last night. In fact, now that I think of it, I didn't see much of him at all."

Monette and I looked at each other, thinking the same thing. Hmm, an interesting observation.

Marc continued innocently on. "So do you have any suspects in mind, Monette?"

"I'll try not to make this sound like a mystery novel cliché, but those at the top of the list are those who stand to gain the most from Rex's death. Darlene Waldron, Brian Keeper, Kip Savage, and Martin Stevers would be up near the top. Vince, perhaps."

"Vince? I just can't imagine that."

"If he stands to inherit a substantial amount from Rex's estate, then he's a suspect. Not a suspect as much as Kip Savage and the rest of the White Party people are."

"Robert says that you've solved two mysteries before, so do I take it that you're going to solve this one?"

Monette turned to me and saw me holding my hands together in prayer and giving her sad face number 43.

"Yes, I'll help. After all, I'll do anything to help Robert and any friend of his."

I gave a hug to Monette, then one to Marc while I whispered in his ear that he'd be okay now. Marc suggested that we sit down and have breakfast, since it was probably a good idea that he remain in the police-protected privacy of his house as much as possible. Among the three of us, we cooked quite an impressive brunch and talked about the particulars of this case. I remembered seeing Rex get two cell phone calls at the party last night, and described in detail the range of emotions that crossed Rex's face as he got the calls.

"So you're saying that he seemed really happy until he got the first call?" Monette asked. She was already piecing the facts together.

"Yes. Everything's hunky-dory until he gets the call; then wham! Face goes down like a deflated beach ball. Then he looks like he's kind of getting his strength together and heading off to meet the bad guys with a smile on his face. Then, second call and down goes the face, and he turns whiter than Michael Jackson."

"Interesting. You know what this could mean?"

Marc and I looked at each other. Nothing.

"What it could mean," Monette explained, "is that anyone who was at the party couldn't have been the murderer, because they couldn't call Rex, since they were at the party."

"What about calling from another cell phone?" I suggested. "I saw Jimmy Garboni talking on a cell phone. I think that Martin Stevers was, too."

Monette shook her head, dismissing that theory completely. "No, too risky, because it would leave a record, one cell phone to another. No, I think it was either someone else we don't know about yet, or someone had an accomplice helping. Two people, or there could be more. There's so much that I don't know. So many people, so many connections. I'm just worried about getting my hands on information that might be difficult to get. After all, you can't always depend on blackmail to find things out."

Marc's face lit up. "I've got just the person to help you, Monette. Actually, two people: Clifford and Grayson."

"Clifford and Grayson?" Monette repeated. "Don't tell me there are parents out there mean enough to give two kids names like those?"

"I suppose so," Marc answered. "I don't think they were named Jim and Mike and purposely changed them to Clifford and Grayson."

"Good point," Monette conceded.

"Clifford and Grayson know everyone in town. Nothing

goes on in this town without them knowing about it first. They can get doors to open all over town for you. Plus, Grayson is the empress dowager of the Most Imperial and Hierarchical Order of Almost-Vestal Virgins."

"Oh, in that case, it would be tasteless to say no to the grand duchess of . . ." Monette mocked.

"The empress dowager of the Most Imperial and Hierarchical Order of Almost-Vestal Virgins. It's the closest thing to a royalty there is in the world of drag."

Monette still didn't believe Marc, and to be honest, I wasn't quite ready to buy his story, either.

"Is this some kind of practical joke?" Monette asked, looking around for a hidden camera.

Marc knitted his eyebrows. "I don't quite understand. A practical joke? Grayson?"

"Robert and I play these practical jokes on each other. I don't know when it started, but from that moment on, it's just escalated out of control. It's just that neither of us know when the other one is going to spring something, so we're always on guard, and this sounds like I'm being set up."

"No, I don't know what you're talking about. There really is a Clifford and Grayson, and Grayson is the empress dowager of the Most Imperial and Hierarchical Order of Almost-Vestal Virgins. I'll give him a call and see if they can talk to you today."

Monette looked disappointed that she hadn't spoiled one of my nefarious plots. "Okay, we'll go see him if you can get us an audience with His Highness."

"You'll like him. He's a real hoot. So is his lover, Clifford. They live in an all-pink house."

Monette stared into her empty glass of champagne and said, "This is turning out to be the weirdest vacation I've ever been on. Even stranger than the Festival of Womyn, in the woods of Michigan, where my tentmate was a woman who swore she was the reincarnation of Sylvia Plath—I guess that's why whenever I fired up the camp stove; she was always trying to put her head in it."

By the time we finished our brunch and cleared the table, it was twelve-thirty. As Marc was loading the dishwasher, he asked Monette if she really thought it was possible that a T-Rex partner could have done Rex in.

"It's certainly possible," she remarked. "You, Leo, anyone. Or Vince, even."

"I really can't see Leo doing such a thing, but he'd have a right to. Not to speak ill of the dead, but Rex would really rip into Leo, treating him like he was a dumb-shit because he was a bodybuilder. I guess that could give him some motivation—that and a few million dollars."

The phone rang. It could be the killer making a telephone threat, so I took the call to protect Marc. Monette and Marc were still discussing the possibility of Leo being Rex's murderer when I put my hand over the mouthpiece of the phone and said they could rule out Leo as a suspect.

"Why is that?" Monette asked.

"Because he's dead. And get this: Michael Stark said he killed him."

8

I Shot Him with My Love Gun

Monette and I rushed over to Leo's, but the paramedics had beaten us to the punch. They had conducted their investigation and were wheeling Leo the Late out to their truck when we drove up to the house. Michael was inside and was telling the police everything he knew—and then some. Monette and I sat back, listening quietly and biting our tongues.

". . . so I was fucking him and his eyes rolled back and his tongue shot out and he died. Let me tell you, it's not the first time, either—I'm trying to be humble here, but I'm good," Michael confessed in earnest. "Ask any good-looking gay man in the capitals of the world. They'll tell you."

"I see," Sergeant Big Arms said, scribbling furiously into a small notebook. "The best in the world."

"Well, I wouldn't say that, but I'm pretty much up there with the best."

"So you say that this has happened before, Mr. Stark?"

"Oh, yes, quite a few times. They just get too excited and poof, their heart gives out. Of course, some of them were doing poppers like they were aromatherapy."

"Poppers?" the Sergeant asked.

"Amyl nitrite. Or butyl nitrite. You sniff them and your head goes flying."

"I understand what they are and what they do, Mr. Stark. Was either of you doing amyl during the course of your lovemaking?"

"No, I never use illegal substances," Michael said, lying through his teeth and causing Monette and me to cough violently. "No, neither of us were doing amyl. Leo was pretty natural, if you didn't count the steroids he does—did."

"How can you be sure Mr. Thomas took steroids?"

"C'mon, Sergeant. Look at the muscles the guy had. You don't look like that unless you're juicing. I should know. Plus, did you look at his balls, Sergeant?"

"Not particularly. Why, Mr. Stark?"

"If you're juicing, your balls shrink. His were so small I could easily get them both in my mouth."

The sergeant coughed uncomfortably as if someone were squeezing his. He stared intently at his notebook, then flipped the pages furiously back and forth. I could tell he wasn't looking for any fact in particular—he was looking for some excuse to change the line of questioning. "Now, tell me, after your bout of all-night lovemaking, what exactly did you do after you went to sleep?"

"I woke up," Michael answered.

(I could just hear the thoughts running through Michael's mind: "Boy, is this cop dumb. What would any person do after they sleep? Sheesh!")

"No, after you woke up. Did you eat, or go out for a run or something like that?"

"Oh, I didn't think Leo would be doing a lot of running after last night. In fact, I'd be surprised if he could walk," Michael said proudly. "Let's see, we got up and had a light breakfast."

Sergeant Big Arms: "Could you tell me what that breakfast consisted of?"

"An egg-white omelet, two slices of cantaloupe, and a potato with fat-free sour cream."

"Good," the sergeant continued. "Then what?"

"We fucked some more," came the reply.

"Yes . . . then?"

"He said he had to go to the gym in two hours. So he had a protein shake, and he wanted to get fucked again. That's the way these bodybuilders are—they act all tough in the gym, but get 'em home and they've got their legs up in the air faster than you can say 'Take it, boy!'"

Another uncomfortable clearing of the throat. "You just said Mr. Thomas had a protein shake, but you did not. Did you have one of these protein shakes?"

"No."

"But you two had the same things for breakfast. Is that correct?"

"Well, not exactly. He had his own plate and I had mine."

"That's not exactly what I meant, Mr. Stark. What I meant to say was, did you both eat the same thing?"

"No, I told you that we had separate plates!" Michael replied, getting a little irritated, undeservedly so.

The sergeant stopped to gather his breath and his patience. "What I meant was, did you both have . . ." he said, checking in his notebook for the facts, "an egg-white omelet, two slices of cantaloupe, and a potato?"

"Three slices of cantaloupe," Michael replied. "Leo had two."

As Monette and I almost bit our tongues in half, the sergeant looked out the living room windows to the pool, probably wondering why he didn't listen to his father and go into real estate instead. Rescuing hostages from a bank robbery was one thing, but trying to coax facts out of a self-absorbed Megaslut who could be outwitted by a tossed salad was another.

"Mr. Stark, could you show me the ingredients Mr. Thomas used to make this protein shake?"

Michael opened a tall cupboard that was cram-packed with bodybuilding supplements, and pointed to a ten-gallon container of whey protein powder.

"Thank you, Mr. Stark. That will be all."

Michael gave us both a quick hello wave, then sat down across from us.

Monette was off and running. "The sergeant suspects poison," she remarked, leaning toward the two of us. "I would too. It would be so easy. The house was full of people last night, and anyone could have waltzed into the kitchen, opened the cupboard, and dumped poison into his protein powder."

"Wait a minute!" I exclaimed. "Remember last night, when I was asking Leo about his workout and eating routines? He remarked that someone had asked him the same thing!"

"He didn't say who it was, did he?" Monette queried.

"No, no, he didn't," I said.

"Shit! I guess we'll never know now, will we? Damn!" Monette stared off into space; then her face lit up. "Robert, you didn't see him talking to anyone last night?"

"I didn't even see him until he came up to us and threw his arms around us. No, I don't remember anyone in particular."

Monette was crestfallen.

"So what do we do now?" I asked.

Michael spoke up. "I don't know about you two, but I'm taking a shower ASAP. I gotta get that dead guy's smell off of me!"

"Michael, it's just so touching when you get sentimental like that," I said, wiping away an imaginary tear with my hand.

"Now, don't go painting me as some kind of insensitive clod. We Starks just don't wear our hearts on our sleeves."

"No, because you've got a round of ammunition strapped there. Michael, if you had it your way, you'd shoot Leo's corpse out of a cannon to get rid of it quickly, just so you could pop open the champagne and get on with the party."

"That is not true, Robert, and you know that. Just because my mother threw a big party two days after she buried my father, people assume the apple doesn't fall far from the tree."

I was aghast. "Your mother threw a party two days after your father's funeral? You never told me that!"

"Well, I'm sorry that I told you now. Besides, she and my father didn't exactly get along," Michael added, trying to justify away family behavior that put the Medicis to shame. "She's not the ice queen that you make her out to be, Robert. She was very emotional over my father's death. In fact, she went into hysterics at the graveside, laughing so hard, I had to pull her off the grave myself and lead her back to the car."

I didn't know what to say. Neither did Monette, who sat there with her mouth open, halfway between being stunned and exploding in laughter herself.

I decided to make amends. "I'm sorry that I ever doubted you mother's intentions, and I will completely forget the fact that she made two attempts on my life the one and only time I stayed at your ancestral home in Newport, Rhode Island."

"Can I help it if you're not used to walking on marble?" Michael fired back.

"I was pushed down the staircase by your mother, Michael—plain and simple."

"She said she saw you slipping and she reached out to grab you and keep you from falling."

"Then I suppose that when she tried to bean me with a four-hundred-pound painting of herself, it was an accident?"

"It's an old house, Robert. Things just give out sometimes," Michael reasoned.

"For fucking crying out loud," Monette interjected. "You sound like two lesbians on the first day of a Rainbow whale cruise of the Blowholes of Alaska."

"He started it," I said, pointing at Michael.

"I did not!" Michael cried.

"Okay, we'll behave, Monette," I promised. "As long as he keeps his hands on his side of the sofa," I said, drawing an imaginary line down the middle of the cushion. Michael's hand darted over on my side, testing our treaty to the limits. I hit at his hand, pushing it back into his own territory while Monette tried her damnedest not to laugh. What are friends for if you can't act juvenile once in a while?

"I can't believe this," Monette said, chuckling. "Two people are dead and we're sitting here laughing and having a gay old time. Life is just too absurd sometimes."

"What do you mean *sometimes*?" I commented. "I think we need to release a little tension. There's an honest-to-goodness murderer in our midst, and we can't seem to figure out where he or she will strike next. It's frustrating."

"I think it's high time we found out who's behind all of this. C'mon, you two; let's go."

"Where?" I asked.

"Back to the casa grande. If anyone knew Rex, it was Vince. I think he could shed a lot of light on this whole mess. Or . . ." Monette said, her voice pausing long enough for me to ask the obligatory question.

"Or what?" I asked.

"Or have him confirm the fact that he's a number one suspect," she said.

9

Let the Games Begin!

When we arrived back at Rex's house, we found Vince sitting on the porch overlooking the pool, martini in hand, staring off into the distance and doing something that I wouldn't think a close friend of a dead person would be doing: smiling. Because I only saw him in a state of perpetual motion, his smiling but motionless body seemed dead, and for a fraction of a second, I thought that this might be true—the killer had struck again. But as Monette and I approached him and I laid my hand on his, I saw him blink. He was alive.

"Vince, is there anything we can do for you?"

"No. I've taken care of everything. I'm having Rex cremated, and the memorial service will be next month—after the Red Party goes down as the biggest sensation in gay history."

"How are you handling Rex's . . . thing?" I asked gently.

"Fine, fine. Rex is on a different plane now."

"American Airlines?" I asked, not quite getting what Vince was talking about.

"No, the plane of the next world. That's where Rex's soul is."

"Oh." I began to wonder what plane Vince was on right now. Maybe he was not on a plane at all but had instead gotten on a bus years ago and ridden it to the end of the line, which ended up in a cornfield.

"I'm not worried that Rex has passed on. In fact, I am glad for him. I'm sure he's much happier now."

I looked at Monette and shrugged my shoulders. What were we supposed to do? Throw a bucket of cold water on him?

"Vince, Monette and I are here to make sure that the Red Party is a success and that we catch whoever it is who did this to Rex. We'd like to ask you some questions, if you don't mind." As I said this, I reminded myself that Vince was indeed a suspect, and a very good one at that. Our line of questioning would either absolve him of that title or merely cement it. But you had to start somewhere.

"Go ahead," Vince said, still smiling with the gods in the next dimension.

I looked over at Monette, waiting for her to start. Once she did, I would jump in where necessary.

"Vince, is there anyone in your mind that stands out as the kind of person who would murder Rex?" she asked.

"Plenty of people. Darlene Waldron for one. I hear she's got money trouble, and I'm sure she wouldn't hesitate to eliminate any competitors."

"Who told you that Darlene has money problems?"

"Rex. He heard it through the party production grapevine that Clothes Circuit was outselling her, plus some Internet sales thing of hers went bust."

"That's very interesting, Vince. That could help a lot. Who else?"

"Jimmy Garboni, because Rex wouldn't deal with him. He said that you have to grease too many palms when you work with Jimmy, and it costs too much to throw a party. He also said that once you give in and work with him, you're hooked. Then if Jimmy doesn't like you using some other supplier, his workers can purposely slow stuff down just when you need things fast. Jimmy's threatened Rex before, too. Plenty of times. But Rex always called his bluff."

"Interesting. Anyone else?"

"This could take all night. Martin Stevers is one person who comes to mind." More smiling.

"Why is that, Vince?"

"Rex and Martin go way back. A few years ago, Rex got a bill from Martin that was way out of line. Thousands of dollars. Martin said there were all kinds of last-minute changes. Rex paid up even though it wasn't the way he did business. Then, next time they work together, Rex gets a bill that's hundreds of thousands over the original estimate. Same story again. Martin points to all kinds of last-minute changes, additions—stuff like that. So Rex refused to pay and Martin sued him—and lost. That incident caused a lot of bad blood between them. I wouldn't put it past Martin to extort money out of Rex and put the Red Party in the red, then kill Rex just to even the score. It would be quite a coup for Martin, the lousy maggot."

"Vince," Monette said, "you haven't mentioned Kip or Brian. Why is that?"

"Because they wouldn't stoop to anything like that. I know Kip Savage and Brian Keeper."

"But how do you know for sure?" I asked.

"Because they helped us the whole way. In fact, when word got out that Rex was planning to throw the Red Party, they telephoned and said that if we needed any help, all we had to do was give them a call."

Monette felt the need to explain my position. "Robert has a point. Of all the people, the White Party has the most to lose if the Red Party takes off."

"I refuse to believe it. Rex told me once that there was some discussion that the two parties should merge—you know, become the biggest party on the planet."

"I see. Anyone else that stands out, Vince?"

"No, that's my list of suspects," Vince said with a great deal of satisfaction and a great big smile.

"Just a few more questions, Vince."

"Fine—it's not like I have a lot of other things to do."

"I'm sorry, Vince. But anything you tell us could solve everything."

"You have my undivided attention," Vince said, still smiling and looking across the pool and into the mountains beyond.

"So Rex never mentioned these threats until they began to hit home, here . . . so to speak?"

"The first time I heard about the boulder incident was when the police came, after the palm tree fell on the house. He never mentioned it to me before that."

"Was that normal? I mean, did Rex tell you everything that happened to him and his business?"

"Yes and no. Look, Rex wasn't going to tell me how many crates of calla lilies he ordered or stuff like that. Not the itty-bitty details. But the big stuff—the big jobs, the gossip—*that* he told me. All the shit with Darlene and Martin—I heard that stuff. He seemed to really hate Martin, probably because of the lawsuit."

"So it came as a surprise that someone made an attempt on his life by trying to flatten him with a boulder?"

Vince shook his head. "It came as a surprise that he was out hiking. But he's been doing a lot of strange things lately."

"What?" Monette asked. "He didn't usually go hiking?"

"No, that sort of thing just isn't—wasn't Rex. He was in great shape because he went to the gym every day, but he wasn't an outdoorsy kind of guy. In fact, the only way I can picture him outdoors is in the pool here or at a restaurant with an outdoor garden."

"You were saying that his behavior was strange lately. What do you mean by that? Could you give me an example?" Monette asked.

"I don't know. It seemed that he was lost in thought all the time. Daydreaming, when he was usually very focused on his work. Stuff like that. Oh, and he took two vacations last year and he didn't tell me where he was going. He said he didn't want anyone to be able to contact him—that he wanted peace and quiet for a change. No phones ringing. No TVs blaring. Oh, yeah; he said that he needed to recharge his batteries, so I assumed it was that New Age resort up in Big Sur that he sometimes visited."

"One last request."

"Whatever you want, Monette."

"Can Robert show me all around the house, both inside and out, so I can see where the palm tree fell on the house? Also, can I look inside your garden shed—if you have one?"

"There's a garden shed out behind the house, but there's nothing in it besides a dozen bags of potting soil and a hand trowel. We have gardeners who take care of everything, and they bring their own tools. I just pot some plants once in a while."

Monette and I got up to leave, but something stopped Monette in her tracks. She pivoted on her heels to face Vince again.

"Are you sure you're going to be okay staying here?" she asked.

"Yes, yes, I'll be fine," Vince replied.

"No, I mean, you're not going to be—how do I put this?—out of house and home now that Rex is gone?"

I smiled at Monette's brilliance.

"Rex made sure I was *well* taken care of if he died."

The emphasis on the word *well* told us all we needed to know: Vince had apparently inherited a bundle from Rex. No wonder he was smiling.

"Oh, that's good, Vince," Monette replied, showing her sympathy with his position. We both thanked Vince and told him that if he thought of anything that might be useful, to tell me or call Monette if I was out. I got the feeling that in the next few days, if you could find Monette, you'd find me there, too.

We stepped outside the house, and I took Monette to the spot where the tree had made its *palmus interruptus* on Michael and Rex. There were plastic tarps and plywood sheets covering the gaping hole.

"I have no idea what it is I'm looking for," Monette confessed. "I guess when one tree falls on a house, it looks just like any other. Wait a frickin' minute!"

"Wait a frickin' minute" is Monette's stock phrase that signals that she is on to something. "What is it?" I asked.

"You said the wind was blowing hard that night. Which way was it blowing?"

"I don't know. What do I look like, a weathervane?"

"Shame, shame, Robert. Use your head; reason it out."

"Monette, dear, the number one problem I have in life is that I'm too cerebral."

"I'm asking you to figure the wind direction out, not to raise your consciousness."

I looked over at the dining room widows and put my little gray cells to work. "It was really windy that night. And . . . I remember a palm frond hitting the window in the dining room that night. Scared the shit out of all of us. The frond hit the window that way," I said, tracing the possible flight pattern with my arm. "So the wind must have been coming from that direction."

"From the northwest."

"How do you know that direction is northwest?" I asked.

"Trust me, my sense of direction is infallible."

"Unlike your driving," I added.

"You try being almost six and a half feet tall and I'd like to see you drive a Metro. Now, can we stay on the subject at hand here? If the wind was coming from the northwest, the palm tree would fall right on the house."

"Which it did. So what's your point, Monette?"

She paused for a moment. "How the hell should I know? Do you think Hercule Poirot got it right the very first time? Let's go look in the garden shed."

"Vince said there wasn't anything in there."

"Yeah, and you believe everything he tells you?"

"More or less."

"Good, when we crack this case, I'm going to reveal myself as the goddess Lakshmi, and you will worship me forevermore."

"I already do," I added, raising Monette's hand to my lips, where I kissed it.

"Okay, let's see what we find in the shed," she said as she flung the door open and entered. "Ten bags of potting soil, one garden trowel, nothing else. Unless . . . unless," she reported, shoving her hand behind the potting soil bags, " . . . unless there happens to be a bow saw here!" she shouted in triumph.

There it was, a saw where there wasn't supposed to be one. She examined it carefully, holding it in such a way that her fingerprints wouldn't land anywhere someone would normally hold it.

"Don't you see, Robert? There are small pieces of sawdust on the blade!"

"I guess that answers the question about *what* cut down the tree. Now we just have to find out *who*."

"Easy for you to say. As you no doubt saw inside the house a minute ago, Vince just proved to me that he has a clear-cut motive for murder. He's a suspect, but he's far from the only one."

"Yes, I saw that. Very clever."

"Thank you. Like taking candy from a baby."

"Well, now what?" I said.

"The sun is about to set behind Mt. San Jacinto, so there's only one thing to do."

"Give Jimmy Garboni the kiss of death?"

"No."

"Break into Darlene Waldron's house and put habanero pepper in her Monistat?"

"No, but it's about as painful."

"You're not going to suggest . . ."

"Yes, I am. I know you'd rather gouge your eyes out, but I think we need to pay a visit to Colorado Jackson. He's one of the few higher-ups with T-Rex Productions we haven't talked with yet."

"Oh, God, Monette, do we really have to? All he's going to do is sit there and snipe at us. My only hope is that someone tries to bump him off. In fact, why don't we do the world a favor and kill him ourselves? We can strangle him with his seven-hundred-dollar drape tiebacks."

Monette gave a small laugh. "Now, now, save it for your bridge game. I know you don't like him—"

"The *world* doesn't like him. Mother Theresa would spit on him if she were alive," I blurted out.

"As I was saying, a good detective doesn't let personal prejudices cloud his or her thinking. You have to keep an open mind and not condemn them just because they're the human equivalent of the Ebola virus. Then, if you're a good little boy and don't kick Colorado in the stomach, we'll stop at the grocery store and buy tequila and all the fixin's for my famous five-alarm nachos. Then we'll head over to Marc's place and give him some company. I'm sure he could use some."

"That sounds like a great way to spend an evening. I like nachos that make my gums and nose bleed! Let me go inside and invite Vince along."

I went into the house and asked Vince if he wanted to join us. He declined, saying that he was going to spend the night at some friends' house. I went into the office and called Marc. He welcomed our idea, suggesting that Monette and I stay the night. I was thrilled. This would be my second night at Marc's, making it a record as far as dates are concerned—if you forgot the fact that I dated a German count last summer. Since Siegfried von Schmidt, I didn't want to date much. And considering the freaks that exist out there, it isn't surprising. As I was zipping up my overnight bag, I noticed a piece of paper under a pair of socks. I pulled it out and opened it up, revealing the folder bearing the architectural drawing of the strange pyramid-shaped building I had found behind Rex's desk yesterday. I looked at the words on the drawing: *Butia A.D.* It made no sense, but I thought it might be of some help. I put the drawing back into my bag, determined to enter the rendering as exhibit A in the Case of the Dead Party Planners.

We followed Vince's directions through Rancho Myass to Palm Desert, where, (surprise, surprise) Colorado lived in a snooty gated community. (Why do they call it a community when people have no contact with each other once they're inside?) His house was a tract mansion with a soaring roofline and inane references to Georgian architecture: fan windows, columns, and a curved stairway that looked more at home in Virginia than the California desert. We rang the doorbell, which Monette and I could hear ringing the tune "We're in the Money." Tacky, tacky, tacky.

The door opened and there stood Colorado, dressed to the nines in trendy microfibers and square-toed shoes with huge buckles.

"Yes?" he asked, convincing himself that we were gardeners having the consummate impudence of rapping our dirty knuckles on his pristine front door. Never mind the fact that Vince had called him up and explained that we wanted to talk to him pronto.

"It's Monette and Robert. Vince called about us seeing you," she said, explaining a fact that was already well known. But Colorado continued to play dumb for a second. Bitch.

"Oh, oh, yes, come on in—and wipe your feet; the carpet's very expensive."

Colorado led us into his home office, a gaudy place done up like a sultan's tent, the walls covered in expensive silk fabric. Every available surface was covered with piles of fabric sample books, bolts of fabric, design magazines, carpet samples, and books of wallpapers. Since there were few places to sit, Monette had aimed her ass at a settee when Colorado screamed like a banshee.

"FOR GOD'S SAKE, DON'T SIT DOWN!" he shrieked, pulling Monette away from the Louis de Hooey sofa. "It's covered in Scalamandre silk! There's over twenty-five thousand dollars in fabric on that piece alone."

Monette stood there in a state of shock, wondering why someone would get so excited over a sofa that looked like a prostitute.

Colorado rummaged through a drawer and emerged with a roll of yellow ribbon, which he unfurled and tied between the two arms of the settee, prohibiting any future asses from parking themselves there.

Monette watched Colorado fuss over the settee, coming to the same conclusion as mine: that while the fabric may be expensive, the upholstery job was mediocre. And even then, a sofa was just a place to sit—not reign.

"Sorry about the sofa," Monette said, stifling a snigger.

Colorado, seeing Monette smirking at him, looked at her with daggers in his eyes. "It's a SETTEE. . . . Don't they teach you anything in Arkansas?" Colorado fired back.

"I'm from Boston," Monette replied with all the grace and decorum of Queen Elizabeth.

I didn't like the sound of this. Monette just sitting there (well, trying to), taking all this bile from this pretentious puff adder. She was being way too nice, too cool about it. Any moment now, her hand would dart out and crack his neck as if she were twisting the cap off a bottle of Gatorade. She did, however, manage to contain herself. Pity.

Colorado motioned toward two ottomans for us to sit on, and we did as commanded. He asked if we wanted to join him for cocktails, and we agreed. If you end up having to throw a drink in someone's face, it's so much handier if you're holding one at the time.

"I'm very busy right now, so could you make this brief? I'm supposed to be draping two miles of scrims at the Red Party, and the goddamn stuff hasn't even arrived yet in Palm Springs."

"I'll do my best to be brief," Monette promised. She gathered up her thoughts, summarizing them in her head in order to get the most mileage out of our audience with Her Highness.

"I suppose by now you know that Rex was found dead in Marc's pool last night—and that Leo died today, most likely by poison."

"Yes, yes, Marc called me a few hours ago and told me. He also said to keep this information confidential for the time being. Like I'm going to go blabbing all this so the Red Party will flop and I won't get paid for my services. Sometimes I think that Marc should put a little Vaseline behind each ear so he can pull his head out of his ass."

I promised myself then and there that I would get Colorado back for that comment.

"Idaho—I mean, Colorado, do you remember what time it was when you left Leo's party last night?"

"I don't know. Around midnight."

"And you came straight home?"

"No, I went to The Zone—it's a dance bar over on Your anus."

"Uranus?"

"Your Anus Street." Colorado let out an exasperated sigh, flustered that we weren't getting the joke. "It's supposed to be Arenas—the gay street—but all the locals call it 'Your anus.'"

"Right. And how long did you stay there?"

"About an hour. Maybe a little more. Then I went home."

"So you said you went to a dance bar when you have all this work to do?"

"I told you," Colorado puffed, "all the shit I've got to hang didn't arrive yet. There's not much I can do until then, and I'm not about to sit around on my hands when there are so many gorgeous boys in town."

"I see," Monette uttered. "Do you have any idea who would've hated Rex enough to kill him—and attempt to destroy the Red Party?"

"I thought you said you'd make this quick. It could take all day to list Rex's enemies."

"So you think he had a lot, eh?"

"Honey, Rex trampled on a lot of people to get where he is today. Martin Stevers could have done it. He lost a lot of money fighting Rex in court. He's still fuming about the whole matter. Kip Savage hates him, too."

I begged to differ on this observation. "Colorado, I saw Rex with Kip and Brian at Leo's party last night, and they couldn't have been nicer and chummier to each other."

"That's just an act! Kip likes to keep his nose clean in public, and Brian is in PR. That says it all. He keeps a smile on for the public, but he'll knife you in the back when no one's looking."

I wasn't about to let this one go. "If Kip hates Rex so much, then why did he offer to help the Red Party out?"

"As I said before, it's all public relations. Look at Darlene Waldron. Don't let the smile fool you. Appearances can be deceiving. These people can be vicious."

The Limoges just called the plate porcelain.

Monette listened to the two of us, composing her next question. "So far, you've named several people associated with the White Party. Why are you so sure these people could have done it?"

"Because they don't know that Rex and Leo are dead," Colorado answered. "More importantly, they don't know the bank account for T-Rex Productions was cleaned out a few days ago by Rex himself."

Monette and I were shocked by Colorado's knowledge. "And how do you know all this?" I asked.

"Because Marc told me everything on the phone a few hours ago. He called the bank and found out. And because Rex and Leo are gone, he doesn't know who to turn to, since there's almost no one left from the partnership."

"You're not part of T-Rex Productions in any way?" Monette asked.

"No, unless you count that I get paid for my services—a fact that looks tenuous now."

"Huh," Monette grunted. "But you didn't answer my question, Colorado. Why does it point the finger of suspicion toward Kip and the rest because they don't know the money is gone?"

"Because . . ." Colorado explained to us as if we were four-year-old children, "if they knew the money had disappeared, they wouldn't be mailing extortion letters like this to people like me. There's nothing to extort—it's gone already, to God knows where."

Colorado extended his hand toward us, his hand bearing a letter with the same words cut out of a magazine. Monette and I looked at each other. I was amazed by this killer's speed.

"But . . ." Monette began, " . . . the killer has no idea that you're not a partner in T-Rex."

"I suppose they think that I'm either a partner or that I have some kind of sway with Rex—*had*, sorry."

Monette looked at the letter closely. "Have you called the police about this letter?"

Colorado finished his gimlet like a child gulping down the last vestiges of a Cherry Coke. "Why bother? I know I'm not liked in this town, and I don't give a shit. But I don't think anyone is out to kill me. I mean, why?"

Monette straightened herself on her ottoman and held the letter out in Colorado's face. "The last two people who got a letter like this are now dead. Marc Baldwin is the only recipient of this letter—besides you—who is still alive."

"See, the killing's stopped," Colorado replied with insanely faulty logic.

"And Marc is still alive only because he's under twenty-four-hour security."

"Honey, I still don't understand why someone would want to kill me."

I thought to myself, *This is too easy*. But I let the opportunity pass.

"Because they're operating under the mistaken notion you're either a partner in T-Rex or that by threatening anyone associated with it, that they can stop the Red Party from ever happening," Monette surmised.

"Listen, I'm a vicious queen and I know it. I had to be. I've faced bigger enemies than this—my stepmother, for instance. That's why I have this huge house, nice cars, clothes, et cetera, et cetera. I was a kid and I had to fight her for my inheritance. And I won. I've learned early on that this is a shitty little world and that you don't get anywhere in this life unless you're prepared to fight for it."

Monette looked exasperated but gave in to Colorado's request. "Fine, if you wind up dead, don't come running to me."

"Monette, darling, you haven't been listening. I don't run from anybody. Don't you and Robert worry your pretty little heads over me. I'll be around to torment the world for a long time, and nobody is going to put a stop to it if I have anything to say about it."

We got up to go. Colorado followed us to the door, then swung it open for us. As we were walking down the sidewalk to the street, Monette turned to Colorado, who was standing in the doorway.

"Colorado, I did my best to warn you. If you go out, be careful."

"Ha-ha-ha!" came the reply. "That's a good one. Someone caring for me!" he shouted, and threw the door closed with a slam. Not a hard one—that would indicate that we had got the better of him. But it was a slam nonetheless.

"I could kill that fucking bastard myself. Maybe it would put him out of his misery," Monette said, her anger finally boiling over after being contained so much.

I took her trembling hand in mine and looked her straight in the eye. "Let's hope that someone beats you to it. Red hair looks awful with those orange prison uniforms."

We rode over to retrieve Monette's things in Rancho Myass, stopped at the grocery store for supplies, and then headed up the hill toward Marc's house. As Monette jabbered on and on about the potential wives she had seen at the Dinah Shore Classic, I thought about how my life could best be described as "keep your head and arms inside the moving vehicle at all times." While other children were watching their hands dip and soar outside the windows of the bus we rode to grade school, I kept mine securely inside the vehicle, not wanting to have my hand torn off by a semi or a telephone post and ending up with a hook or a mechanical arm. I wanted to participate, to break free, but the horrific alternative kept rearing its ugly head in my mind. "That's what you get," I could hear my mother saying, chastising me for sticking my hand out the window to let it flutter in the wind and feeling the flood of freedom. "Now, how are you going to throw a football with a mechanical arm like that?" I could see my mother with her hands on her hips, cigarette dangling from her lip, playing the role that parents relish more than life itself: the I-told-you-so parent. "And what is the pope going to think when he sees you cross yourself with that arm? I'll tell you! Another child who did-n't listen to his parents!"

I came out of my daydream when we roared up to Marc's house, the hood of the Metro stopping a menacing two inches from Marc's garage door.

"I think I'm going to turn into a gay man and marry Marc and live up here in a desert paradise forever—that is, if you don't marry him first."

I smiled. Even my best friend was confirming that a rela-tionship was quickly forming between Marc and me. But I, the hopeless romanticist, was way ahead of Monette. In my mind, I had already moved in with Marc. I was a famous writer of offbeat comedies of my upbringing in the Midwest, which were the toast of the world, and Marc had quit his job since he and I could comfortably live off just my income. As we sat by the fireplace in his living room on a crisp winter morning, I could see myself throwing stacks of hundred-dollar bills into the fire to keep it roaring. We traveled around the world, where we collected hands of Buddha stat-ues, drank exotic cocktails made from local herbs, and did anything we damn well pleased. I was about to partake of a delicious cereal made mostly of thin twenty-four-karat gold leaves when a door hit me in the head.

"Watch out for the door," Monette cautioned, a little too late to stave off the knot that would undoubtedly rise on my forehead. A lump is never as sexy as a fencing scar, but I in-tended to milk it for all it was worth.

"Thanks for the advance warning about the door, Mo-nette."

"I couldn't help it. The wind caught it and it just flew out of my hand. Anyway, if you were watching where you were going, this wouldn't have happened. You looked like you were somewhere else."

"Somewhere in Thailand, if you must know."

"Well, come back to Cathedral City for a little while, if you don't mind. We're going to have a little fun."

"And a little gossip, you mean."

"They're the same thing, aren't they?"

We made our way into the kitchen, where Marc had a plastic bag filled with ice cubes waiting for my aching head. He tenderly applied the ice with loving hands, making me feel warm and cold all at the same time.

"Before I can get to work, I need an important ingredient," she said as she reached into a grocery bag and pulled out a bottle of tequila that needed two hands just to lift. "There," she said, staring at the bottle in a self-satisfied way, as if she had given birth to it. "Come to Mama, you precious. Marc, could you make some margaritas? There's margarita mix in one of these bags. Make 'em good and strong. So, Marc, we talked with Vince and Colorado today."

"Boy, no wonder you're looking forward to a drink," Marc commented. "Not that Vince is much trouble, but Colorado—whew!"

"Don't worry, Robert and I knew how to handle him. I have a few questions, though."

"Whatever helps. Go ahead and ask."

"Good. Now, jump in anytime, Robert, if I leave anything out. Colorado told me that his part of the Red Party has something to do with swags."

"Scrims."

"Oh, right—scrims. What else does he do?"

"As far as I can tell, not much more than that," Marc answered. "He tells everyone he's responsible for the event's overall theme and look. It's something a half-wit could do, but Rex seemed to tolerate him. Why, I'll never know."

"So he's not a partner in T-Rex?"

"No, thank God."

"So the only partners are you, Rex, Leo, and David McLeish?" I chimed in.

"That's right."

Monette paused while cutting her vegetables. She pointed the chef's knife she was holding at Marc, to emphasize her point. "So how did Rex withdraw all that money without the consent of the rest of you partners?"

"Because T-Rex is a general partnership. Rex structured it that way because there aren't a lot of assets with party production, so there's not much value in it to protect from lawsuits. In the agreement, Rex had control of a larger part of the partnership, so he worded it so he could sign checks without the rest of us approving them. Stupid of us, huh?"

"Don't be so hard on yourself, Marc. Rex was a very shrewd businessman. I don't think there was ever a moment when he didn't know what he was doing."

"Except when he went to pay off his killer to ensure that the Red Party went off without a hitch. I don't think he figured that he—or she—could turn out to be a cold-blooded killer," I theorized.

"Now, that's another thing that's bothering me," Monette said, pointing the knife at me this time. "You and I are saying 'he or she' all the time. What's preventing the killer from being *them*?"

"Monette, that's brilliant!" I almost shouted.

Monette tried to be humble. "I wouldn't exactly say it was brilliant, but it's something we've been overlooking until now. It makes a lot of sense. I mean, we have a whole handful of people who want Rex and his party out of the way. What's to say that they didn't all work together, huh?"

Marc shook his head in agreement. "It's so simple and obvious. Someone had to place those calls to Rex at Leo's party; someone had to poison Leo, then meet Rex at my pool and receive the money and finish him off. It's going to take a lot of people to carry something off like that," Marc added, as if the case had been solved.

"It's a distinct possibility," Monette responded. "After all, they're the people with the most to lose. I think tomorrow we need to see this Clifford and Grayson you mentioned. We're getting into unfamiliar territory, and we need people who know their way around town. Do these guys know the White Party people?"

"No," Marc replied, "but don't let that stop you. Grayson may be small and elderly, but he's got a lot of nerve. You had to in order to be a man and wear a dress out in public back in the forties."

"The forties! Wow!" I exclaimed.

"Oh, yeah. Nowadays, no one would even bat an eye if you walked down Market Street in San Francisco wearing a dress, but back then you were taking your chances."

Monette again: "So tell us about this Clifford and Grayson. They sound like a hoot."

"You have no idea. For starters, they live in a pink house. Totally pink, from the pool to the Formica in their kitchen. They even have a vintage pink Rolls Royce. You can spot it all over town."

Monette and I laughed hysterically.

"You think I'm kidding, don't you?" Marc asked, swallowing a fair bit of laughter himself. "And you know what the funny thing is? They didn't come up with that color. The straight couple they bought the house from had a thing for pink."

"No!" came the reply from both Monette and me.

"Yes. They tell everyone they were going to change the color immediately after they moved in—which was ten years ago, but they discovered that the color did wonders for their skin. At least that's what they say."

"Oh, my God. That's wonderful," Monette said as she chopped away. "I cannot wait to meet them. This makes my whole trip worthwhile!"

I was instantly intrigued with Clifford and Grayson, even though I hadn't even met them. "So tell us a little more about them. What do they do?"

"Right now, nothing. They're retired," Marc reported. "Apparently, Grayson is loaded because his family used to own a huge sausage company—ironic, huh? He did a lot of drag in San Francisco, and he does a charity drag show here in Palm Springs now and then—he's quite hysterical. Let's see, what else have I heard?" Marc asked himself, racking his brain for any more tidbits. "He invented the title for himself: empress dowager of the Most Imperial and Hierarchical Order of Almost-Vestal Virgins. Oh, yeah, he used to be very active in gay rights in San Francisco. Most of the mayors have been afraid of him, and he hasn't lost much of his spunk since he landed here. The city council members used to be a bunch of old Republican farts who never wanted anything to change here, but Grayson used the political tactics he learned in San Francisco and really shook up things at City Hall. More than one council member's ass has Grayson's heel mark on it."

"So what about his partner, Clifford?" Monette asked.

"Complete opposite. Quiet, cute as a button, sweet as can be. It's amazing how opposites attract. Grayson will be up there at a city council meeting, spitting fire at the members, and Clifford will sit there quietly."

"I love this town," I said. "And drag queens . . . God love 'em! They're so . . . so . . . bigger than life."

"Some of them are bigger than a ship, if you remember Rotunda in *The Battleships: Aground in New York*. That was quite a show," Monette recalled. "I prayed that the stage was specially reinforced. Plus, you neglected to mention that for a brief and shining moment in Provincetown, you were one."

"Just to solve a murder," I defended myself, especially in front of Marc. "I'm proud of my part in solving a murder and as a drag superstar opening to rave reviews."

"You had one line, and you never got the chance to speak it," Monette said, pricking the balloon of the one time in my life that could truly be called exotic.

"You gotta admire them."

"Who?" Monette asked.

"Drag queens," I said. "They're so colorful, so unafraid.

They don't care what anyone thinks about them. I could use a dollop of their courage sometimes."

Marc nodded his head. "I guess that's where the term *fierce* came from. Oh, I was going to ask you what you found out from Vince and Colorado."

"Vince is now very comfortable, and Colorado received an extortion letter similar to yours," I said.

"No kidding. Colorado?" Marc asked. He seemed stunned.

"Yes! He showed it to us," I remarked.

"What is he doing about it?"

"Nothing," Monette added.

"Nothing?" Marc asked. "No police or anything?"

"No, Marc, nothing," I said.

"Well, that sounds like Colorado. He does whatever he wants. It just seems foolish."

"I guess his reasoning is that the killer has the wrong impression that he's a partner in T-Rex," Monette said. "I have another question, Marc. How much space does two-point-five million dollars fill up?"

"What do you mean?"

"Will that much money fit in a suitcase?"

"I can answer that question because I've already tried to figure it out. The answer is yes. The bank teller told me that hundreds are bundled in packs of a thousand, five thousand, and ten thousand—thousand-dollar bills aren't in circulation. Now, you see dollar bills in stacks of one hundred all the time. It's not even an inch thick. So if we figure that a stack of one hundred hundred-dollar bills equals ten thousand dollars, then it would only take two hundred fifty stacks to equal two-point-five million dollars. I would think that would fit in a suitcase or a large briefcase."

"I wonder if Vince knew what Rex was doing," Monette mused. "Withdrawing the money, I mean."

"Why, are you looking for incriminating evidence against Vince?" Marc asked.

"I don't have to," Monette replied. "We don't know where

Vince was after he left Leo's party in search of Rex, plus, Vince had ample opportunity to pull all three attempts on Rex's life. He knew where Rex was hiking; we found a bow saw in the potting shed—with sawdust on it, so he could have cut the tree down. Hey, wait a minute. Robert, was Vince with you every minute before the tree fell on Rex's bedroom?"

"Let's see," I said, trying to reconstruct the dining room in my head that night. "I was sitting at the table, Rex and Michael went to go hide the salami, and Vince was either with me or in the kitchen preparing the next course. Come to think of it, he did disappear into the kitchen for extended periods. He could have run out to the tree and cut it down while I was waiting in the dining room."

"That seems a little far-fetched. Even if the blade was sharp, to cut down a sizable palm would take at least ten minutes—that is, unless it was partially cut already. Then, Vince would only have to disappear from the kitchen for a few minutes to finish the job. And look at the third attempt," Monette pointed out. "The exploding barbecue grill. Vince had easy access to that."

Marc was listening intently to every word Monette said. "I hate to agree with you, Monette, but you've made some very good points. I don't want to think that Vince could be the murderer, but facts are facts."

I was watching Monette's breathtaking examination of the case thus far, when her face suddenly changed its expression. She shot me a worried look and then pursed her lips, as if a thought were struggling to escape her lips but she wouldn't let it. She waited a minute and then spoke.

"I don't know about you two, but I've had enough talk about these murders for now. Why don't we put a moratorium on this kind of talk and just have fun for a while—and go for a swim?"

"That sounds wonderful," I said, wondering if Marc had

added more chlorine to the pool since Rex was found floating in it.

"I second the motion," Marc added cheerfully. "I think we should dine outside under the stars and have your famous five-alarm nachos."

Before you knew it, the three of us were seated outside under a canopy of stars, in a breeze that was so warm and soft, it caressed your skin like silk. We had a pitcher of margaritas, Monette's famous fire-hot nachos, and the bicarbonate of soda nearby just in case. As usual, Monette's nachos made my nose bleed, meaning I had to sit at the table with my head tilted up to the sky, which wasn't such a bad position to be in. At least there was plenty to look at.

Marc carried some of the plates into the house, ordering us to sit and enjoy while he did some washing up.

"Robert, can you hear me?" I could hear Monette asking just above a whisper.

"Yes," I replied, my head still tilted up. "It's my nose that's bleeding, not my ears."

"Oh, right," she conceded. "It looks like you are really falling for Marc—and vice versa."

"That's right."

"I'm so very happy for you."

"Thank you, Monette."

"You do realize that he could have killed Rex—and Leo."

"Yes, I reached that conclusion about an hour ago, when I saw your face turn ashen white, a feat that isn't easy with your freckled complexion. Oh, and thank you for reminding me about this fact. I will remember it clearly when I'm sleeping next to him in the same bed tonight—if I don't bleed to death first."

"Just keep your head back. What I said was that Marc is a suspect—I didn't say he is the killer. The one thing in Marc's favor is that whoever made attempts on Rex's life, then killed him and Leo, seems to have done his or her planning—that or there's more than one person involved. It's like the murderer is everywhere. It just seems impossible for one person to have done it all."

I was looking up at Betelgeuse, the center star in the Orion constellation's belt, when I heard the telephone ring in Marc's kitchen. "I know what you mean—either this killer is very cunning, or we have more than one person to contend with."

"Yes, it could be like in *Murder on the Orient Express*, where everyone on the train had some part in the murder of a very unlikable person."

As Monette and I pondered this prospect, Marc came and sat at the table; the pupils in his eyes were black and fearful.

"That was the police on the phone just now. It seems that someone took a shot at Colorado while he was driving down Highway 111. He's in the hospital."

10

Think Pink

"**N**o shit!" Monette exclaimed.

"Yes, the police said he was driving along 111 when a bullet hit his car. The car ran off the road and into a ditch, and he was knocked unconscious. They took him to Eisenhower Medical Center. Thank God he's in stable condition."

"Boy, that's a statement you don't hear every day," I said.

"What's that?" Marc asked.

"That someone's concerned for Colorado's welfare. I'll bet he was trying to run some elderly woman off the road when he picked the wrong senior to cross. She pulls a snubnosed thirty-eight out of her purse and blows him away."

Monette was musing something in her head. "I guess that pretty much eliminates Colorado as a suspect."

"Now you and David McLeish are the only partners left to T-Rex," I said. "Are the police still out front in the car, Marc?"

"Are you kidding? As soon as I hung up the phone, I checked. We're safe. If it weren't for the steep cliff behind that wall, and the tall hedge, I'd ask that we move this party inside while I go hide in a closet until this is all over."

"I think that is a good idea, actually," Monette said. "It's been a long day, and I need to get some sleep."

"You don't want to go for a swim?" Marc asked.

"No, I'm just bushed."

Marc looked Monette right in the eye. "I put more chlorine in after they hauled Rex out."

"Maybe tomorrow," Monette said. "I've got to get some sleep. Good night."

We were alone. The night was so pretty and the sky so magnificent, that Marc and I sat out on chaise lounges by the pool and talked late into the night. And the more we talked, the more we realized how much we had in common. It was almost spooky. When I confessed a developing attraction to policemen, Marc looked at me with surprise. Perhaps, in the rising heat of passion, I had confessed a little too much. I said that you only had to spend some time around Michael and you ended up thinking the same way. Or, perhaps Michael unleashed what was already inside me.

"Really?" he said. "Me too!"

Could this get any better? I thought to myself. A guy with the same turn-ons as myself?

We talked further. I discovered that Marc, like me, knew a million pointless facts. He knew, for instance, that yak milk is pink. He knew what an event horizon is on an interstellar black hole. And most impressive was the fact that he loved the ribald songs of Rusty Warren. It's not like my boyfriends had to be *Jeopardy* champions, but it was nice to know that your heartthrob has a desire to know things just for the sake of knowing things. Marc also preferred watching black-and-white movies on Friday night instead of going out, he swooned over the smell of a fireplace on an autumn night, and linguine with pesto sauce was his favorite dish. They say that there's someone out there for everybody, and I was beginning to feel as if this might be that someone. I know I was maybe jumping the gun, but I understand that when people have waited so long for the special person, it's only natural to be gunning the engine instead of just sitting there in idle.

But what if this one was a murderer? I didn't even want

to think about this possibility—a possibility that was made more remote since Marc was with Monette and me when someone took a potshot at Colorado. Of course, Marc could be working with someone else who actually did the shooting, but I didn't think so. I've been wrong before, but Marc was the type of person who didn't want two and a half million dollars. He knew that it wouldn't make him any happier.

Nonetheless, after we went inside and just fell asleep in each other's arms, I waited for him to drift off before I closed my eyes. Then, in the darkness, a thought came to me. *Take a chance. Just let go.* And I did. I have to say, I never slept better in my entire life.

The next morning, I heard Monette's voice in the kitchen. Marc was in the shower, so I got up and poured myself a cup of coffee. I sat down next to her at the kitchen counter, watching her scribbling maniacally on a notepad as she held the phone against her ear.

"So he never told you that he had withdrawn the two and a half million? Uh-huh, you stayed at the setup . . . he took the car . . . gone an hour . . . uh-huh, had a briefcase with him . . . not his normal briefcase . . . I see . . . and when you left the party that night, did you go straight home to look for Rex? . . . I see . . . yes, uh-huh . . . Did anyone see you come home? . . . Did you remember what time it was when you got home? Okay, thank you so much for answering these questions at a difficult time like this."

She hung up the phone without looking at the handset, which missed the base and fell on the floor with a clatter of technology. She didn't even look up, her hand struggling valiantly to keep up with her thoughts.

"Boy, did I get a bunch of information just now. I'll be with you in a minute. I just have so much to write down. Could you be a darling and pick up the phone for me?"

I complied and poured myself another half cup of coffee while I waited for Monette to come down from the natural high she got when she was hot on the trail of a murderer.

"Whew! Okay, I'm done. Listen to what I've found out. The day of Rex's murder, Vince and Rex went to the Red Party setup site in the same car. Rex takes the car and leaves for an hour, then returns. The briefcase he went to the Red Party site with wasn't in the car when Rex came back to retrieve Vince."

"I know," I said.

"How do you know?" Monette asked. She couldn't believe that I could be a step ahead of her.

"Because he came back to the house in the afternoon before Leo's party, briefcase in hand. A larger-than-normal briefcase. He was trying to get into his office when I was snooping around."

"You didn't tell me that!" she whined.

"Because it didn't seem abnormal at the time. Carrying a briefcase isn't a federal crime, you know."

"So he came back and caught you snooping?"

"No, the door was locked—I said I was changing."

"And you let him in and he had a briefcase in his hand?"

"Yup, he put it in the corner."

"God, just think, there was enough money in that briefcase for us to never work again, and it was just a few feet away!" Monette commented excitedly.

"Don't remind me, Monette. Even I would probably kill someone if I could get out of writing advertising copy for feminine hygiene products."

"I thought you weren't on that account anymore," she said.

"I was writing brochures for WorldCom, but you can imagine where that ended up."

"In the crapper along with their worthless shares," Monette replied.

"Exactly, so it's back to vaginas."

"That's just where a gay man wants to be," Monette said, smiling at the irony.

"Wait a minute, we were just talking about Rex's office, and I remembered something that I want to show you—and Marc. I think it could really be important!"

I went to Marc's bedroom, where he had just finished dressing. I retrieved the architectural drawing from my overnight bag and grabbed Marc by the hand and dragged him down the hall to the kitchen. I laid the drawing down, asking Monette and Marc what they thought about it.

"Not bad, Robert," Monette replied, "but don't give up your job writing about douches. It's tough making a go of it in architecture."

"Very funny, Monette. This is a drawing of something I found in Rex's office. It was in a folder that had fallen behind his desk. See, it's marked 'A.D.' After death. Get it? It's some mystical tomb or something he wanted to be buried in."

Monette's eyebrows, which had been raised in raw disbelief, now furrowed as if to get a better look at the drawing.

"Marc," she started, "does this mean anything to you? Butia? What's a butia?" she wondered out loud.

"I have no idea," Marc explained.

"Did Rex ever say anything about a tomb or a pyramid?"

"No, never," he answered.

Monette clearly wanted to get to the bottom of this mystery. "And this doesn't have anything to do with a project, past or future, that T-Rex did, or bid on?"

"No, I've never seen this before. I have no idea what it means."

"Let me ask another question, Marc."

"Go ahead."

"Was Rex mystical in any way? I mean, did he believe in psychics or wear charms or believe in superstitions?"

"Now that you mention it, when he came back from a vacation about a year ago, he was wearing a chain around his neck."

"A chain? What kind of chain?" Monette probed.

"A gold one, with an ankh on it."

"The Egyptian symbol of life?"

"Yes, that one."

"Was that unusual for him, Marc?"

"Monette, if you knew him, he would never wear jewelry. He never even wore a watch. It was like he just knew what time it was—like there was a clock built into his head."

"What do you suppose it means, Monette?" I asked. "Maybe it was a talisman, perhaps to ward off wicked event planners."

"Perhaps," Monette answered, never wanting to be prejudiced too much by any one theory. She liked to take everything in, then sift the clues endlessly, waiting for one theory to emerge. "These threats might have been going on a lot longer than any of us have thought. I think that today Robert and I need to pay a visit to Clifford and Grayson. As out-of-towners, there's only so far Robert and I can get without a little inside help. Marc, could you phone ahead and find out a good time for us to stop by?"

"Sure," said Marc, who was just about to pick up the phone when the instrument rang. "Maybe it's Grayson—he's supposed to be psychic."

"Hello? Julie? Yes, uh-huh . . . What? Really, what did they say? . . . Well, we should thank our lucky stars that's all they said. . . . They want to talk to me? . . . Oh, that's right . . . Rex and Leo would've handled that. . . . Okay, I'll call them later. Just give me their number. . . . Uh-huh. Okay, just stay cool. . . . We'll pull this one off. . . . Okay, call me if there are any other problems. Bye."

From the conversation, I could tell that the newspaper or the local news people had gotten their mitts on the story.

Marc confirmed my hunch. "Well, the newspapers have a front-page story about Rex and Leo this morning. And now the local news team wants to talk to me. I guess by default, I'm the new president of T-Rex, and PR man as well."

"Good, you handle the Red Party, and Robert and I will visit Clifford and Grayson; then we'll go talk to Darlene and Brian and everyone else, since they obviously know by now what happened to Rex and Leo . . . and Colorado—I almost forgot him. At least we can ask questions since everything's out in the open. Do you mind if we have a quick breakfast, Marc?"

"How about cereal?" Marc replied. He went to the cupboard and grabbed a handful of cereal boxes, one being Monette's favorite, Count Chocula. She ate three bowls, no doubt fortifying herself for a grueling day. After breakfast, Marc secured an audience with Clifford and Grayson at ten A.M. Monette and I left and drove over to the South Canyon Country Club area in South Palm Springs, where large and crazy 50s- and 60s-style houses sat nestled between the San Jacinto mountain range and the beginning of the Santa Rosas. As I looked at the mountains on either side of us, I thought that this was exactly our predicament right now: we were between a rock and a hard place.

Shortly after ruthless land-grabbers and developers had swindled the native Cahuilla Indians out of choice parcels of their own land and given them less-than-satisfactory parcels in the windy north end of Palm Springs, Palm Springs spent a brief bustling period that brought Spanish haciendas, mission revival and Italian villa-style buildings to what would soon become the city of Palm Springs. For a brief time the city grew, then fast-forwarded itself to become the mecca of mid-century modernism. The early modernist architects Richard Neutra and Rudolph Schindler were followed by others such as Albert Frey, John Porter Clark, and William F. Cody, who created houses that exemplified the modern idea that housing could be light, bright, sophisticated, and modern. At the very peak of their craft, they created some of the most enduring monuments of the modern style: the

John Porter Clark house, the Kaufmann house, and the Raymond Loewy house, to name a few.

Clifford and Grayson's house was not one of those monuments. True, it had been built in the true spirit of modernism and was probably quite daring in its day, but had been sadly remodeled at some point in its history, with mansard roofs, plaster half-columns topped by fruit baskets, and other French touches added to the mid-century modern frame. But the bad facelift that it had endured wasn't the first thing that struck you about Clifford and Grayson's home. What hit you immediately upon entering the driveway was the fact that it was pink on the outside, and that wasn't the half of it. It was pink through and through—a fact that became clear once the door to the house opened and we were greeted by a man of about seventy who looked like he could be anyone's grandfather. He was wearing a Hawaiian-style shirt covered not with parrots or palm trees, but numerous images of Michelangelo's *David*. His gray hair was carefully coiffed in precise swirls, and was more than ample for a man his age. Maybe too ample. In total, he was as cute as a button, and his gentle mannerisms made you want to scoop him up and put him safely on a sofa like a precious doll.

"Clifford or Grayson?" Monette ventured. "Monette and Robert—I called earlier about asking your help in something important. Marc Baldwin sent us."

"Clifford," our host said, daintily shaking our hands and waving us inside. "Grayson, Monette and Robert are here!" he called out toward the back of the house.

"Oh, wonderful," came a voice that was followed by a short, elderly man carrying a potted orchid. He was dressed completely in yellow, including yellow half-moon eyeglasses with yellow-tinted lenses hanging on a chain around his neck. "Clifford?" he said to his partner. "Could you take this plant and put it back in the greenhouse with the other chocolate orchids? I think she's pregnant and ready to start showing any day now."

As Clifford circled behind Monette and me to retrieve the orchid, I suddenly let out a tiny but unexpected yelp. I tried to excuse my sudden exclamation as nerves, but there was no doubt about it. Clifford had pinched me. Once I got over the suddenness of Clifford's attack, I was actually touched that in this violent and emotionally distant world, there was still someone left who engaged in something as tame as pinching. Clifford was living proof that while there was snow on his roof, there was a roaring fire in the oven down below.

Clifford complied and ferried the delicate orchid away, its leaves shuddering as he took tiny, measured steps in the direction of the back of the house. Before he turned a corner and disappeared, he flashed me a look that said, "How's about tonight, baby?"

It was just too cute.

"Come in and sit down." Grayson motioned to Monette and me, choosing for himself a large chair with elaborate carvings and several throw pillows, which, true to their name, Grayson took and carelessly tossed onto the floor. "You're in search of information that might lead to the arrest of whoever killed Rex Gifford and Leo Thomas," he pronounced like a fortune teller. Indeed, he certainly looked the part. His neck was adorned with what seemed like a dozen gold chains, each containing either a crucifix, a horn, or some other talisman. "I'm not sure I can be of much help, but try me."

Monette started. "We need your help in opening some doors in Palm Springs, because it could be a matter of life and death."

Clifford came back into the room and sat down in a Chippendale armchair—just the sort of furniture you'd need in a mid-century modern house.

"Clifford and I are all ears," Grayson said majestically.

Monette proceeded to tell our dynastic duo as much as she knew about Rex, Leo, the Red Party, and everyone connected with it. When she finished, Grayson sat back in his chair as if he needed to digest the facts. Clifford sat there motionless, holding his hand over his mouth like he was trying desperately to stifle a scream.

Grayson was the first to speak. "From what you've told me, the people associated with the White Party are your number one suspects—they have the most to lose. Fortunately, there are three things working in your favor. One, I do know quite a few of the people you've mentioned who work with the White Party. And two, Clifford and I have solved more than a few incidents in our time. And three, I never give up."

"We appreciate your kind offer, Grayson—and Clifford—but I must warn you that one of these people is a murderer—a killer who has struck twice and botched a third attempt at murder," I said, jumping in.

Grayson smiled coyly. "I'm not worried about anything, honey. I've worn dresses right down Market Street in San Francisco in the forties—long before you were born."

I didn't see how wearing a dress in San Francisco provided the fortitude needed to face up to a cold-blooded killer, but I once met a drag queen dressed like a nun who swore that a Chanel handbag had saved her life. Female readers and drag queens everywhere, take note.

"Robert and I and a lot of people are very thankful for your help," Monette said. "It's just that in the past, we've been able to *coerce* people into giving us information. But Palm Springs is all new territory for us. I'm afraid that we don't know anyone here."

Grayson shifted in his seat, pulling himself to the edge of the chair as if he were about to share privileged information with us.

"Monette, darling . . . you and Robert may not be able to resort to blackmail to find things out, but I can. How do you think I know what's going on in this town? Sometimes you don't even have to do that: people just love to talk in Palm Springs—it makes for excitement. Let me ask this: have the police been any help yet?"

"Not really, Sergeant Big Arms doesn't trust us."

"Who is Sergeant Big Arms?" Grayson asked, his eyes getting bigger than saucepans.

"That's what one of our friends named him, and the name stuck."

"But you don't remember his name?" Grayson asked.

"No, we've been calling him Big Arms so long," Monette confessed.

"Well, not only did he help me with my luggage at the airport two years ago, but I know who he is. His name is Mike Gorski and he used to be a trainer at the local gym before he became a police officer—I know, because I trained with him for a while, but it didn't do much good," Grayson reported, pinching a roll on his waistline. "He's married now, but I think a phone call from me will loosen his tongue. Give us a few minutes and we'll be ready to start our investigation. We'll take our car," Grayson said.

11

Now Begone, Before Someone Drops a Convention Center on You!

Exactly thirty minutes later, we were ready to go. I can't imagine what took Clifford and Grayson thirty minutes to get ready, but I didn't question it. Clifford had changed from his Hawaiian shirt to a white Izod polo shirt and white polyester pants so sheer that you could see his pants pockets and 2xist underwear—bikini—clearly from Mars. Grayson kept on his yellow outfit. We clambered into their vintage 1970s Rolls Royce, the cracked leather upholstery creaking under our shorts as we sat down in the backseat.

Clifford drove, which gave new meaning to the word *terror* and put Monette's driving skills to shame. It's not that Clifford was reckless. It was hard to call twenty miles per hour reckless, but Clifford meandered along so slowly that at times I felt that we weren't moving at all. People in pickups would whip around us aggressively, some of them flipping us the bird because we were going so slowly. Yes, I was fascinated by the fact that, like in the advertisement, the only thing you could hear was the sound of the clock ticking as you drove, but that was about the only excitement we experienced. Although the car was probably capable of doing 300 miles per hour, I wasn't sure that I wanted Clifford pushing the car to that limit. He could mow down a crowd of nuns and wipe out a gaggle of circuit boys by the time his brain registered that he had run a red light back on Vista Chino. Better to lumber along at twenty miles an hour.

If you didn't count Grayson's shouting directions to Clifford constantly and Clifford's becoming flustered on several occasions and missing the convention center—which was almost a block long—my first ride in a Rolls Royce was uneventful.

We pulled up to the Palm Springs Convention Center and disembarked. We figured that it would be a great place since we could talk to all of our primary suspects at one time, since they would all likely be there setting up. Our party reassembled at the center and headed toward Circuit Toys for Party Boys.

The first person we encountered was Darlene Waldron, gritting her teeth over some slipup. When she saw us, she broke into a forced smile that reminded me of Laura Bush, her crocodile grin reminding me not to venture too near the water's edge. Crocodiles can move faster than you give them credit for.

"Darlene, we're investigating Rex's death in a sort of unofficial way, so we're wondering if you'd mind answering a few questions for us," Grayson politely asked.

"Unofficial!" She snorted. "I've already been questioned by the police. I'm really busy, so if you'd keep this short . . ."

"Fine," Grayson stated. "So the word is out that your business is in heap-o trouble and you need every sale you can get to keep your henna-ed little head above water."

Jesus! This guy didn't fool around. A quick two-by-four blow to the head and it was done. I was used to Monette's cat-and-mouse way of playing with the perpetrator, coaxing him—or her—out of their lair to strike at the bait. Monette and I stood back, waiting for the reaction, which came swiftly and caustically like a beaker of tossed acid. She turned away from us, pretending to be involved in something, which made her response all the more startling. We had been warned, but it still didn't prepare us for the controlled explosion that burst from her mouth like a thousand shrieking bats.

"Listen, I don't know who the hell you are, but whoever told you such a crock of horseshit is sadly misinformed, and if I discover who said such a thing, I will be talking to my lawyer if she or he doesn't watch it. Besides, my business is none of yours, so I would advise you to keep your nose out of places where it doesn't fuckin' belong."

The four of us stood there, shocked at the storm surge that issued from Miss Waldron's potty mouth. It was as if she were ready at any moment to detonate and blow her enemy to bits. Since Grayson started this "dialogue" with Darlene, the rest of us seemed more than willing to let him stand in the line of fire. What Darlene didn't realize was that Grayson was no newcomer to the world of caustic comebacks.

"Miss Waldron, I asked you a blunt but simple question. There are lives at stake here, and my group and I intend to get to the bottom of who killed Rex Gifford and Leo Thomas and took a potshot at Colorado Jackson. So if you don't mind . . ."

"Listen," Darlene broke into Grayson's conversation, slashing the air with her voice, "I told you that you are misinformed and I've already talked to the police, and I don't care to stand around talking to a bunch of jerk-ass sleuths with too much time on their hands."

"One other question," Grayson asked as if he hadn't heard a word that Darlene hissed at us. Perhaps he hadn't. "Rex complained that people like you were colluding to keep other vendors and suppliers from working with the Red Party."

Darlene, who was checking the contents of a box with such intensity as to convey the impression that she couldn't hear us, replied without even looking in our direction. "It's a load of fuckin' crap—the same that Rex was filled with. Now get out of here before I call Security."

And that, as they say, was that. Grayson wordlessly motioned to us that we should go, but as we did, there was a series of huge crashes behind us, causing our group to stop in its tracks and turn on its heels. A large display of glow-stick hand sabers had fallen over, causing them to domino into another display, which fell into another display. Grayson shrugged his shoulders as if he had nothing to do with it.

"Well, that went over like Smellovision," Grayson said.

"Not exactly," Monette commented. "I learned quite a bit from our brief encounter."

"Oh, and what did you pick up—besides the fact that I'd rather face a wolverine with PMS instead of Darlene?" Grayson commented as he tottered along.

"The most obvious is that she's a desperate woman."

"I'll say," I chimed in. "I'm sure that she'd be lucky to get even a eunuch to come near her."

"That's not what I meant," Monette responded.

"Oh."

"But that was good. What I meant is that her manner suggests that she would do anything to keep what's hers—or make something hers. In other words, she seems quite ruthless . . . a person easily capable of murder."

"Who is next on our list?" Grayson asked eagerly.

"May I make a suggestion?" Monette asked the four of us.

"Go ahead, Monette; we're all ears," I said.

"If we split up, we'd cover more ground and we'd also be less intimidating."

"Yes, Monette," I replied. "I think that we frightened Darlene, fragile little flower that she is."

Monette smiled at my comment and continued. "I just think our suspects would be more willing to talk if they didn't have eight pairs of eyes breathing down their necks, if you'll excuse the mixed metaphor."

"That sounds like a fine idea," Grayson concurred.

"Okay, how about if Grayson and Clifford take on Jimmy Garboni and Martin Stevers, and Robert and I question Kip Savage and Brian Keeper? Remember, the one thing they don't know about is the missing money. It's the one fact that the newspapers and TV stations didn't pick up on yet. So mum about the missing money, okay? We'll meet up here at the car in an hour? Everyone, synchronize your watches."

Monette and I went off in search of our prey. It didn't take long for us to find Kip. He was watching as workmen were hoisting speakers the size of a Range Rover to be hung on a huge steel scaffold over the dance floor.

"Mr. Savage?" Monette asked politely.

"Yes? Are you with the riggers?"

"No, my friend Robert and I met you the other night at Leo's party."

"Oh, gosh, wasn't that tragic!" he said, shaking his head. "First Rex, then Leo. They were both such terrific guys." Kip waited for the obligatory number of seconds to pass, grieving for his competitors, then looked up at the scaffolding again. This guy was as cool as a cucumber. Real cool. "So what can I do for you?"

"Well, if you don't mind, Robert and I are working in a semi-unofficial capacity for Marc Baldwin and the other partner in T-Rex Productions."

Kip snorted a little laugh at our title. "Semi-unofficial, huh? Well, I've already talked to the police."

"Oh, so they talked to you already?" Monette asked.

"They'd be fools if they didn't. After all, I am the most likely suspect in Rex's death. If anyone wanted Rex dead, I suppose I'd be right up there on the top of the list. But I would never do such a thing. I mean, why jeopardize what I've built up over the years? There was no way that Rex was going to push us off the map. At best, he'd be about as successful as I am. But I don't think so. White Party followers are very loyal."

"That's funny, I always thought of gay men as very fickle. Dangle something shinier in front of them and they'll follow it anywhere."

"That shows how little you know about the party circuit, Ms. . . ."

"O'Reilley, but call me Monette, please."

"Okay, Monette Please. Rex had it in his mind that the Red Party was going to be bigger and flashier than the White Party. There's only one flaw in that plan."

"And what's that?" she asked.

"He wouldn't break even. You see that speaker going up over us?" he said, pointing to the behemoth that looked like it could blast Mt. San Jacinto into pea gravel. "That one speaker is costing me about three thousand dollars to rent for just three days. And that speaker is just one tiny part of the White Party. It's not just the equipment that costs money, but it takes an army of people to get this show on the road. Electricians, security, DJs, sound system crew, lighting, bartenders, janitors—you name it."

Monette nodded her head as if she understood. But her question showed that she didn't completely buy Kip's reasoning. "I guess that Rex was going to charge more for tickets, thereby making up the costs."

"I warned him to keep an eye on costs. I helped him on a lot of things, Monette. Now, why would I spend so much time helping him if I wanted to kill him?"

"You have a good point," she answered.

As Monette and Kip sparred with each other, I took mental notes of Kip and his reaction to each question Monette asked. He was friendly and helpful, while underneath he was as cool as ice—a poker face must come in handy in the rough-and-tumble world of party production.

I could see that Monette was adding things up in her head. "Kip, I have just one more question—if you don't mind?"

"Not at all."

"Thank you. Rex made quite a commotion that people were conspiring against him—I mean, that your vendors and suppliers and perhaps even you were conspiring against him to stall services or items that he needed for the Red Party. Any comments?"

"It is completely untrue. I gave Rex all the help I could give, and he took a lot of it. I'm very disappointed that Rex would say such a thing."

As I was watching Kip, I heard a crack above my head and had only a fraction of a second to push Monette out of the way before the one-ton speaker landed just a foot away from where we were standing.

"Jesus Christ, George, you lunatic!" Kip yelled as he got up and dusted himself off. "I told you to double that right side. It's holding twice the load as last year! You could've killed us!"

I got up on my feet first and helped Monette up.

"Are you two all right?" Kip asked with genuine sympathy for our plight. Or was it?

"I seem to be in one piece," Monette replied. "How about you, Robert?"

"Still here," I reported.

"Shit, I'm really sorry that happened. Why don't we move over here, where we'll be out of harm's way. Listen, I've got a conference with the DJs in fifteen minutes. If there aren't any more questions, you'll have to excuse me. Nice meeting you two, and I hope that you find whoever did this to Rex and Leo," he said, waving at us and marching off. "Good luck," he added.

I looked over at Monette, who seemed to be in the same dazed state as I. "The guy tries to drop a speaker on us and then wishes us good luck."

"Well, you have to say one thing about the guy," Monette conceded.

"And what's that?"

"He has good manners."

* * *

We met back at the car to trade stories, and everyone was brimming over with exciting things to tell. Grayson led the way.

"We didn't get the chance to talk to Martin Stevers, but we had quite an encounter with Jimmy Garboni!" Grayson crinkled his nose in disgust. "We asked him if he knew anything that could help solve the mystery of Rex and Leo's death, and he clammed up like an oyster."

"So he didn't talk at all?" I inquired.

"Oh, he opened up a little, but not much. But he denied trying to blackball Rex with vendors and suppliers—which, I guess, doesn't mean a lot if you consider that he's got ties to organized crime. It's difficult to believe a person who breaks people's knees when he doesn't get his way."

"That's interesting," I commented. "Kip Savage had the same answer to Rex's conspiracy theory."

"So did Darlene," Monette said. "That leads me to think that either Rex's paranoia was getting the best of him after the extortion letters started to arrive, or . . ."

" . . . everyone was telling a well-rehearsed lie and we have a genuine conspiracy going," Grayson said, pouncing on the truth.

"We didn't get a chance to—wait a minute . . . Isn't that . . . ? Yes, it is!" Monette said, spotting Brian Keeper at the same time I did. "Clifford, Grayson, that's Brian Keeper, the PR man for the White Party. Could you go over and question him while Robert and I try and find Martin Stevers?"

Grayson gave a quick nod and grabbed Clifford by the shirtsleeve and dragged him in the direction of Brian. When they had jumped on their prey, Monette and I started on our quest, and Monette spoke to me.

"This conspiracy thing seems to make a lot of sense. I think if we talk with Martin Stevers, we will find some very interesting things. Not even Darlene could hate Rex as much as Martin. Martin not only lost money to Rex on a job, but he lost a big lawsuit to Rex. I'm sure Martin is still fuming to this very day. Let's ask someone where we can find him."

We chanced upon a woman carrying enough electrical cable to wire New Guinea. When she turned her head and looked right at us, I was immediately reminded of Ellen DeGeneres. The resemblance was uncanny. To complete the picture, she was wearing a T-shirt that said, *I'm not a lesbian, but my girlfriend is.*

"Excuse me," Monette asked gingerly, "could you tell us where we could find Martin Stevers?"

"I sure could—I work for him," the lesbian replied.

"Did anyone ever tell you that you look like Ellen DeGeneres?" Monette inquired. Of all the women in the world, Ellen was the one who really got Monette's soccer shoelaces tied in knots. Her fascination and love of Ellen had gotten her into trouble more than once. She claims that she had once been arrested for following Ellen too closely. Monette's obsession with Ellen sometimes caused her to stretch the truth a bit, so there was no telling what really happened, but one thing was clear: Monette was in love with Ellen.

"Only about fifteen million people. The truth is, I *am* Ellen. I'm just working here because it's the only place Anne Heche won't find me. Plus, I need the money."

Monette broke out into a great big grin. "That's good, real good. Where'd you get a quick wit like that?" she asked, clearly engrossed in this woman.

"I grew up in a family of seven kids—you had to be quick."

"My name's Monette. Only child."

"Glad to meet you. I'm Djuna. It's spelled *D-J-U-N-A*, but pronounced 'Juna.'"

"Interesting name," Monette commented.

"I'm named for a famous American lesbian expatriate, Djuna Barnes, who wrote in Paris in the twenties. I guess my parents knew I was going to grow up to be a dyke when I was born, so they named me appropriately."

"Well, I'm Irish but named for no one in particular. My mother thought I was going to grow up to be a famous ballet dancer, but my height kind of got in the way. Listen, my friend and I—oh shit, I forgot to introduce you to Robert."

"Nice to meet you, Djuna. I'm Robert."

"Nice to meet you," she replied.

"My friend and I have to see Martin, but could I stop back and talk?"

"Martin's behind that van over there. I'll be wiring the sound over on that scaffold—the one that almost fell on you. That was a close one! Listen," she said, bending toward us and lowering her voice. "George isn't the sharpest knife in the drawer. I don't stand anywhere near him when he's setting something up. Anyway, you know where I'll be. Stop by," she said with a wink that suggested that Djuna was interested in plugging her cables into Monette's socket.

"I'll take that under consideration," Monette said as the two of us headed toward Martin.

"Did you see that?" I said, grabbing Monette's arm excitedly. "She's really hot for you. I could almost see the sparks flying. Who'd ever think that you'd find a potential date at the largest gathering of gay men in the U.S. besides a Margaret Cho concert?"

"You never know when love is going to fall right into your lap," she said.

"Or dance around once they get there," I added, winking in my own suggestive way. "I'm so happy for you, Monette!"

"Now hold on," she cautioned. "We haven't even had dinner together yet!"

"Yes, but this was meant to be."

"Wait a minute. You, Robert Wilsop, the world's biggest skeptic and unbeliever, telling me that I was fated to meet Djuna?"

"Yes, look at the Ellen DeGeneres resemblance—your

all-time favorite. She's been sent to you to make up for your last girlfriend."

"The one who looked like Ricardo Montalban? Yes. That's an interesting theory. I will ponder that thought—after we talk to Martin. Here goes," she said, not without a little trepidation.

We approached Martin who was inspecting some plans rolled out before him. He must have been about the same age as Rex, his flattop haircut and carefully trimmed goatee showing just a hint of gray here and there. His muscular figure clearly showed through the tight, white T-shirt and skin-tight jeans. A *daddy* type if I ever saw one, and a sexy one at that.

"Mr. Stevers?"

"Yes," he replied without even turning his head to see who was calling his name—shades of Darlene.

"We're friends of Marc Baldwin, and if you don't mind, we'd like to ask you a few questions that could help us catch the murderer of Rex Gifford and Leo Thomas."

Martin turned around with a slow, almost theatrical motion.

"Why would you even think I would want to help find the guy who whacked Rex? On the contrary, if you find the guy, would you give me his name and address so I could send him ten thousand dollars?"

Rex was by no means an angel, but to treat a dead person with such disrespect seemed a bit too much. I defended Rex but wasn't quite sure why—maybe because Marc was a partner in T-Rex, and whatever slimed Rex slimed Marc as well. "Mr. Stevers, I know Rex and you locked horns in the past. I don't blame you for harboring a grudge against him and wishing him harm. But Rex wasn't the only one who was killed. Leo Thomas is dead, and attempts have been made on the lives of Marc and Colorado. We're trying to stop the killer before he strikes again."

Martin looked at me with pity, the scorn plainly showing

on his face. "You just don't get it, do you? You haven't the slightest idea of what that man did to me! I got tired of him cleaning me out."

"But . . ." I tried to get in.

"You're right—I do hate Rex, and reading about his death in the newspapers was one of the most enjoyable things I've done in a long time. He deserves to be dead. So does his helper, Colorado. He's a bitch who deserves to be shot."

"I'd be careful about saying things like that about Rex, Mr. Stevers," Monette warned Martin.

"What do I care? I have an airtight alibi."

"And that is . . . ?" Monette gently probed.

"I left Leo's party and went to The Zone. It was a real slow evening, so I talked to the bartender for over an hour, paid for several drinks with my credit card, then, when the bartender knocked off work, we went home together. If MasterCard doesn't back up my alibi, then Jeff the bartender will."

"This all sounds very convenient for you," I admitted. "Very."

"It is—very. Just luck, I guess. I have great sex with a handsome bartender and Rex gets killed at the same time. What more could a guy want? Now, if you don't mind, some of us have to earn a living, even though shit-heads like Rex will take it all away from us. If you want any more questions answered, go talk to the police."

And with that, Martin turned away from us and went back to his work. As soon as we were out of earshot, I confessed to Monette the hopelessness I felt.

"I feel like we didn't learn a thing."

"To the untrained mind it may look futile, but you have to sift through the information, no matter how sparse, to find the tiny grains of truth that lie buried in all the chaff. Remember what Ptolemy—or someone—once said: 'He who wishes to eat the nut must first crack the shell.'"

"My Lithuanian grandmother used to say that if you beat

a rabbit on the head long enough, he'll eventually learn to smoke a cigar."

"What the hell does that mean?"

"I think it means she had ninety-five percent arterial blockage. So what do we do now?"

"We go back to your house, see if there are any messages from Sergeant Big Arms, and go from there. Oh, but first I have to make a pit stop and visit Djuna for a few minutes. Do you mind, Robert? I'll meet you back at Clifford and Grayson's car."

"Enjoy yourself—and good luck," I said, crossing my fingers in the air for her to see.

She headed off for Djuna, humming to herself—a good sign. Monette was off in search of love, I had already found it, and Michael was off—getting off, I assumed. I couldn't imagine him doing anything else. Michael was a member of that class of gay men whose lives revolve completely around dancing, shopping, and fucking. Put them in a remote cabin without a telephone, television, or a CD player, and they'd go stark, raving mad. I tried to make a correlation between the evolution of a person's mind and the reliance on electronic appliances for one's very existence, when I heard Grayson's voice call out my name. He was standing next to the Rolls Royce with Clifford, who was looking at me with smoldering bedroom eyes. I kept a safe distance.

"So did Martin say anything of interest?"

"He said he's glad Rex is dead."

"Hmm . . ." Grayson contemplated the fact. "It seems to be the standard response around here. You should have seen Darlene eyeing Clifford and me from a distance. I could feel the daggers from clear across the center. She must really be under the gun."

A thought occurred to me. "Grayson, I told myself that I wasn't going to ask you this question, but I can't stand it any longer."

"Yes, what is it, dear child?"

Now I was being called a child. I guess from Grayson's perspective, I might be considered an ovum. I continued. "Did you knock over that display of Darlene's?"

"My dear, I did nothing of the sort," he said with an air of theatricality that didn't exactly convince me of his innocence. "My shirttail must have caught the edge of the display. I would never do such a thing!" he stated. He held his hand up to shade his eyes from the sun, scanning for something in the distance.

I think I had my answer. After a life of making the outrageous the everyday, I had the feeling Grayson would do just about anything if he could get away with it.

12

A Call to Arms

Monette eventually returned to the car with a piece of paper held triumphantly above her head. She had indeed secured Djuna's cell phone number and was beaming with pride. The way she danced back and forth, waving the piece of paper in joyous celebration, you would have thought it had Jesus' autograph on it.

Clifford turned the key, and the Rolls purred to life. Clifford pulled out onto Amado Road and crept slowly back to Pink House, where we were soon deposited near our not-so-luxurious Chevrolet Metro. We thanked the two of them and assured them that we would keep in close contact. Ten minutes later, we pulled in through the gate into Rex's former compound, now Casa Vince. Since I had met and fallen in love with Marc, I hardly spent any time here. I felt guilty about leaving Vince on his own, but he assured me that he was just fine. Michael, of course, was not there either and probably didn't feel guilty about it at all.

"Don't worry about me," Vince said to the two of us. "I've been over at Greg and Minnie's. They're a straight couple who love to cook like I do. We've been cooking up a storm—it keeps our minds off things."

"I understand completely," I replied, patting Vince on his bare shoulder. I turned to Monette, who stood there trying not to stare at Vince's body hardware, since she had seen it before, but she was shocked to see it all the same.

"Vince, I gotta ask you this," Monette said, smiling with amusement.

"Oh, about the body jewelry?" Vince remarked.

"Yeah, do you avoid magnets?"

"That's a good one," Vince replied, actually coming back to this dimension and chuckling."

"Vince, have you seen Michael?" I asked. "I haven't seen him all day."

"He's over there on the sofa, taking a nap. Or at least I thought he was."

"I was—until you three started stomping around and making all kinds of noise," Michael said with not a little irritation in his voice.

"What's wrong with Princess?" I asked Vince, thumbing toward Michael.

"From what he told me, he's had very little success in getting laid. If you don't count his encounter with Rex and the palm tree."

"To set the record straight—if you'll excuse the expression—I've had several encounters already. It's just that they weren't up to my standards of depravity. Too vanilla. But I did have sex on the tram," Michael added, making reference to the cable car that ascends to an 8,000-foot ledge on Mount San Jacinto.

"You had sex at the top of the mountain?" I asked.

"Not on the mountain—in the tram itself," Michael boasted.

"And how, pray tell, did you manage that?"

"Well," Michael said excitedly, "I was so bored, I took the tram up for something to do. Well, on the way down, I was the only person going down."

"Figuratively speaking, I suppose."

"Going down—oh, yeah." Michael chuckled, finally getting the joke. "So the tram operator was giving me bedroom eyes, and before I knew it, he unzipped his pants and, well, you know. I had to hurry, because the ride down is only fifteen minutes long."

"Michael, are you sure you're not a member of the Kennedy family?" I commented.

Vince cleared his throat and continued. "Grayson DeVallier called and said that Sergeant Big Arms wants to talk to you at his house."

It was as if Michael had been hooked in the mouth and landed like a graceful Marlin at our feet.

"You know," he said, slithering from the couch to my side so quickly it startled me, "I was thinking that you two are in over your heads in this case. You could use a little help from someone big and strong, in case things got a little rough," Michael said, flexing his biceps to show us that he wasn't just a glamour boy.

"Michael, you are so transparent, you should be wrapped in cellophane."

"I've done that before," he said, making a reference to some past kinky episode that Monette and I didn't want to hear about.

"Michael, I will not have you gawking and drooling over Sergeant Big Arms," Monette said, standing all six feet, four inches of her ground.

"Oh, c'mon, I really want to help," Michael said, lying through his capped and bleached (twice a month) teeth.

While the two of them argued it out, a thought sprang into my head. This thought sent an electrical tingle down my right leg, causing me to lift my leg and kick Monette in the shin ever so slightly.

"You know, Monette, I think that Michael is right. He should come along since we can use his help. And if all else fails, if the bullets start flying, we can use him as a human shield."

The electrical signal sparked by my kicking Monette's leg raced up her leg and alerted her brain that I was trying to set Michael up for something. She made an abrupt change of thought and looked at me for more clues.

"Listen, I think that Michael could work closely with Grayson—*and especially Clifford*—to help us solve this case," I said, jerking my head ever so slightly at the name Clifford.

"Yes, yes, I see what you mean. Michael could be a very valuable member of our team."

"Fine, then it's settled," I replied. "I'll give Grayson a call and let him know that we can meet Sergeant Big Arms right away."

I called Grayson and discovered that Sergeant Big Arms would meet us at Pink House in half an hour.

"Vince?" Monette asked.

"Yes?"

"Do you mind if we use Rex's computer for a few minutes?"

"No, go right ahead. I can't imagine what harm it would do," he replied.

"We're not going to look at any personal documents. I just want to have access to the Internet for a few minutes."

"It's all yours," Vince answered.

"Vince, do the words *butia* or *A.D.* mean anything to you? Did Rex ever mention them?"

"No, I have no idea what a butia is."

"Robert, could you go get the drawing that you found behind Rex's desk?" Monette asked.

"Sure," I replied, fetching the folder containing the drawing of the strange pyramid-shaped building, which I had copied and put back in its original spot behind the desk. I brought it to Monette, who opened the folder and showed the drawing to Vince. I watched his face carefully—not even a glimmer of recognition.

"I have no idea what it is. Rex never mentioned it to me. Offhand, I would say that it's a studio party for some Egyptian movie opening. You know, that was the bread and butter of

T-Rex: movie premier parties. But I know for a fact that it isn't."

"How can you be so sure?" I asked.

"Because the drawing was in a red folder. That means it's a personal item. Rex was very anal about that kind of stuff. Proposals were always in blue folders, current projects in green, and so on. Red always meant personal. Did you ask Marc if it meant anything to him?"

"Yes, we showed it to Marc and he's never seen it before," I added.

"Well, it was worth a try," Monette said dejectedly.

Monette and I went into Rex's office and fired up the computer. A couple of clicks later, we were on the Internet, trying to find out what the hell a butia was. And we found it.

Monette was hunched over my shoulder, looking at the computer screen with me.

"It looks like it's a palm," I remarked. "*Butia capitata*. It's native to Brazil, Uruguay, and Argentina. Slow-growing with edible fruits. Well, I guess I stumbled on a folder of landscaping ideas—a dead end."

"But that doesn't explain the *A.D.* part. *After death* is all I can come up with," Monette mused. "I can't help but think this folder was something he prepared in case he was killed. But what the hell does a palm tree have to do with it? Wait a minute, what kind of palm tree fell on the house?"

"How should I know, Monette? I killed every plant I ever tried to grow."

"Let me go ask Vince if he knows," Monette said, then left the room for a minute and returned. "*Phoenix Daffytickera* or something like that, Vince said. Nope, no connection. God, this is bugging me. This means something, but I don't know what."

I was trying a few more Web sites under *A.D.*—nothing really significant—when Michael stuck his head in the door and told us that it was time to go. Half an hour ago we couldn't drag Michael to Clifford and Grayson's, and now he was hurrying us along. I had turned off the computer and followed Monette out to the tiny Metro when we both laid eyes on Michael. With what he was dressed in, he could've been arrested. He was wearing a muscle tank shirt that scooped so low in the front, you could almost see his navel, and his white shorts were so brief that I don't see how they could support pockets. On his feet, he wore his favorites: black combat boots, the long laces tied completely around his calves (the way straight boys laced their boots, Michael once told me—it was very butch) with just a hint of white socks peering out at the top of the boot. *Playboy* centerfolds showed off less flesh.

"Michael, you're a disgrace to the gay race," I said, offering my only comment on his outfit.

"You're a slut, Michael. Plain and simple, you're a slut," Monette added, heaping another all-too-true statement on Michael's shameless head.

Michael looked down at his clothes, not having a clue that his intentions were so blatant. As we crammed ourselves into the sardine can on wheels, Monette and I could hear Michael still trying to keep up the charade: "What do I have to do to convince you guys that I'm really interested in solving these murders?" he said.

When we arrived at Pink House, there was a Palm Springs Police Department cruiser in the front driveway. Michael was magnetically drawn to the car, and he was still pressing his nose against the windows of the black-and-white car when Monette and I rang the doorbell. It was amazing that Michael had such a fetish for authority figures, because in everyday life he ignored them completely.

Clifford answered the door, his face lighting up on seeing me, but I almost had to pick up his eyeballs off the ground and put them back in this head when I introduced Michael.

"So nice to meet you, Michael! My, you are a handsome one, aren't you?" Clifford drooled, his paper-thin hands running all over Michael's ample shoulder muscles. "My goodness, they grow 'em big in New York nowadays," Clifford said while giving a quick pinch to Michael's ass.

Michael spun around to find Clifford grinning lasciviously at him. The hunter was about to become prey.

We were ushered into the living room, where cocktails were offered and heartily accepted by all but the officer. After all, it was way past noon by now. Like the pro that he was, Michael sat right next to Sergeant Big Arms. Michael, however, was outdone by Clifford, who waited for him to sit down, then planted his delicate grandfatherly frame right next to him.

Grayson started things off. "Sergeant Gorski, could you tell everyone what you know, and then Monette and Robert can add their two cents. Why don't we go down the line of suspects one by one, shall we?"

Sergeant Big Arms—I mean Gorski—started us off. "As you probably found out, I talked to several suspects before you did. I first talked to Kip Savage and Brian Keeper. Kip Savage has a long record of living up to his last name, which is miles from the happy and helpful exterior he puts on. His first conviction was for slashing the tires on the van of a rival party production company back in nineteen eighty-eight. Since then, he's had a host of charges against him—all of them eventually dropped—for similar acts, including a charge of arson at a competing event planner's warehouse, destroying most of the planner's props. He pointed to the fact that he offered to help Rex with the Red Party, but upon further questioning, it turns out that before Kip extended a helping hand to Rex, he tried to buy Rex out when he realized that Rex was going through with his plans. And get this: Kip has kept his nose clean for a decade now, but his event planning company has had no competition to speak of."

"That's *very* interesting," Monette commented. "The things people will say when there's a badge staring them in the face."

"That's so true," Michael added. "I practically turn to Jell-O when a guy in a uniform is standing over me."

I could see Monette rolling her eyes. The remark had a profound effect on Clifford, who got up from his position next to Michael and disappeared down a hallway.

Sergeant Gorski continued. "Brian Keeper has a clean record, but he previously worked in public relations for several of the major studios in Hollywood, so you can imagine, uh . . ."

". . . so you can imagine the sleazy stuff he's capable of," Monette said, completing the thought that the sergeant seemed reluctant to say himself for fear of appearing biased.

Gorski smiled, then continued. "Darlene Waldron is facing money problems. The dot-bomb she teamed with on the Internet went under a year ago and took a hundred twenty-five thousand dollars of hers with it. She can't afford to lose any sales to the Red Party—or anyone. She tried to make things look rosier than they are, but several people I talked with said she's in desperate straits."

"And her alibi?" Monette asked.

"Like several of the others, she went home the night of the murder by herself."

"Big surprise," Grayson interjected. "A convict with sexual-compulsive syndrome just completing a thirty-year sentence would run the other way from that woman."

Another smile from Sergeant Big Arms—no comment, however. "No witnesses saw her return to her hotel room—she's one of the few who don't have a second home here in the desert," the sergeant replied. "Jimmy Garboni has ties to organized crime. He muscled his way into catering about ten years ago. He controls a big part of the catering and linen supply business in Los Angeles. He doesn't like competition—ask his competitors, if you can find them. I figure most of them are at the bottom of the Pacific or are out in the desert pushing up cactuses somewhere. I couldn't get much out of him and probably wouldn't without a warrant."

I looked over at Monette and grimaced. Perhaps we were getting in over our heads. Monette raised her eyebrows and bit her lip—a sure sign that she was feeling the same way, too.

Big Arms was about to continue as Clifford returned to the room and retook his seat next to Michael. He folded his hands in his lap and told the sergeant to continue.

"I also talked to Martin Stevers and questioned him about the lawsuit he lost to Rex."

"We found that he was angry enough to say that he wished he could pay the guy who bumped Rex off," Monette added.

"Wait until you hear what I discovered," Gorski said with pride. "He has plenty of reason to wish Rex dead."

"Rex stole a big event from Martin?" Monette asked quizzically.

"Nope," the sergeant said casually. He was still beaming with pride. I suppose that being a police officer in Palm Springs, you didn't often get the excitement of a big case like this one. I assumed he spent more of his time chasing down hustlers who stole gold watches from old gay men, or handing out fines to businesses with unauthorized pots of geraniums on their doorsteps.

"There was more than one lawsuit?" Monette guessed again.

"Nope. Martin and Rex once were lovers."

The sergeant's pronouncement produced a stunned silence and even one or two whistles of amazement. This was big news. In fact, this could, in Monette's words, break the case wide open.

"You see, Rex and Martin were in business years ago together," Gorski said. "According to Martin, Rex fell for a younger guy and decided to split with Martin. When he did, Martin said he took the bulk of the business and the furnishings in the house."

"Martin told you this?" I said, astonished since he had revealed almost nothing to us. Or had he?

Monette nodded her head in an of-course manner. "So that's what he meant when he said that Robert and I had no idea what Rex had done to him and how he got tired of Rex cleaning him out. Now it all makes sense. There was much more than a lawsuit gone bad."

"Don't forget that he has a very compelling alibi," Gorski warned us.

"Can I make a bold suggestion?" Monette proposed.

"Go right ahead," the sergeant said.

"I've had this idea in the back of my mind that perhaps the murderer is someone like Martin—in fact, could be Martin Stevers. But, there was an accomplice who actually carried out the deed. It just seems that the killer was all over the place, as if two people were carrying out the deed separately. I mean, spiking Leo Thomas's protein powder with poison—I assume that's what killed him . . ."

"That's correct."

". . . then getting ready to line up his next target, Marc Baldwin, then shooting Colorado Jackson—it all seems like too much for one person to handle!"

Gorski's face looked flushed, as if Monette had outguessed him. Yet, despite the fact that Grayson had unearthed some dirt on him to get him to come over here and spill his investigation, he attempted to play it cagey. "That would explain another strange fact that's come to light just a few hours ago."

"And what might that be?" she asked.

"The threat letters. We sent all of them, including the ones sent to Marc Baldwin and Colorado, to our forensic lab in Riverside, and something strange turned up. The first batch, sent to Rex, were from a magazine using very cheap paper."

"Like *Spunk* magazine?" Michael suddenly hinted, then realized that he shouldn't have. "Oh, never mind. I was just thinking out loud."

"I'm not acquainted with that publication," Gorski said in complete innocence.

"Oh, never mind. You can only pick it up in Amsterdam. Please, continue."

"The second batch of letters came from a very slick publication. Very expensive paper."

"So what I think you're concluding, Sergeant Gorski, is that two different people sent out those letters. Or, maybe the explanation isn't quite so sinister: that the killer, or killers, ran out of letters from the first magazine and went on to another, different magazine."

"Perhaps."

"Do you have a copy of all the different letters?" Monette asked. "I never saw the ones sent to Rex or Leo."

Sergeant Big Arms reached inside a briefcase and pulled out several photos of the letters. "I took the precaution of having the lab make copies for you."

"That's very kind," Monette responded, and she meant it. I could tell by the sound of her voice. The sergeant was now considering her an equal in the proceedings. What Monette longed for was to be taken seriously, and not just as the only woman who claimed to have read every mystery ever written.

Since I was an integral part of this investigation, I got up and stood next to Monette, receiving the photos as she perused them and handed them to me. The room was silent while Monette and I shuffled through them.

"The only one I didn't see was the one sent to Leo." We both stared closely at the photo that was labeled with the words *Leo Thomas* and bearing the date the letter was received.

AlMOsT ToO LatE!
Stop nOW or DiE.

"There's something about these letters . . . I don't know . . . that bugs me," Monette finally said as she continued shuffling back and forth. "It's right in front of me, but I don't know what it is. I think I'm either getting psychic about this case or I'm just going batty." She shuffled back and forth through the photographs again. "Can your lab find out what magazine these came from?"

"It depends. We have some obvious magazines we can check, like event planner magazines and general-interest news magazines like *Time* and *Newsweek* that everyone gets. But it's going to take time, because it's like searching for a needle in a haystack. There might be clues on the back of each letter that was cut out, like another word or words that might give us a clue. But it's going to take time."

"Which is something we don't have," Monette said starkly. "Marc Baldwin is under police protection with a killer after him, and Colorado is in the hospital. Oh, by the way, how is he?"

"He's going to pull through, no problem. The doctors said they could release him in a day or two. The bullet shattered the window but didn't hit him. He lost control of his vehicle and it hit an embankment pretty hard. It's a good thing his car had an airbag."

"Sergeant, could you give me a map of the area around where the killer shot at Colorado's car? I want to look for vantage points where the killer could have stood."

"Here's a copy of the accident report filed with the Rancho Mirage Police Department," he said, handing the document to Monette. "Oh, one last thing: I'm checking on the phone calls placed to Rex's cell phone the night of the party, especially the last two. Mr. Wilsop here, I remember, saw Rex's disposition change radically when he received them, perhaps prompting him to leave the party to meet his assailants. I'll have the phone numbers that those calls came from by early tomorrow.

"That's all I can tell you now. When I get more information, I will let you know. I want everyone present in this room to know that the information that I've shared with you is privileged and is not to leave this room. I trust that you will let me know if you learn anything. As I see it, this is a partnership. Thank you for your time," Sergeant Big Arms said as he flipped his notebook closed, got up, and let himself out the door.

No one in the room moved or even said anything for a few minutes. While our silence could be put down to everyone digesting the facts just given to us, there was a much more imposing reason: We all wanted to know what Grayson had dug up out of the sergeant's past to make him open up and sing like a canary.

"So what was it that made him tell?" Monette said, asking the question that was on everyone's mind.

Grayson adjusted himself in his chair, pulling a pillow from behind his back and tossing it on the floor. "I just happened to find out that Sergeant Gorski did some gay porn years ago. I found pictures of him purely by mistake on the Internet. I just reminded him that his wife might not be so appreciative of his pictures as his clients at the gym used to be."

"You scalawag," I said.

Grayson was somewhat repentant. "I hate to do things like that," he said, throwing another fringed and tasseled pillow onto the floor, "but when it's a matter of life and death, you can't let anything get in the way."

"I think that's about all my head can hold for one day," Monette said, standing up and giving the signal that it was time for all of us to go.

We said our good-byes as Grayson led the way to the door. Clifford, who hadn't taken his eyes off Michael, reached inside the cardigan that he had donned to fend off the chill of the air-conditioning (it was freezing in their house—no energy crisis here). Clifford withdrew what looked like a photograph, placed it tenderly in Michael's hand, winked at him, then stepped back into the house and watched us go. As our tiny car drove away from the Mansard-roofed desert minimansion, I asked Michael if I could see what it was that Clifford had given him.

"Here," he said, listlessly dropping the photo over the seat into my lap. "Keep it. I've got my eyes on the sergeant."

I picked up the five-by-seven glossy photo and began laughing so hard that I choked and was left gasping for breath. When I recovered, I handed the photo to Monette. Never mind that Monette was a terror on the road when she had her eyes on it, so I guess it didn't matter that she was looking at a photograph at the same time. In it was Clifford, dressed in a police uniform, legs spread in a defiant stance, brandishing a nightstick menacingly and flashing an evil grimace as if he were about to break down the door of a noted Colombian drug lord and go in single-handedly in a blaze of testosterone-slick machismo. At the bottom of the photo, preprinted, were the words *"Officer" Cliff Lockwood. (760) 555-5521.*

13

Mission Implausible

It was getting late, and we were all hungry and felt that we should go out and get a bite to eat. I called Marc, who was answering phone call after phone call from his setup people at the convention center. He said he couldn't join us, because there was too much to do: there were just two days left until the opening festivities.

We all went out to a local diner and polished off burgers and fries. While we were eating, Michael spoke up.

"It's obvious that Martin Stevers is one of the murderers," he said with a sly look in his eyes.

"Yes, for once I think you're right," Monette conceded. "I just wish there was some way of proving it."

"There is," Michael replied like a cat dangling a piece of cheese in front of a starving mouse.

Monette was clearly amused. Michael with an original idea? This she had to hear.

"And pray tell, Michael, how do you intend to procure this proof? Break into his house here in the desert?"

Michael didn't even have to utter a word, because the answer was clearly yes.

Monette slapped the table in unbelief. "Now, how to you think you're going to pull something like this off?"

"Because I've done it before," Michael answered, revealing a side of him that I had never before imagined. "Plenty of times."

"Where?" I asked.

"In New York. I know how to break into a house or an apartment, for God's sake. I belonged to the In and Out Club!" Michael interjected proudly.

"Please promise me this isn't the kind of club I think it is," Monette replied, expecting the worst.

"No, it's not a sex club. The In and Out Club was a bunch of us guys in New York who'd break into houses and apartments just for fun. We never took anything. We just did it for kicks—to see if we could do it and not get caught."

I couldn't believe what I was hearing. "Why is it that I never hear about this kind of stuff?"

"Listen to this—this is really great," Michael said, priming me for what he was about to dish next. "We got bored just breaking into places, so we started sabotaging things. You know John McMannus, the real estate developer? He goes around sucking cock all around town, then goes home to his wife and puts on the hetero act. So we broke into his apartment and left Polaroids of us naked—from the neck down, no faces—all around his apartment for his wife to find. Stuff like that."

Monette and I were flabbergasted.

"Michael, I think I'm really getting to like you," Monette confessed. "This sounds like fun, but what if Martin has a security system?"

"I have something that will get me past that. It's so simple a child could figure it out—well, a child who lives near a beach."

Monette and I looked at each other and, in a moment of instant understanding, nodded our heads in agreement. We both had come over three thousand miles for a vacation in this desert paradise, but it seemed like the only thing we had done was watch people get killed and have head-on encounters with oversize dildoes. This seemed like fun.

And just like that, we took leave of our senses and drove back to Casa Vince, where Monette and I changed into the darkest clothes we could find. Michael wore a bathing suit and nothing else, telling us not to worry, that there was a method to his madness. He was also carrying a small suitcase.

It was dark now, and we headed toward the Deepwell area of town, following Michael's directions. The wind, true to its reputation, was whipsawing the palm trees to and fro.

"So how did you get Martin's address?" Monette asked Michael.

"I just went into Rex's office and got it off his Rolodex. Okay, turn here and slow down—I need to see the house numbers."

Deepwell was a well-kept neighborhood with the unmistakable signs of fairy dust everywhere. Yes, the faggots had moved in and claimed one of the best areas in town—like they always did. The houses were updated, and the yards planted with so much greenery, some of the properties looked like they belonged in upstate New York. My heart was racing with the sheer excitement that I would be, for a brief time, a cat burglar. I pictured myself as the debonair Cary Grant in *To Catch a Thief*, leaping from rooftop to rooftop, eluding the idiotic French police.

"This is it," Michael proclaimed. "Pull around the corner and park the car. We'll go across the lawn and make a preliminary inspection of the house and all points of entry."

"And how do you know that Martin isn't home?" I whispered, even though we weren't out of the car yet.

"And you guys think you're hot-shot detectives? I used an old technique called ringing Martin's house and hearing the answering machine saying that he'd be over at the convention center all night and leaving his cell phone number there. Easy. Okay, since you're amateurs, follow me to the house, and for God's sake, be quiet."

We slipped from the car and stole across the lawn. Despite Michael's warning, Monette and I started laughing and struggled to stifle our giggling. We couldn't help it, since it all seemed so silly. Here we were, dressed in black, and Michael in a bathing suit. It was ludicrous. Michael told us to stay put while he examined the windows. He disappeared for about five minutes, during which Monette and I laughed quietly to each other, finally getting our snickering under control only to look up at each other and start the laughing all over again.

Michael returned and told us that a window on the side of the house was open a crack. We followed him to our point of entry, wondering what he had in the suitcase that would ensure our safe passage into the house and past the security system that was clearly indicated by the signs planted amid the vegetation around the house.

Michael laid the suitcase on the lawn and opened it, lifting out a body suit in black.

"This is what all the secrecy is about? A wet suit?" Monette exclaimed—quietly.

"You see, Monette, you take great pride in solving mysteries because you've read a lot of mystery books. But that's not the real world. This is," he said, pulling and tugging the suit on. "The neoprene keeps the cold from getting in. Well, it also keeps body heat from escaping, too. So when I walk in front of a motion detector, I won't give off any infrared body heat for the detectors to pick up. I can walk freely throughout the house," he explained, tugging on a hood that covered his face almost completely.

"And what about dogs?"

Michael tapped his head to indicate his superior brain. "Martin doesn't have any. I asked Vince. Okay, I'm going in, and I want you two to stay here and keep an eye out. Whistle if you see anyone," Michael said, lifting the window screen out with the skill of a surgeon and sliding the window open. He hopped over the ledge and in seconds was inside the house. "Now, remember, whistle if you spot anyone," he said, and disappeared into the bowels of the house.

"What I want to know is, what is Michael doing with a wet suit in the desert?"

"Don't ask," I warned her.

"Surfing in the sand dunes?"

"I said, don't ask," I repeated, starting to laugh again, when all hell broke loose.

Michael came tumbling out of the window like a Hungarian acrobatic act, followed by a viciously barking dog, who snapped his jaws at the now-empty window. As if that weren't bad enough, a siren started to whoop and holler, no doubt raising the interests of the neighbors and, soon the police. The three of us ran across the lawn and jumped into the Chevrolet Metro, which Monette gunned into a series of fishtailing squeals that were surprisingly loud for such a small car.

"I don't fucking believe it," Michael shouted between gasps. "That goddamn Vince told me that Martin didn't have a dog. See what happens when one link of the chain is weak?"

"Michael?" I managed to wheeze out between breaths.

"You know what I'm thinking?" Michael continued. "I'm thinking that Vince is our culprit and he set us up so we'd get caught! That's what I think. Ladies and gentlemen, we have our murderer."

"Michael?"

"Yes, what the fuck is it, Robert?"

"What was the address that Vince gave you for Martin's house?"

"Forty-eight twenty-seven South Driftwood, like it says on the piece of paper you're holding."

"That's correct. But that's not the house we just broke into. We were at forty-eight twenty-three."

"Are you sure?" Michael asked, not believing a word I said.

"As sure as this car is too small for the three of us. I remember seeing the numbers painted on the curb, because they're the last four numbers of my telephone in New York."

"Oh. I guess that explains the dog!" Michael said, as usual, getting ready to shift the blame like a congressman.

"Yeah, so what happened to the neoprene suit?"

"It worked perfectly for me, but I opened a door to a room and this beast from hell came flying out of the room and chased me. I guess he's the one who set off the alarm."

"Michael, it was a cocker spaniel that was chasing you. I know because I caught a glimpse of it. All you had to do was stare it down and it would have peed on the floor and run away."

"I don't believe it!" Michael replied, trying to squirm out of a first-class botched burglary. "It was dark, but all I could see were these glowing red eyes that burnt like the flames of hell."

"It was a hyperactive cocker spaniel," I asserted. "I saw it."

Monette was laughing quietly to herself as she steered the car back to Casa Vince. Michael said he had to lie down for a while and he would probably go out and get laid that evening—at least that was something he couldn't fuck up. Vince left a message in the office for me, saying that Marc had called and wanted some company for the evening—and that meant Monette, too. It wasn't difficult getting her to stay the night. The lesbians she was staying with in Rancho Myass were still arguing and were no fucking fun—her words exactly.

We drove up to Marc's house, noting the police cruiser parked reassuringly out front. Good, Marc was safe.

We sent out for a pizza and sat down to watch a schmaltzy made-for-TV movie about the life of Jackie O.

"Oh boy, this movie stinks like the Salton Sea on a hot

day," Monette said as we half-watched the film and told Marc of our misguided cat burglary adventure.

"So Michael is going into the wrong house in a wet suit in the middle of the desert!" I reported to Marc, who was holding his stomach and laughing hysterically. "The house we wanted to break into was actually next door! We were so close!" I said as I was hit by a bolt of lightning inside Marc's den.

At first I thought I had been hit by an assailant's bullet, but it turned out to be a thought that had far more impact.

"What—what is it, Robert?" Monette exclaimed, reaching over and shaking me.

"I'm okay, but it was like . . . there, then it wasn't there."

Marc stared at me, not knowing if I had snapped my cap or had suffered an epileptic fit. "Are you okay?" he asked, grabbing my hand and looking at me with deep concern.

"Oh, I'm fine. It's just something—like a great awareness that played hit-and-run with me. I guess I'm still a little dazed."

"I know exactly what's happening, goddamn it," Monette said. "You're on the cusp of solving this whole damn mess! You're going to figure it out before me!"

"Oh, I'm not so sure about that. It was weird. Like I know what I was thinking, but it wasn't completely clear. Like a foggy idea. It just didn't crystallize yet."

"That's how it happens for me," Monette indicated. "You fill your head with all the facts, then you let it sit and stew, and whammo! It hits you. But you have to be careful and not disturb it while you're in this state. Let's just sit back and watch this stupid movie and maybe it will come back to you."

So we did just that. We watched Jackie bumble along as a photographer until she met Jack Kennedy and fell in love with the cheating scoundrel. Nothing. No solution came to my mind. Nothing. Jackie was just about to go down the aisle of the church to get married for the first time, when the screen froze and went to black, and up came the words that hundreds of faggots across America probably yelled in agony: *To be Continued.*

"Oh, shit," Marc said, thumbing through a *TV Guide.* "This is a two-parter," he complained. "They get you hooked on the gloves and the hats; then they pull it away from you and tell you to come back tomorrow." Marc turned off the television and asked what we wanted to do next.

"I'm going to make a suggestion," Monette said.

"As long as it doesn't involve breaking into a house," I said, drawing a line in the sand.

Monette smiled. "You two haven't had much time together, so why don't you go off and I'll go take a swim in the pool or sit out and watch the stars or read a book. Don't worry about me—I can entertain myself. Go, now, off with you two."

Marc looked at me. I returned his gaze. Wordlessly we grabbed each other's hand and started down the hall to Marc's bedroom.

"Just remember one thing, Robert," Monette's voice came from behind us. "While Marc is handling the Red Party from here tomorrow, you and I are going for a hike. After all, we gotta start checking out some facts. So, Marc, make sure Robert can walk tomorrow."

14

Happy Trails to You

Unlike Michael Stark, I like to keep my sexual life private. So I'm not going to go into any detail about another night with Marc. Suffice it to say that when I got up in the morning, I felt like I could climb straight up to Mount San Jacinto's 10,800-foot peak.

In fact, I was beaming over with contentment and pride when Monette and I squeezed into our minuscule Metro, heading out for our hike. Already Monette had an ace up her sleeve.

"Sergeant Big Dick—"

"Sergeant Big *Arms*," I reminded her.

"What did I say?" she asked.

"Big Dick."

"Oh, that's not like me to be thinking about big dicks—or any, for that matter. Anyway, Sergeant Big Arms called me this morning, and you're not going to believe this."

"Believe what?"

"About the calls that came to Rex's cell phone."

"Oh, yeah. And . . . ?" I pleaded.

"The first one came from his own house, Casa Rex," Monette stated, knowing that this information would send my head reeling.

It worked.

"What?" I replied. "From his own house? You mean someone was there?"

"I don't think a ghost made the call."

"Well, offhand, I would say that this would make Vince the number one suspect, but he was at the party with Rex that night."

"That's right," Monette agreed. "Are you confused enough, or do you want to hear where the second call came from?"

"You've just blown all my shaky theories out of the water, but go ahead."

"Call number two came from Leo's own house."

"None of this makes any sense."

"Yes, it does," Monette said. "It means that there were two callers."

"Our double-murderer theory?"

"Could be," Monette said, squealing around a corner. "There's still so much we don't know. Plus, there's something about those letters."

"Other than the paper?" I asked.

"Yes, but I can't quite put my finger on it."

"So why are we going on this hike? I suppose this has something to do with the first attempt on Rex's life?"

"You are correct-a-mundo. Plus, I'm stuck—we might as well start somewhere," she said, flying down a rather desolate road and coming to a screeching halt off to the side of the road and raising a great cloud of dust that enveloped our tiny sardine on wheels. "This is it. Spitz Trail."

"Do you know where this leads?" I said, looking at the rugged terrain.

"Hopefully, to some answers," Monette responded.

The trail was narrow, so I followed single file after Monette, hoping that if we chanced upon any rattlesnakes, she would know what to do. After hiking for about an hour, Monette turned to me and said, "Do you see what I see?"

"Obviously not," I said, trying to scan the landscape for

the cougar or dead body that Monette had spotted but I had somehow missed.

"Rex said that someone threw a boulder down on him when he was hiking. There's not a hill overlooking this entire trail. It's almost as flat as a pancake."

"There are some cliffs over there," I objected.

"Robert, if you wanted to kill someone, it's a million-to-one shot for anyone to roll a boulder from those cliffs, make it jump two deep washes, and just happen to roll all that way and hit Rex. George W. Bush would have a better chance of getting a degree from Harvard."

I cracked open the trail guide that Monette had handed me earlier, and read again the description of the trail. "The trail guide categorizes the Spitz Trail as easy. It says there are no significant hills or inclines on the way. Maybe the evildoer didn't want to kill Rex. Remember how they wanted money?"

"It still makes no sense. If you wanted to scare someone into paying you off, wouldn't you want to have a near miss with your intended target? The way this trail goes, you'd need a catapult to hit Rex from any of those cliffs. Plus, I want to add that I can't believe that you're huffing and puffing on a trail that a two-year-old could handle. You have to get out of smoky bars and out into the fresh air."

"I do the stair-stepper machine at the gym. Michael says it gives you buns like two cherry tomatoes," I answered. "So what have we learned here?"

"We've learned that none of this makes any sense."

"Maybe a boulder just kinda rolled by itself, and Rex, his mind already being in a suggestive state, imagined that someone threw the rock at him."

"Close, but no cigar, Robert. A more plausible theory was that the boulder incident never happened. In that case, where did Rex go instead? Or, another possibility is that Rex was on a different trail and got the names mixed up.

Oh, fuck it all. I don't know anything anymore. We might as well go."

We walked back toward the car, with Monette and me rearranging the facts of the case in our heads. Suddenly, a thought came to me.

"Monette, I think we should find out from Vince who had keys to Casa Rex. If we could just find out who could have made that call, we might have our answer."

Monette turned around in her tracks and gave me one of her rib-cracking hugs.

"Great idea. You're learning, kiddo. Someday you'll be almost as good as me."

The trouble with most theories is that they look good on paper, but when put to the acid test they fall apart faster than a set of Firestone radials. My great idea sounded terrific until Vince gave us the disappointing news that all the higher-ups had keys to Rex's house office.

"Leo, Marc, Colorado—even David McLeish—had keys. Rex holds his meetings here; the plans and most of the paperwork is here—so people need access to this stuff. Plus, Rex writes off part of the house on his taxes because of the home office. But no one comes here in the middle of the night, if that's what you mean."

"Well, someone did," Monette said, trying to set the record straight.

"What do you mean? The palm-tree incident?" Vince asked.

"Never mind," Monette responded so abruptly that I knew something was up. "Do you mind if we look around in Rex's office some more?"

"I don't know what you're going to find," Vince added. "Just don't disturb things too much, because Rex might want to come back, and he hates it when things are out of place . . . from beyond, I mean."

Monette shot me a this-guy's-cuckoo look.

"Thank you, Vince," she responded, grabbing my hand and tugging me down the hall into Rex's office, closing the door, and locking it behind us. "Vince is really starting to give me the creeps."

"And you wonder why I don't want to sleep here?" I said.

"Do me a favor. Turn on his computer and let's do some snooping," Monette suggested.

I did as I was told, and in few minutes we were sifting through what was left of dear, departed Rex. True to what Vince had predicted, his filing system was as neat as a pin. Everything was filed in tidy folders that ranged from *Personal* to *Proposals*. We searched every file and document we could, but we found nothing out of the ordinary. The file marked *Personal* was off limits to us and protected by a password.

"What is that blinking light at the top of the screen?" Monette asked, pointing to a blinking icon off the side of the screen.

"Let's click on it and find out," I said. "Oh, it's a fax thing. He's got messages in there he hasn't read."

"And I guess he never will, unless we run an Ethernet cable into Heaven where he can download his messages," Monette replied, dripping with sarcasm.

"Oh, you are evil, Monette!"

We looked at each other and laughed, two skeptics sharing a little joke.

"Let's look at the faxes. Maybe there's something in there," Monette prodded me.

We did. Nothing. Just invoices, business correspondence, and a joke involving a man with a strawberry up his ass.

Monette, not satisfied with what she found, studied the computer screen carefully.

"Ah!" she exclaimed in triumph. "We were looking at the *in box*. What we need to look at are the *sent* faxes." She clicked on the *sent* icon and the screen was aglow with a list of all the faxes sent in the last few weeks. "Bulls eye!"

"I don't see it," I confessed to Monette. "It's just a list of the faxes Rex sent, the phone numbers he sent them to, and when he sent them. What's so special about that?"

"Let me print out this list and I'll bet that we find something highly significant—if my guesses are right," she replied. "Okay, where do we look next?"

"Oh, Monette?"

"Yes?"

"Marc wanted to know if you wanted to come over and watch the rest of that Jackie O movie. He's going to order some wonderful food from a restaurant and have it delivered, champagne included."

"Champagne? Count me in," she said, just before she got hit by a bolt of lightning.

It's one thing when people of my height, five feet eleven, get a breakthrough idea. We look surprised and may clap our hands. When a six-foot-four-inch Monette gets a eureka, she jumps up and down and dances around like a quarterback making a touchdown in the last few seconds of a game.

"That's it? Oh, goddess, I've been so stupid. It was right there all the time! And it was so simple! Thank you, Robert. Thank you, thank you, thank you!"

This was it! The answer. I was about to explode, waiting to hear about the clue that would blow this case wide open. "What? What's the answer?" I begged.

"Jackie O," she said, grinning from ear to ear.

It was a while before I moved or even breathed.

"This is one of our practical jokes, isn't it?" I asked. "I know that you've been here about a week and you haven't played one on me yet. And, I haven't played one on you yet."

"You've been too busy falling in love," she explained. "No, I'm quite sure about my idea; I just don't know how to prove it yet. But I will. Do me a favor, will you? Turn Rex's computer on again, and I want to make up a list of questions that I need the answers to. Then we can fax them to Sergeant Gorski."

I did as she wanted. The questions left me stumped when I saw them appear on the computer screen as she typed:

1. What *exactly* did Martin Stevers see at The Zone bar the night of Rex's death?
2. What alibi did David McLeish give the night of Rex's death?
3. What was the result of Rex's last physical?

I couldn't see her logic in solving this mess, but I was gaining some insight into how a good detective surmises what really happened and then looks for answers to questions that will prove his theory. The all-important skill is in coming up with the *right* theory—that's the kicker.

Monette printed out her list of questions and went over to Rex's fax machine and faxed her list of questions to Sergeant Gorski. Or at least she tried to.

"The thing's broke," she said, looking at the fax machine as if staring at it intently would fix it.

She went to the door and shouted down the hall to Vince, "Vince, is there something about Rex's fax machine that I don't understand? It doesn't seem to be working."

Seconds later, Vince popped his head in the door.

"It's not working because Rex threw it against the wall a week ago when the paper jammed. What do you want to send?" he asked, trying to see what was on Monette's piece of paper.

Monette's hand flew behind her back, keeping her list of questions safe from Vince's hands—the second time she seemed to be keeping something from Vince. She suspected Vince, and so did I—in a way, he had the most to gain.

"Just one sheet of paper," Monette replied.

"Did you print that out on the computer?" Vince inquired.

"Yes, I just printed it."

"Oh, you can fax it right from the computer. Just click on the 'Just the Fax' icon and follow the directions to send your document."

"Thank you, Vince," Monette said, shooing him out the door and locking it quietly behind him. She sat down at the computer again and sent the fax to the phone number on Sergeant Gorski's business card.

"You don't trust Vince, do you?"

"No, Robert, but I don't trust anyone until we have all the facts in the case."

"Everyone's guilty until proven innocent." I put on my sad cow eyes and tried to look pitiful. "And you're not going to tell me who you think did it, are you?"

"Nope. I want you to figure out what I'm doing and why. You need to guess if you ever want to become a first-rate armchair detective. I'll give you a clue that will help and will make cases easier to solve: don't spend your time watching the smoke like most people do—keep your eye out for the fire."

"Thank you for that sage piece of Zen advice, oh, mistress of the sound of one hand getting the clap," I responded. "Do you want me to visualize world peace, too?"

"Don't get smart with me, missy," Monette said coyly. "Now, we have to get busy ourselves."

"So what are we doing next?"

"Guess."

"You gave the sergeant a list of questions that you either can't or don't want to dig up, so we're going to search for stuff we can find out for ourselves."

"Very good!" she replied, heaping praise on my first real step in the art of solving mysteries.

"Don't ask me what our next step is, because I don't know," I confessed.

"We're going to ask Vince the name of Rex's travel agent."

"I see," I said, lying through my teeth.

"Then we're going to grill Marc. First and foremost, we need to know if Leo Thomas had a boyfriend. Why would I want to know the answer to that?"

"To eliminate the possibility that Leo was murdered for an inheritance by a lover."

"Very good!"

"So even though Leo is dead, you suspect that he might have killed Rex?"

Monette smiled. "I'm just trying to eliminate another theory. Soon we'll be down to one. Let's get the name of Rex's travel agent from Vince and then head over to Marc's house so we can grill him. Then we're going to take an excursion down some remote roads."

"A desert scavenger hunt?" I suggested.

"What I'm looking for is far from worthless. In fact, if I find what I'm looking for, I'll have all the evidence I need."

15

A View to a Kill

We drove over to Marc's house, where Monette made a quick call to Grayson.

"Grayson, Monette here. I have the name of a travel agent here in town. John Haggerty. Do you know him? Vince said he's the number one gay travel agent here in town. . . . You do? Good! . . . You use him? . . . Excellent! Could you give him a call and ask him if he's made any travel arrangements for Rex in the last year? . . . You could? Good! As soon as you get the answer, call me here at Marc Baldwin's house. . . . Yes, the number I gave you the other day. . . . Fine. . . . Okay, good-bye."

She then placed a second call.

"Sergeant Gorski? . . . Oh, good. I was afraid you were out. Did you get my list of questions? . . . You did? Good. . . . They're cryptic, you say! . . . Oh. But you say you already have the answer to the third one? . . . Oh, really! . . . No! . . . That's just what I thought. . . . The question about what Martin Stevers saw? . . . Yeah. . . . Yeah. . . . Well, that's what I meant. . . . Uh-huh. And you're still trying to locate David McLeish to check out his alibi? Well, did you try setting out a dish of Alpo? . . . Just a private joke; never mind. . . . Okay, call me here at five five five, six seven six nine—it's Marc Baldwin's house, in the Cathedral City Cove. And don't plan anything for tonight. I've got an assignment for you. I'll explain later. . . . Okay, bye. What's that? . . . You did! Oh, that's wonderful. . . . So that's the magazine, huh? Your forensic people are pretty good. . . . But just the first batch—not the second. . . . Okay, call me when you know about the others. . . . Okay, we'll be talking."

We were all sitting in Marc's home office, me watching Monette in action and Marc poring over plans for the Red Party with an assistant, Marcia Brandon.

"Marc, could we talk to you in private for a minute—in the other room?" Monette asked, jerking her head toward Marcia.

"Oh, sure," he replied, wondering what she was up to.

He wasn't the only one.

When we got to the kitchen and pulled the folding doors closed, Monette began. "Marc, give me a rough idea of what each person's financial stake is in T-Rex Enterprises."

"Well . . . Rex has the biggest, fifty-one percent, followed by David McLeish, with about twenty-five percent. Then Leo and I have—had—oh, fuck, *have* roughly twelve percent."

"Okay, good. So if Rex dies, his share looks like it might go to Vince, right?"

"I don't know the contents of Rex's will, but he was awful fond of Vince. Plus, Rex is estranged from his family. They wouldn't have anything to do with him after he told them he was gay years ago."

"Okay, next question. Do you subscribe to a party production magazine? You know, a trade publication dealing with event planners?"

"Yes, I do. I get *Party Production* magazine," he stated. "Wait a minute, you don't think I sent those threatening letters, do you?"

"I'm just asking a question, Marc," she replied.

"Everyone at T-Rex had a subscription to that magazine!" said Marc, his defenses up. "For a while, Rex had the only copy, but he kept complaining that everyone was always borrowing his, so he bought subscriptions for Leo and me. Do you want to see mine?" he said, getting up, preparing to retrieve them to prove his innocence.

"Marc, I said that it wouldn't be necessary."

"That's the magazine that some of the letters came from, wasn't it."

"Yes, it is," Monette stated.

"But it's not just us at T-Rex that get *Party Production*. Everyone with the White Party probably subscribes to it, too," Marc answered.

"Yes, that's the trouble. Too many people get it, so by itself it isn't a great clue. But when someone subscribes to that magazine and several issues are missing, then it becomes meaningful."

"And you're looking for someone who's missing a few issues?"

"The way you say it, it sounds so funny," Monette remarked. "Yes, yes, we are."

"We?" I asked.

"Sergeant Gorski and me," Monette replied. "And Robert, once he unravels the twisted clues in this case. He's getting close; I can tell. Now, Marc, if you'll be so good as to excuse Robert and me for a few hours, we're going in search of a good place to shoot at cars."

"Excuse me?" Marc asked, sounding like Monette had flipped her wig.

Monette clarified her statement. "I'd like to see the spot where someone took a shot at Colorado."

A half-hour later, Monette and I were parked on the side of the road, looking at the spot indicated on the police report of Colorado's "accident." On the way over, I told Monette my theory and she reached out across the front seat to shake my hand. I was so proud that I had figured this caper out, a small tear escaped the confines of my eyes.

"Nope," came the deflating reply. "But keep trying," she advised me. "You'll get it. Just don't give up; keep going. So what am I looking for?"

"Uh, evidence that the killer left, just before he squeezed off a shot at Colorado's BMW."

"That correct. And where do you think that evidence is?"

I looked at the map in the police report, noting the streets that led off of Highway 111.

"I think that place over there would be a good place to look," I said, pointing to a side street on the map. I then turned around to survey the general area where the street lay.

"Why?"

"Because, if my directions are correct, that road looks like it goes up in the hills, and it looks like there aren't any houses around—so no one could hear a shot."

"An excellent guess. Let's go," she said as she put the car into drive and took us up into the hills. The desolate road was only about a half-mile off busy Highway 111, but it was the perfect place to look and the perfect vantage point. We got out of the car and walked along the cracked pavement, studying the ground for our sacred clue. And lo and behold, after just five minutes, we found it. Monette handed me an envelope in which to put our find.

We headed back to Marc's house, to watch the second part of the made-for-TV movie about Jackie Kennedy. On the way back, Monette made me promise not to reveal anything to Marc just yet. She said it could jeopardize our investigation. Plus, she said Marc had a part to play in this mystery yet. She wouldn't elaborate further.

The food arrived from nearby Desert Moon, and we were very impressed by their culinary output. Marc made some exotic martinis, and we had a wonderful evening eating, drinking, and making fun of the movie, substituting our own dialogue for the actors' words, making a bad movie much better. We were disturbed briefly by a phone call from Colorado. Marc spoke briefly with him, then hung up.

"I'm sure that you're all going to be relieved. That was Colorado. He'll be out of the hospital tomorrow."

"Oh, joy," was Monette's response.

We stayed up until after midnight, talking and laughing. Considering that there was so much negative energy around us, I felt good. Here I was with my two soul mates, Monette and Marc. The only regrettable thing was that in a matter of a week, I would be on the other side of the country with one of my best friends, but Marc would still be here. I tried not to think about it. *Just stay in the moment*, I told myself, repeating what my therapist told me: most people stood with one foot in the past and one in the future, while pissing on the present. I resolved to just be Robert, right here, right now. But to ensure that there was a future for Marc, I resolved that I would do anything to catch the homicidal maniac—or maniacs—that were threatening him.

Eventually, we were too tired to go on any further, so we retired for the evening. Marc and I were settling down to just snuggling and talking; then our conversation was interrupted when the window at the foot of the bed shattered and a large rock tumbled across the carpet. I threw Marc under the covers and covered his head with a pillow, waiting for a hail of bullets to come flying into the bedroom, but there was only silence.

The rock might have been the end of the attack, but I didn't plan on taking any chances. Marc reached under his bed and pulled out his slippers (he said he kept them there in case of earthquakes—and broken glass). I liked how this guy's mind worked. He was prepared for anything, just like me. He gave one slipper to me and put the other on his foot, telling me to hop until we got out of the room. We were both hopping on one foot into the hallway when we were met by a hulking presence looming in the dark. We both froze. We knew how to get out of the room with our feet intact, but meeting a stranger in the hallway was something we hadn't expected. A light flicked on, causing us both to yell and hold on to each other.

The stranger was Monette.

"I know I don't wear a lot of makeup, but I'm not that ugly."

"Oh, fuck," I said, relieved that the end was not near. "You scared the shit out of us."

"Let me guess. You were both playing one-slipper leapfrog and Robert knocked over a vase."

"The window, Monette! Someone threw a rock through the window!" I managed to get out between breaths.

"Oh, thank goodness," Monette said.

"Thank goodness?" was my reply.

"I'd say a rock is better than a bullet."

"I guess you're right," I replied, picking up on the clue right away. "But it's puzzling."

"Puzzling?" Monette asked.

"Yes, because it's inconsistent. The first threats were far more deadly, and—forgive me for being so blunt—ended in death. So why a rock now? Did our killer run out of bullets?"

"I don't know," Monette replied. "Obviously, someone is still trying to keep the Red Party from opening. Robert, go out front and tell the nice policeman outside what happened, and tell him to keep a sharper lookout."

"Where are you going?" I asked as Monette turned and walked sleepily down the hall.

"Back to the guest room. I'll move my stuff into your den and you two take the guest room."

Marc protested, but Monette wanted us to be together—comfortably. We moved a few things across the hall and got in bed together. I knew we were relatively safe, but just to make sure, I pulled Marc tightly up against me before I closed my eyes.

* * *

I woke the next morning and was overjoyed for the simple reason that I had woken up. No one had killed Marc or me in the night. Except for the broken window, the house seemed intact. Life was good. Of course, unbeknownst to me, this was the day we would come face-to-face with murder.

After breakfast, Monette asked me to help her swing her plan into action, but it was Grayson who started things off with a phone call.

Monette found out that Rex had taken three trips to Buenos Aires in the past year, unbeknownst to Vince. Monette instructed me on what to do next.

I then called Sergeant Big Arms and relayed the information to him. He checked the dates against credit card records that Vince had provided to the police. Neatly corresponding to Rex's trips were three charges to a ferry company. I only had the amount of each charge (all for the same amount), so I figured that if I called them, I could tell from the amount of the charge where Rex had taken the ferry. I spoke very little Spanish, so this effort took a great deal more time than I had imagined. From what I could tell, Rex got off at one of the many fishing villages before Montenegro. But why? Was he transporting drugs? Or making deals to bring cocaine into the United States? For the first time during this whole sordid affair, I had the inkling that maybe Rex's business was just a cover for something else. But what?

About noon, a fax came through on Marc's machine. It was from Sergeant Gorski, and it contained the answers to Monette's questions. Her mysterious questions were answered in the same mysterious language, as though coded against prying eyes. The answers were scribbled next to Monette's questions, then faxed back. In response to Monette's first question, *What exactly did Martin Stevers see at The Zone bar the night of Rex's death?* Big Arms simply replied that Martin didn't see anything out of the ordinary. The second question: *What alibi did David McLeish give the night of Rex's death?* The answer: *He was in a puppy pile, playing with eight other puppies and their trainers. Mr. McLeish asked that we keep this information confidential, because of his career in Hollywood.* Last question: *What was the result of Rex's last physical?* Answer: *Can't get any information on this. Rex apparently switched doctors a few months ago and I was unable to find out who he was seeing. He complained to his regular doctor of abdominal pains, but when he was referred to a specialist, he never showed up.*

It seemed the more I learned, the more confused I got. I got so frustrated that I took a walk down the hall to Marc, who was talking to two assistants from the Red Party. I watched him taking command and making tough decisions on the spot. He looked so heroic, so in control. It was a characteristic that I admired in others since it was something that I lacked. But things were changing. I was making strides with my therapist, my past and all its baggage were unraveling like a cheap sweater, and I was learning to stand up for myself—I was learning my worth.

I padded back down the hall to Marc's office. Monette was searching the Internet for information about Uruguay, flipping from page to page in a frantic search for something I couldn't yet deduce.

"Ah, there it is," she said in triumph.

"There's what?" I asked.

"It's right there. Don't you see it?"

"No. What am I looking for?"

"I can't tell you that any more than I can tell you the telltale clues I found in the letters sent to Rex."

"You know, Monette, I've stared at the letters for hours, and I still don't see what's so special about them. Despite the fact that Big Arms informed us that they're from different magazines."

"That's not what tipped me off. You don't need to be a forensics expert to see the clue."

"I am still in the dark," I admitted. "Although I did deduce from the fax from Big Arms that David McLeish has an alibi. Don't ask me what a puppy pile is, unless it's something that you pick up with a plastic bag and put in the trash."

"Please, Robert, I beg you—don't go there."

"Believe me, I won't."

"There's just one question that I need answered. The whole case hinges on this, more or less."

"And what's that?" I asked.

"Where is the fuckin' money that Rex paid to his extortionists?"

They say that time flies when you're having fun. They also say that you can lead a horse to water but you can't make him drink. I don't know what either of these two sayings have to do with what was about to take place, but my general state of confusion about the point of them perfectly mirrored the state of my mind at that moment: lots of things made sense on their own, but I just couldn't put them in the context of the larger picture.

Monette told me not to worry, because I would soon figure things out. But in case I didn't, she promised that "the end was near"—words that I felt could have been better chosen.

We had a very late lunch outside by Marc's pool. Monette and I threw some things together and came up with a very respectable Italian alfresco lunch, with the requisite bottle of Italian wine.

Monette was starting in on the pasta when she looked up and dropped the bombshell I suspected she had been harboring for some time.

"Marc, I need you to do something for me tonight. It's sorta dangerous."

Marc looked stunned. I, however, wasn't going to let my chance at happiness be blown away by a maniac with a gun. "What you do mean, 'sorta'?" I asked.

"You'll have protection," she said, smiling between bites of penne, arugula, and radicchio.

"A condom or a gun?" I inquired.

"Several of us, plus Sergeant Big Arms."

Marc turned to me with the look of a trapped animal. The pleading in his eyes told me that he desperately wanted my opinion. I shook my head no, which he repeated to Monette, shaking his head vigorously.

"Okay," Monette ventured further, "before you say no," she started.

"Before?" I blurted out. "We said no."

"But you haven't heard what it is that I want Marc to do."

"Monette, please don't put Marc in danger," I said. "If anyone, it should be me," I added, putting myself in harm's way for my boyfriend. It was not only a chivalrous gesture but a genuine one.

Monette shook her head. "It won't work with you. You're not a threat to the killer. Now, just listen up. The killer—or killers—aren't going to stop just because they might have their hands on the money. Sooner or later, they know that Marc or anyone else associated with T-Rex is going to figure things out. And with only circumstantial evidence so far, the killer—or killers—are going to make sure that the person who figures things out never gets to that point. And next time, they won't miss. The rock is a desperate warning by desperate people. They didn't kill you, but they showed that they can get past the police."

"I noticed that you said 'killer' *and* 'killers,' Monette," I pointed out.

"You think I'm going to tell you when you're probably close to solving the case, Robert? But Marc will soon. Please,

Marc. You'll be safe, because the police will be hidden about the place, but there is a small element of risk. It's the only way to get this thing put to bed forever."

Marc turned to me and put his hand on mine. Looking me right in the eyes, I felt him reach way down inside my soul and tell me that everything would be all right.

"Okay, Monette, you win," Marc said.

"No, not me. Just every innocent person involved," she answered. "Especially Rex and Leo."

16

Dial M for Moy-der

Fortunately, few of us on this earth have ever had to get ready to be murdered. It is no easy thing, let me tell you. I myself was a nervous wreck, so I could imagine what Marc was going through. Sergeant Big Arms arrived at six o'clock with several burly policemen in tow. They spread out over the house and grounds, taking note of every point of entry, placing concealed recording equipment about the kitchen, and conferring with Gorski about their plans.

When they had set up, Gorski talked with Monette in the kitchen. I tried to eavesdrop, but the only thing I could hear was "we've got the warrant and we're standing ready" and "terminal cancer."

Gorski and Monette helped Marc get fitted into his body armor suit, over which they had Marc wear a long-sleeved shirt.

"This will stop anything," Gorski said, smiling at the genius of its inventor. "I took a bullet once wearing one of these. Kicked me back a few feet, but I survived. I was bruised for a month, but these babies work like a charm."

Kicked me back a few feet, I thought. I pictured Marc taking a bullet from a faceless assassin and flying through the air like a stuntman in an action picture. Unfortunately, there were no wires involved in this stunt, and this was something the stuntmen's union would never agree with.

I was scared shitless—a fact that I shared with Marc.

"How do you think *I* feel?" Marc said, grinning. "I just don't want to crap my pants, because I'm afraid I'll explode in this suit. I'm afraid I'll pepper the house with shrapnel."

He was being so brave.

"Listen, this is something I have to do—for Rex and Leo. Rex could be a real prick sometimes, but he took me under his arm and gave me a job and taught me a lot. And Leo, well, he was just a good guy. I have to do this for them. And you know, it's bigger than even that. I'm standing up for those who refuse to be frightened by others; I'm going to make this Red Party a success. For Rex and Leo, yes, but for me too. To show to myself that I can do it."

And just like that, I saw in Marc something that was more admirable than the daring architecture of his house, the way he took command of the Red Party all by himself, or the fact that he still had the original album of *Petula Clark's Greatest Hits*. No, Marc had become heroic right in front of my eyes. He was going to prove to himself that he could do the impossible. It was an idea that appealed to me more than life itself.

Monette approached the two of us.

"You ready?" she asked.

"Yes, yes, I am," Marc said, pulling himself up to all five feet eleven inches.

To me, however, he stood much taller than that. In a room filled with a six-foot-four-inch lesbian, Sergeant Gorski, and several burly policemen, he looked like he could pierce the clouds.

Monette took him into the study and counseled Marc on what he was going to do. I stayed a safe distance away, not wanting to disturb Marc's concentration. After an eternity went by, Marc rose and went to the phone. Monette and Gorski motioned for everyone to remain quiet.

Marc dialed the phone.

"It's Marc. Marc Baldwin. . . . Yes, *that* Marc Baldwin.

I'm calling because I know you killed Rex Gifford. But that wasn't enough, was it? You killed Leo, too, didn't you? I know all about how you called Rex from Leo's party. Yeah, called from a phone in Leo's house the night of the party. You lured him up here to my house, took the money, and pushed him into my pool. Then you threw an electric cord into the pool. . . . Fuck you! . . . No, you listen to me, you fuck-wad. And I saw how you poisoned Leo's protein powder the night of Leo's party. I know you talked to Leo at the party and asked him about his workout routines. . . . How do I know? He told Robert, my boyfriend, that someone else asked him about his nutrition program at the party. That person was you. . . . Yeah, well, I *am* pretty smart. I knew what you were up to, so I watched you as you put the poison in Leo's protein powder, knowing that he wouldn't drink it until the next day. . . . Huh! I also know that you sent the threatening letters. You cut them out of some of your magazines—you know, the ones that have the glossy, expensive paper. . . . Oh, don't fuck with me, asshole! You have those magazines because you use 'em in your line of work! . . . Oh really! You're a pretty sloppy killer, you shit-head; you left a telltale clue that night on Hillview Road. . . . Uh-huh . . . That's right! Before the auto hit the embankment. You're not a very good shot are you? Or are you? . . . What? . . . The cops? No, they couldn't find their asses to wipe 'em," Marc, said, winking at the five of us standing there. "What do I want? Boy, you aren't very smart, are you, dick-wipe? I want money! You come over here and bring one-point-five million with you, chowderhead. You can keep the rest. After all, you did the murders yourself; consider that your pay. . . . No . . . no . . . the cops aren't here anymore. They think the killings have stopped, so they dropped the twenty-four-hour protection. . . . No, there's no one here. . . . What!? . . . Do you think I'm stupid? I've busted my ass for T-Rex and Rex gave me squat for all my hard work! So now I'm going to get my fair share for all my work, and you're going to give it to me. It's a far cry more than I would have made working for that prick. So get your pretty ass over here pronto and give me the money I earned!"

He slammed down the phone and looked at our crew. "How did I do?" he asked.

"Perfect," Gorski answered. "Now we wait."

Everyone took their positions as darkness worked its way into the valley, leaving everything in its inky blackness. Gorski oiled the hinges on the door leading to Marc's walk-in pantry (so it wouldn't squeak, Gorski informed us) and Monette, Gorski, and I got inside, leaving the door open a crack. The other cops went somewhere inside the house, and one went out the front door and disappeared into the night.

And we waited. It was dead quiet for a long time as we huddled in the pantry. There was the boom-boom of a car stereo that passed by outside, then faded away like a radio going dead.

Gorski's walkie-talkie squawked suddenly, scaring Monette and me with its outburst.

"Car pulling into driveway. This is it, everyone!" a voice said on his walkie-talkie.

Gorski reached around and turned a switch on the communicator, and the device went silent with a static click.

Marc left the kitchen and disappeared. He must have switched on his stereo, because we could hear music thumping from the living room. And then the doorbell chimed. My pulse raced as I heard Marc open the front door, exchange some muffled words with the killer, and close the door. I heard footsteps on the polished concrete floor and saw two forms enter the kitchen.

"I'm so glad you could come over on such short notice, Colorado," Marc said coldly.

"You didn't give me any alternatives, did you?" Colorado shot back—not literally.

"I see you brought the money. Good. You had me

stumped for a while there. But the magazines you used to send the threatening letters gave you away. They came from *World of Interiors*, didn't they? That's a very expensive paper they use."

"What are you, some kind of cop?" Colorado asked.

"No, I just have my sources."

"But you're wrong about all the letters. I only sent them to myself, you, and Leo. Rex sent the first few to himself."

"To himself?" Marc wondered.

"Yes, your fucking prick of a boss had terminal pancreatic cancer. He found out almost a year ago. So he hatched a plan where he'd make it look like someone was going to stop the Red Party unless he paid up. The White Party people had nothing to do with any part of it, but Rex made it look like they did."

"Uh-huh."

"Yes, so Mr. T-Rex decided to rip off his own company to get his hands on everyone's money by making it look like he went to pay off his tormentors. He planned to abandon his car on a side road and disappear, making his way across the border to Mexico, where he'd fly to Uruguay and live the last days of his life."

"But you found out about Rex's plans, probably by snooping around his office, and you told him you'd tell the police if he didn't meet you—at my house," Marc deduced.

"Very good, Markie, baby. I called him on his cell phone from Leo's bedroom and told him I was on to him."

"But why kill Leo? He never hurt you."

"I needed to keep the finger of blame pointing at the White Party people. Kip, Martin, Brian—it didn't matter. All of them had enough motive to threaten Rex."

"But they never did, did they?"

"No."

"So why stage the accident with your car?"

"I thought you were the smart one, Marc," Colorado snapped. "As a victim, no one would consider me a suspect.

I was just like you—out of the running. And just to make sure I was in the clear, I planned that accident so I'd be in the hospital and beyond suspicion."

"I figured that out already," Marc admitted falsely. "You drove up Hillview Road, knowing it was deserted. You shot out your own windshield, then drove a short distance down Highway 111 and swerved off the road and into the wash, knowing that your air bag would save you. After all, you can't drive far with a shattered windshield before someone notices, so I figured the spot where you shot out your windshield couldn't be far from your accident. That's where I went looking for shattered glass, and I found it. Very good. You were a perfect victim."

"Like you're about to be," Colorado remarked with an icy coldness that sent chills down my spine.

I couldn't see everything from my vantage point crouching beneath Sergeant Gorski (a position that I found strangely erotic), but I could catch glimpses through the slit of light that entered the pantry. Colorado had a gun and was brandishing it about.

"How stupid do you think I am, Markie? Did you think I was going to go to all this trouble and let you come in and walk away with most of it? This is where you finally get yours."

A lot happened in the next few nanoseconds. I could actually hear the sergeant's lungs fill quickly with air, readying his body for action. At the same time, I prepared to spring out the door and tackle Colorado myself—that is, if Michael Stark hadn't entered the kitchen door behind Colorado.

"What the fuck is going on here?" Michael asked, suddenly coming out of the blue, startling even me in the safety of the pantry.

Colorado spun 180 degrees to face Michael. As he did, both Sergeant Big Arms and I shot out of the pantry at the same time, tripping each other and collapsing in a pile like a third-rate circus act. Behind me, Monette burst out of the pantry and delivered a gut-wrenching kick to Colorado's groin, sending him down like a sack of potatoes. Like a person who had done this every day of her life, she calmly stepped on his hand and lifted the gun from his limp digits, holding it carefully to avoid putting her fingerprints on it.

Michael, who was clearly impressed by what he had just seen, shook his head and put his hands in his hips. "Huh . . . and I thought *I* was the one out having all the fun," he snorted.

Several hours later, we were all gathered at Clifford and Grayson's house, recounting the high-voltage evening we had all just been through.

"Thank you so much for having us over so late . . . and for fixing this magnificent dinner," I said.

"After what you've been through," Grayson said, snapping his napkin in the air to release it from the swan it had been folded into, "Clifford and I thought you could use a little celebration dinner. Clifford, could you open the champagne?"

Clifford, the cute but libidinous grandfather, got up and uncorked a bottle of champagne, the cork flying across the room and hitting a porcelain Russian wolfhound that stood guard at the entrance to the dining room, separating its right ear from its head with a clean cut.

"Oops!" Clifford exclaimed.

Grayson rolled his eyes. "Merv Griffin gave us that," he confided to us in a whisper, not wanting to upset Clifford. "Oh, well, life is precarious, I suppose. So, tell me, Monette, apparently you were the first to get to the root of this affair."

"*Affair*." I thought the word was a little underwhelming in comparison to what had actually happened, but like many things in life, I let it slide.

Monette, who loved to be onstage almost as much as

Michael—almost, I said—brightened whenever her talent was recognized.

"The clue that tipped me off was in the notes," she started.

"Monette," I interrupted, "I have been over those notes a hundred times, and I still don't see what was so telling. I read the words backwards; I looked at the colors of the letters, how they were combined, everything. And I turned up a great big nothing."

"And you call yourself a writer," she shamed me ever so gently.

"I work in advertising, Monette. What I do is prostitution, not writing. Plus, what does that have to do with the letters?"

Grayson added, "Monette, dear, I looked the letters over all day and I didn't see anything amiss about them, either."

Monette smiled her Cheshire-cat smile. "I spotted the difference even before the forensic department noticed that the letters came from two dissimilar magazines—which isn't a good clue in and of itself. Perhaps the killer just changed magazines."

"And . . . ?" I pleaded.

"The letters sent to Rex had no punctuation in them between sentences. Not even commas. The ones sent to Leo, Marc, and Colorado did. No one changes their grammatical style like that. Punctuation is so ingrained in people, they follow a certain style whether they realize it or not. It's almost subconscious. So I knew we had two people involved. Then, when Marc and Robert and I were all watching a bad made-for-TV movie about Jackie O, we discovered that it was a multipart movie. Eureka! I thought; that's what was going on here. Plus, we discovered that for a while, Rex had the only subscription to *Party Production* magazine, which would have meant that suspicion for the letters—however slight—might be shifted to Rex. That's why he bought subscriptions to *Party Production* for everyone at T-Rex: to make them all possible suspects."

Grayson leaned forward. "So what got you thinking it was Colorado?"

"Just a hunch, but my hunch was confirmed when Sergeant Gorski got a crucial piece of information from Martin Stevers. My question was, what did he see at The Zone bar the night of Rex's death? And the answer was, nothing."

"But how did that lead you to zero in on Colorado?" Grayson continued.

"Because," Monette stated, "Colorado said he was there that night. It was a slow night, so Martin would have mentioned if he had seen Colorado there. After all, they hated each other—Martin would have noticed if he were there."

"Okay, so you've told us how you figured out that Colorado was involved. But how did you come to the conclusion that Rex was the other person involved?" Grayson puzzled.

"When Robert and I checked out the first attempt on Rex's life—well, nothing checked out. Even Rex's naked houseman, Vince, was shocked that Rex had claimed to be hiking. When Robert and I hiked Spitz Trail, we found it would have been impossible to roll a boulder at a victim from above. The second attempt—the palm tree—was too easy to arrange. Rex probably precut the tree earlier in the evening, then slipped out the door that leads from his master bath outside, cut the tree some more, and then let the wind do the rest. And the grill, cutting the propane hose—a kid could've done it."

"Okay, so now we know about Rex and his part in it, but where does Colorado come in?" Grayson asked, pausing from daintily devouring his goat-cheese tart.

Monette continued, "About a year ago, Rex learned that he had terminal cancer. The problem is, so did Colorado, who probably scoured through Rex's office on a regular basis. I mean, everyone at T-Rex had access to that office. So Colorado found out about Rex's illness and probably told Rex he'd use it against him somehow, like telling Rex's clients, who wouldn't book with him since he could die, leaving them in the lurch. In fact, almost no one associated with T-Rex could see how Rex could tolerate someone as repulsive as Colorado. But the answer was easy if you asked the right question: Why was Rex tolerating him and paying him to do almost nothing?"

"Okay, so how does South America come into this?" Grayson challenged.

"Well," Monette continued, "Robert found a drawing of a building labeled with the words *Butia, A.D.*"

"So this was his plan for after death. Was it a mausoleum?" Grayson asked, riveted by the unfolding story. In fact, even though most of us who were at Marc's house in the recent fracas knew most of the story by now, it sounded even more exciting as we heard it in its entirety. Michael was the only one who looked uncomfortable, sitting there and keeping a close eye on Clifford, who sent an occasional sly wink in his direction.

"No, it was a house he had built in Uruguay. *Butia* is the name of a native palm that grows in the region, and its fruit is made into a jelly by the inhabitants of a small fishing village on the Atlantic coast called Aguas Dulces. A.D."

A collective "Ohhhh" rose up around the table as everyone finally understood the significance of the two initials.

"I think," Monette mused, "that Rex also probably found it ironic that the initials also stood for *after death*."

"So Rex planned to rip off his own company and head to Urlugay?" Michael finally jumped in, mangling the name of our South American neighbor.

"Yes, he withdrew the payoff money the day of Leo's party and planned to pay off his tormentors, who didn't exist. He would then disappear and head to *Urlugay*," Monette said, making fun of Michael's pronunciation without his even realizing it. "But Colorado was on to Rex's plan for months now, and he set in motion a plan of his own. Earlier that day, he sent a threatening letter to Leo and Marc, knowing that they'd arrive at their destinations the next day, after Rex was dead and Leo was already—or about to be—dead.

"At the party, Rex gets a call from his supposed extortionists, asking for the payoff. He conducts a heated conversation in front of Robert, Marc, and me so there would be witnesses. What happened was quite ingenious. Rex had programmed his computer to call his cell phone at a specific time, trying to send him a fax. We know this because Robert and I found a list on his computer that confirms this. So, when Rex received the fax, he just talked excitedly into his cell phone, acting like there was another person on the line. Colorado then swung into action, knowing that Rex was just minutes away from heading to Mexico with the money he had in the trunk of his car. Colorado went into Leo's bedroom and called Rex's cell phone, threatening to expose Rex's grand theft if Rex didn't meet him at Marc Baldwin's house with the money. Colorado gets there first, plugs an extension cord into an ungrounded outlet, and hides the cord behind some bushes. When Rex arrives, Colorado takes the suitcase full of money, pushes a surprised Rex into the pool, and then tosses the extension cord in after him. In a few minutes, he withdraws the cord and puts it back behind the bushes where it was found. Colorado is now a wealthy man, and the finger of blame is pointed in the direction of the White Party."

Grayson asked the question that all of us wanted answered next. "So where is the money? You have Colorado's confession, but without the money, the affair isn't resolved."

Monette tapped her head, indicating that her little gray cells had sniffed out the hiding place.

"It was almost under my ass!"

This comment produced puzzled looks from most of the table, except Michael, who twisted his mouth in disgust.

"The money was hidden in a sofa—sorry, a S-E-T-T-E-E—

in Colorado's home office. In fact, the day we went to question him—that was before his staged accident—I almost sat down on it. He threw a hissy fit, not because of the expensive fabric on it, but because I might have discovered that a twenty-five-thousand-dollar settee wouldn't have been that lumpy."

"But how do you know this, Monette?" I asked.

"Because I figured it out as we apprehended Colorado in Marc's kitchen. When I stepped on Colorado's hand and relieved him of his gun, I thought to myself that I was getting revenge for when he snapped at me about his goddamn settee. Right then, I knew."

"Ah, yes, my dear," Grayson intoned, "but *did* you get revenge?"

"Of course I did," Monette answered. "When I figured where the money was hidden, I had Sergeant Gorski call his men who were searching Colorado's house. I had him relay the information that the money was in a sofa in the living room, and to slit open all the furniture to find it. When they didn't find it, I told them to do the same in the bedroom. And so on. Then, miraculously, I remembered that it was the settee in his office with the ribbon on it. I'm sure by the time they finished, Colorado's house must have looked like he kept three hundred cats in there." Monette smiled the smile of a triumphant victor.

"And what about you, dear boy?" Grayson said, turning to Marc. "You were so brave, staring, right down the barrel of a gun, at death."

"Aw shucks, t'weren't nothing," he replied.

I loved this guy more and more by the minute.

"Grayson," I said, "if you think he was good then, you should have heard him on the phone earlier this evening, when he was threatening to blackmail Colorado. He talked like a pro, baiting him with every cussword I could imagine. He said things like 'You're not so smart, shit-head,' 'I figured you out, dick-wipe,'" I said, changing my voice in imitation of Marc's. "Baited him like a pro."

Marc, who was silent for most of the evening, spoke up. "That wasn't baiting him. I just can't stand the evil queen."

Epilogue

I Love a Man in Uniform

And that, as they say, is that. Colorado was arrested for first-degree murder, and the Red Party went on. It was spectacular from the opening ceremony to its closing party. We danced, we partied, and we had fun. Even better, hordes of men bought tickets to both parties, filling the coffers of both production companies. Marc donated a substantial portion of the proceeds to AIDS organizations.

The Red Party was billed as a "once-in-a-lifetime event," and the tag was prophetic because Marc said he would not continue it the following year. His reasons were simple. First, he had proved to himself that he could carry it off in the absence of Rex and Leo. In fact, he dedicated the party to the memory of Rex and Leo. But his second reason was even more touching: he said that it took him away from time spent with me.

Monette had a great time, she said. Of course, how could she not? Djuna spent as much time with Monette as she could during the party, dancing and talking and sharing a beer or two. She even wore the T-shirt Marc and I had quickly made up for her—the one that said, *I can't tell the difference between a sofa and a settee.* I did, however, confront her on one item that needed to be addressed.

"I may not have guessed the identities of the people involved in this case, but I did guess one thing," I said.

"Oh, yeah? And what might that be?" Monette responded.

"I figured that you were the one who threw the rock through the window of Marc's bedroom that night I was staying there."

"And how did you deduce that?"

"I said it at the time. It was too out of character for the killer. I mean, a rock through a window? It didn't have the same signature, the same cunning and planning as the murders. But I know you did it for a noble reason. Your motives were that if this case wasn't solved, Marc would be in danger because he was too close for Colorado's own comfort—which was exactly what you said before he agreed to be bait in your trap for Colorado."

"I guess there's not much more to say," she answered.

"I have something to say: thank you. Since Marc made that decision to catch Colorado, he's been . . . well, heroic. I think it's been good for his ego, and I've learned a lot from it, too. Thanks," I said, giving her a hug and spurting out a tear or two.

Michael, well, was Michael. He cavorted and seduced and toyed as usual. He did, however, spend an inordinate amount of time with a strangely handsome man who, upon later inspection at a hotel room, turned out to be a woman. How could Monette and I resist? We hadn't played one prank on each other the entire trip, because we were so busy. So why shouldn't Michael end up the recipient of one of our jokes? We had help, however. If you're reading this right now, dear and helpful Grayson, thanks for the male impersonator. She did a splendid job. We didn't stop there. There was one more score to settle. To David McLeish, we sent one plastic fire hydrant to the publicity department at the studio where he films his soap opera, with a note attached: *Here, David. Now you'll never have to run down the hall to pee again.*

* * *

By Monday morning we had packed up, and Monette, Djuna, Marc, Michael, and I sat waiting in the Palm Springs International Airport. I was fighting back tears because I didn't want to leave Marc. I wanted to stay in this gay paradise, to wake up and see the mountains every morning with Marc, to look up at the endless carpet of stars overhead every night, and to have him lying close to me every night and to be there every morning when I got up.

As the flashing monitor signaled that our plane was now boarding, I got up, wiping back a flood of tears that welled up in my eyes and burst over the dam. I reached under my seat and pulled out the present I was obviously saving for Marc for last.

"Here's the gift that you couldn't keep your eyes off, Marc. Go ahead; open it," I commanded him.

I handed the beautifully wrapped gift to Marc, and he opened it as carefully as I would, untying ribbons and pulling off the wrapping paper as delicately as a surgeon. He opened the box.

Inside lay a police uniform with honest-to-goodness Palm Springs Police Department arm patches (thank you, Sergeant Gorski), complete with a shiny name badge with Marc's last name engraved on it.

Marc closed the box, put it down on a chair, and hugged me so tightly and lovingly that I thought he would come out the other side of me. We hugged for what seemed like an eternity (perhaps it was); then we released each other. We had our own worlds to go back to . . . for the time being. I turned, took one last look and fought back a tear that I promised I wouldn't let escape, and headed down the corridor to the plane that would take me back to New York City. But just before I was out of earshot, I turned back to Marc and yelled, "Don't forget to pack that when you come visit me in New York, Sergeant Baldwin."